"If you will just stand on the step, Miss Ross, I will carry you across to the horses," Lord Weston instructed.

The previously assured figure before him seemed to shrink back into herself. "My lord, I should tell you...I am five foot ten and one quarter inches tall."

"Indeed, ma'am? I am six foot three. And one half," he added after a moment's thought. "I would be charmed to stand here all day exchanging shoe, glove and hat sizes, but I really feel we should be making a start."

There was a muffled choke of laughter from her maid behind her and Decima realized she was being teased. *Teased* about her height! Why, no one did that; no one considered it grounds for anything but the deepest shame and gloom.

He swept her up. "Can you put your arm around my neck?" he asked.

Decima did as she was bid. The viscount turned and began to wade back through the snowdrifts. The movement of his torso against her body was...disturbing. Something was making her feel quite strange inside: melting and flustered.

For heaven's sake, Decima, pull yourself t—

The
Harlequin® H...

the VISCOUNT'S BETROTHAL

Louise Allen

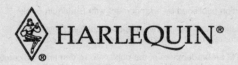

HARLEQUIN®

TORONTO • NEW YORK • LONDON
AMSTERDAM • PARIS • SYDNEY • HAMBURG
STOCKHOLM • ATHENS • TOKYO • MILAN • MADRID
PRAGUE • WARSAW • BUDAPEST • AUCKLAND

Recycling programs
for this product may
not exist in your area.

ISBN-13: 978-0-373-29582-1

THE VISCOUNT'S BETROTHAL

Copyright © 2006 by Louise Allen

First North American Publication 2010

www.eHarlequin.com

Printed in U.S.A.

Chapter One

In a charming breakfast parlour overlooking a sweep of wintry parkland in the county of Nottingham, three people were partaking of the first meal of the day in an atmosphere of quiet refinement and elegance.

Miss Ross placed her slice of toast neatly upon her breakfast plate, wiped her fingers in a ladylike manner with her linen napkin and smiled at her sister-in-law.

'Over my dead body.'

'Dessy!' Charlton spluttered into his morning coffee. Decima felt dizzy, as though something inside her had snapped. Had she really just said that?

Charlton put down his cup and wiped his lips with an irritable dab. 'What is the reason for that outburst? Hermione merely suggested that we should pay a visit this afternoon to our neighbours the Jardines. I told you about them—they have only been at High Hayes for six months and are a most charming family.'

'Who just happen to have a most charming and eligible gentleman staying with them, if what Hermione told me last night is correct.' Some stranger was inhabiting her body, uttering all the things she had always thought and had never dared articulate.

Nine years of increasingly desperate attempts by her family to marry her off had left Decima with an acute sense of when another 'suitable' match was threatening. She always did as she was bid and trailed along obediently to make painful conversation to the unfortunate gentleman concerned.

Obediently and spinelessly, she told herself, staring blankly at the platter of ham and eggs before her half-brother. Now, without any conscious volition on her part, it seemed the spineless worm was finally turning.

'We could have visited them at any time in the past fortnight, but I collect this gentleman only arrived two days ago and therefore we must go now,' she added, heaping coals on the blaze.

She glanced out of the window, suppressing a shiver despite the warmth of the room. The lowering sky was threatening snow after a week of dry, cold weather, but to escape this fresh humiliation she was quite ready to pack her bags and set forth at once. Why had walking out never occurred to her before? It was hardly as though she were a prisoner with nowhere else to go.

'Why, yes, Mrs Jardine's brother. An unmarried, titled gentleman as it happens, but that is not why I suggested we call.' Lady Carmichael, an unconvincing liar at the best of times, faltered to a halt as Decima's grey eyes came to rest on her and looked imploringly at her husband for support.

'One does not wish to intrude upon family Christmas gatherings,' Charlton blustered, slapping down his newspaper. His wife jumped. 'Naturally we could not call before.'

Decima regarded her half-brother with a calm that she was far from feeling. What she *wanted* to do was enquire bitterly why he persisted in humiliating her by parading her in front of yet another potential suitor whose lukewarm attempts at civility were bound to remind her yet again why she was still a spinster at the age of twenty-seven. But even her new-found rebellious courage failed her at that point.

'We have made upward of a dozen calls this holiday, Charlton, and have received as many,' she said mildly. 'Why should the Jardines alone be so exclusive?'

Really, Charlton's expression of baffled frustration would be amusing—if only she did not know that he was quite incapable of understanding her feelings and would most certainly plough on with his insensitive matchmaking come hell or high water.

'It is nothing to do with Mrs Jardine's brother,' he stated with unconvincing authority, ignoring her question. 'I don't know why you cannot oblige Hermione by accompanying her on a social call, Dessy.'

'Well, Charlton, one reason is that I will be leaving today.' Decima put the lid on the preserve jar, concentrating on stopping her hand shaking. Never before had she been able to stand up to his bullying, but then, she saw in a flash of self-realisation, never before had she been legally and financially free of him. At least, she would be in two days' time, on New Year's Day.

'What! Don't be absurd, Dessy. Leaving? You have hardly been here a sennight.' Around the walls the footmen stood, blank-faced. Charlton ignored their presence as usual; it never occurred to him that browbeating his sister before an audience of what he considered to be menials might cause her distress, or them discomfort.

'Two weeks and a day, actually,' Decima interjected, and was ignored.

'I made certain that you would stay here at Longwater for at least a month. You always stay a month at Christmas.'

'And I told you when I arrived that I intended staying for a fortnight, did I not, Hermione?'

'Why, yes, but I did not regard it…'

'And Augusta will be expecting me. So I must finish my breakfast and set Pru to packing or the morning will be well-advanced before we set out.' Charlton was becoming alarmingly red. Decima took a last bite of toast she found she no longer had any appetite for and turned to smile at the butler. 'Felbrigg, please will you send to the stables and ask the postilions to have my carriage at the front door for half past ten?'

'Certainly, Miss Ross. I will also send a footman up with your luggage.' Decima suspected that Felbrigg rather approved of her; he was certainly able to ignore his master's infuriated gobblings with aplomb.

'You will do no such thing, Dessy! Just look at the weather, it will be snowing in a minute.' As she got to her feet Charlton glared past her in frustrated rage to a portrait of his own father, side by side with the petite figure of their mother. 'I can only assume that you get this stubborn, disobliging streak from your father, along with so much else. You certainly do not inherit it from our dear mama.'

Decima glanced at Hermione's distressed face and bit back the bitter retort that was on her lips. The worm that was turning seemed to be a full-grown adder, but to let it loose now would only wound her sister-in-law. She forced a smile. 'It was a lovely stay, Hermione, but I really must be leaving now or Augusta will fret.'

Decima made herself walk calmly to the door. As Felbrigg shut it behind her, she heard Hermione say with disastrous clarity, 'Oh, *poor* dear Dessy! What *are* we going to do with her?'

Six miles away Viscount Weston raised a dark and sceptical eyebrow at his youngest sister. 'What are you up to, Sally? You know I said this was a flying visit and I was leaving by the end of the week.'

'Up to? Why, nothing, Adam dear, I only wanted to know if you were going to be here in case our neighbours, the Carmichaels, call.' Lady Jardine fussed with the coffee pot. 'Another cup?'

'No, thank you. And what is the attraction of the Carmichaels?' Sally assumed an air of innocence, belied by her heightened colour. Adam smiled slightly—Sal had always been as easy to read as a book. 'An eligible daughter?'

'Oh, no, not a daughter,' she replied, with what he could tell was relief at being able to deny something.

'An ineligible middle-aged sister,' his brother-in-law put in suddenly, emerging from behind his *Times* with an irritable rustle of newsprint. 'Carmichael's desperate to get her off his hands by all accounts. I do not know why you let yourself get drawn into this silly scheme of Lady Carmichael's, Sally. If Adam wants a wife, he is more than capable of finding one himself.'

'She is not middle-aged,' his affronted wife snapped. 'She is under thirty, I am certain, and Hermione Carmichael tells me she is intelligent and amiable—and very well-to-do.'

'Adam is in no need of a wealthy wife,' her loving spouse retorted, 'and you know as well as I do what *intelligent and amiable* means. She'll be as plain as a pikestaff and probably a bluestocking to boot.'

'Thank you, George, a masterful piece of deduction if I may say so. I gather neither of you has set eyes on the lady?' Adam flicked a crumb off his coat sleeve and thought about what his brother-in-law had said. He was certainly in no need to hang out for a well-dowered bride, but as for finding himself a wife, he was not so sure.

Not sure whether he ever wanted to be leg-shackled and not sure either that the woman for him was there to be found in any case. With a ready-made and eminently satisfactory heir already to hand, the matter was one that could be very comfortably shelved.

'No, we have not met her.' Sally sounded sulky. 'But I am

sure they will call today—look at the weather, anyone can see it is about to snow soon and tomorrow might be too late.'

'It will certainly be too late, my dear.' Adam stood up and grinned affectionately at his favourite sister. 'In view of the weather, I will be setting out for Brightshill this morning.'

'Running shy?' Sir George enquired with a straight face.

'Running like a fox before hounds,' Adam agreed amiably, refusing to be insulted. 'Now, don't pout at me, Sal; you know I said this would only be a short stay. I've a house party due in two days, so I'd have to be leaving tomorrow morning at the latest in any case.'

'Wretch,' his loving sister threw at him as he left the room. 'I declare you are an unrepentant bachelor. You are certainly an ungrateful brother—you *deserve* a plain bluestocking!'

Decima stared unseeing out of the carriage window at the passing landscape. It gave her no pleasure to be at outs with Charlton and Hermione; she would have quite happily stayed another week at Longwater if only they had left her in peace. Cousin Augusta, the placid eccentric whose Norfolk home she shared, would greet her return with pleasure, or her absence for a little longer with equanimity—just so long as she had her new glasshouse to occupy her.

This ability not to fuss was much prized by Decima, although she did wish sometimes that Augusta could comprehend how miserable her other relatives' attempts at matchmaking and their scarcely veiled pity made her. But then Augusta had never had any trouble doing exactly what she wanted, when she wanted to, and found it difficult to understand Decima's compliance.

Widowed young with the death of her elderly, rich and extremely dull husband, Augusta had emerged from mourning and scandalised all and sundry by declaring that she was devoting herself to gardening, painting—very badly, as it turned out—and rural seclusion.

At the age of five and twenty Decima, in disgrace for failing to please when paraded in frilly pink muslin before a depressing dowager and her equally depressing and chinless son, was sent to rusticate in Norfolk. The cousins formed an instant attachment and she was allowed to stay there.

'Out of sight and out of mind,' she had said hopefully at the time. Although not, it had proved, completely out of mind. She suspected that Charlton and her various aunts made notes at regular intervals upon their calendars that read 'Marry Off Poor Dear Dessy', and took it in turns to summon her to stay while they produced yet another hapless bachelor or widower for her. And always, meekly and spinelessly, she had gone along with their schemes, knowing each and every one was doomed to failure. And each and every one left another scar on her confidence and her happiness.

Enough was enough, she had decided while helping Pru fold garments into her travelling trunk. Why it had taken until breakfast this morning for the penny to drop and for her to realise that, by coming into control of her inheritance, she had also come into not just the ability but the *right* to control her own life, she did not know. It was part and parcel of the passivity she had shown in the face of her family's constant reminders of what a disappointment she was to them. Of course, the kinder of them agreed, she not could actually help it. She was a sweet girl, but what, with her disadvantages, could one expect?

Decima bit her lip. If she looked critically at her life since she was seventeen she could see it as a series of evasions, of passive resistance aimed at stopping people doing things *to* her. Well, now it was time to start being positive. Just as soon as she had decided what it was she wanted to be positive about—that was the first thing.

She certainly had much to learn about taking control of her life. Why, it had just taken three months, since her twenty-seventh birthday, for her to realise that the fortune, which she had always known she possessed, was the key to more than financial independence. Charlton had been very cunning, giving her a generous allowance that more than covered her needs and her occasional fancies—nothing to rebel against there, no reason to grasp the prospect of access to her entire capital with desperation.

After today, Decima decided, she would leave immediately on each and every occasion in the future when her relatives tried to matchmake. If she was not there to hear them, what did it matter how much they lamented her shortcomings?

She was reviewing this resolution, and deciding that it was an admirable one for New Year, when Pru exclaimed, 'Look at this weather, Miss Dessy! This is taking an age—we only passed that dreadful ale- house, the Red Cock, twenty minutes ago.'

Startled out of her reverie, Decima focused on the view. It was indeed alarming. Although it was only about two in the afternoon, the light was heavy and gloomy as it fought its way through the swirling snowflakes. Great mounds of snow hid the line of roadside hedges, the verges were an expanse of unbroken white and the trees, which at this point formed a little coppice, were already bending under their burden.

'Oh, bother.' She scrubbed at the glass, which had clouded with her warm breath. 'I thought we would make Oakham for a late luncheon quite easily, now we will be lucky to arrive there for supper. I suppose we will have to stay at the Sun in Splendour overnight.'

'It's a good inn,' the maid remarked. 'It will be no pain to stay there, and in this weather I don't expect there'll be that many folks out on the roads. You should get a nice private parlour with no trouble.' She sneezed violently and disappeared into a vast handkerchief.

The prospect of a roaring fire, an excellent supper and the Sun's renowned feather beds was appealing. And there would be no one to nag her. She could kick off her shoes, drink hot chocolate curled up in a chair with a really frivolous novel and go to bed when she felt like it. Decima contemplated this plan with some smugness until the carriage came to a sudden halt.

'Now what?' She lowered the window and leaned out, receiving a face full of snowflakes. 'Why have we stopped?' Through the snow she could just make out that they had halted at a crossroads and that another vehicle, a curricle and pair by the look of it, had stopped on the road that intersected with theirs.

One of the postilions swung down from his horse and made heavy weather of stamping back through the snow to the door. 'Can't go no further, miss. The snow's too deep, drifting right across the road. Look.'

'Then we'll have to go round.' The snow was blowing down her neck now and she pulled the velvet collar of her pelisse tighter.

'Round where, miss?' the man asked bluntly. 'This isn't just some little local shower, it's a regular blizzard—I'll wager it's this bad right across the Midlands. Only thing to be done is to go back to the Cock—the horses won't manage to get further than that, not until this lets up. There's nowhere else for five miles.'

'The Cock?' Decima stared at him, horrified, the vision of the Sun's snug private parlour dissolving like a snowball in a muddy puddle, into an image of the squalid alehouse. 'That is out of the question. They have no bedchambers, let alone a private parlour, and we could be stranded there for days, in goodness knows what company.'

The man shrugged. 'Not much option, miss. We'd better be getting back now, before the place fills up with other travellers in a like fix.'

'Might I be of assistance?' The man's voice reached them

clearly, despite the snow, and Decima strained to make out the speaker through the thickening whiteness. The voice sounded reassuringly deep and pleasant, but as the figure loomed up she gasped. It was a giant.

Then he came nearer, wading through the drifts, and she realised that he was simply a particularly tall gentleman wearing a many-caped driving coat and low-crowned hat.

'Ma'am.' He doffed the hat, revealing dark hair that instantly became spangled with white, and came right up to the carriage. 'I suspect, like me, you have come to the conclusion that the road ahead is impassable for carriages.'

'Indeed, sir. My postilion is convinced that the only shelter is the alehouse back a mile or so, but—'

'But that is quite unsuitable for a lady, I could not agree more.' What Decima could see of him was reassuring. A formidable breadth of shoulder, a pair of level grey-green eyes, a determined chin and a mouth that, although serious now, seemed ready to smile. And he agreed with her, a definite point in his favour in a world of men who all seemed determined to point out to her that she was just a foolish woman.

'Yet there seems no alternative, unless you know of some more reputable hostelry in the vicinity, sir.'

Adam dug beneath his greatcoat and found his card case. What a lady with only a maid as companion would make of his proposal, goodness knows, but as her alternatives were to be snowed up in a flea-ridden drinking den or to freeze to death in her carriage, he suspected that all but the most strait-laced would agree.

'My card, ma'am.' She took it and studied it, giving him an opportunity to study her. Large, wide-set grey eyes, now masked by thick lashes as she read; brown hair peeping from beneath a stylish green velvet bonnet; a generously wide mouth, set in serious lines, and a wild sprinkling of freckles all across her nose and cheeks.

Her maid began to sneeze violently and she glanced across, a slight frown between her brows. 'Bless you, Pru.' She turned back to Adam, eyes frankly searching his face as the snow blew between them, her mouth now set in a thoughtful pout that made him want to lean forward and nip its fullness in his teeth. Adam blinked away the snow and took a grip on his imagination.

'Lord Weston. I am Miss Ross and this is my maid Staples. If you have some alternative suggestion to make, I would be extremely glad to hear it.'

There was no point in beating about the bush. 'I am travelling to my hunting box near Whissendine, about five miles distant. I do not believe I can drive any further beyond here with these drifts, but my groom is with me and two of my hunters. I propose that we unhitch my carriage horses and use them to carry our valuables and essential baggage. My groom will take up your maid on one of the hunters and I will take you on the other. It will not be an easy journey, but I can promise you a warm refuge at the end of it. Your postilions can take your carriage and our remaining baggage back to the alehouse where they can take shelter until the weather breaks and they are able to collect you and take you on to your destination.'

Miss Ross looked down again at the card and then up at his face. He saw her lips move slightly, *Adam Grantham, Viscount Weston.* Behind her the maid went off into another paroxysm of sneezes. 'Who else will be at your box, my lord?' A pleasant voice, even now when it was constrained by both formality and caution.

'Today, my housekeeper, a maid and a footman. Tomorrow I expect a small house party consisting of two married couples, one of whom is my cousin, Lady Wendover, and her husband.'

'If they can get through.' She sounded thoughtful rather than dubious. 'Very well, my lord. Thank you for your most kind suggestion. Could you ask the postilions to pass my luggage down into the carriage so I can decide what to take?'

He gave the order and trudged back through the drifts to the curricle where Bates stood huddled, holding the carriage horses' lines in one hand and the reins of the two hunters in the other.

'We'll take the women up with us on Ajax and Fox and the baggage up on the greys. Let me sort out a valise—is your gear all together?'

Bates grunted and gestured abruptly with his head towards a battered bag strapped on behind the curricle seat.

'Good, then unhitch the greys and shorten the reins off.'

Adam rummaged rapidly through his bags and reduced his essentials to one valise, thankful for a lifetime's habit of travelling light. Goodness knows what a lady with that taste in bonnets would consider she could not do without, and how many bags that would involve. He hefted the rest down and carried them back to the carriage. The snow was deepening by the minute; this was going to be a nightmare of a journey.

'We are ready, my lord.' By some miracle the two women were swathed in heavy hooded winter cloaks with not a sign of a fashionable bonnet. On the seat were two valises and a dressing case.

'I congratulate you on both your dispatch and your packing, Miss Ross. Now, if you will just stand on the step I will carry you across to the horses.'

The wide grey eyes stared at him, then, disconcertingly, she coloured deeply. Now what had he said? Surely a lady willing to go with a stranger on trust was not going to baulk at being carried through a snowdrift?

'Ma'am?'

The previously assured figure before him seemed to shrink back into herself. 'My lord, I should tell you...I am five foot ten and one-quarter inches tall.'

Chapter Two

It might, after all, be better to spend days shut up in the Cock rather than to face the shame of being lugged through the snow like a sack of coals. It would probably take both men to achieve it. No previous humiliation lived up to the prospect of this. Obviously the viscount had no idea when he suggested this scheme that he was dealing with a lady who was freakishly tall.

Adam Grantham was looking serious, although it was difficult to read his expression through the swirling snow. 'Indeed, ma'am? I am six foot three. And one-half,' he added after a moment's thought. 'I would be charmed to stand here all day exchanging shoe, glove and hat sizes, but I really feel we should be making a start.'

'But you misunderstand me, my lord…'

His expression changed to one of chagrin. 'You mean you think me incapable of carrying you, Miss Ross? I have to say I resent that slur upon my manhood.'

Completely thrown into disarray, Decima hastened to reassure him. 'Lord Weston, I did not for a moment mean to imply any lack of strength on your part—' There was a muffled choke of laughter from Pru behind her and Decima realised she was being teased. *Teased* about her height! Why, no one did that, no one considered it grounds for anything but the deepest shame and gloom.

Furious with herself, and with him, she threw the door open and stooped to step out. The wind hit her like a cold douche of water and the snow caught her breath in her throat, effectively stopping the stinging remark she was about to make.

She had hardly straightened when he swept her up, one arm behind her knees, the other across her back. 'Can you free your left arm and put it about my neck?' Apparently he did not even have to breathe deeply to cope with her weight.

Decima disentangled her arm and did as she was bid. It involved a fair amount of wriggling around and she was perversely gratified to observe a slight flush under the skin of the cheek her nose was so close to. *Possibly you are not as strong as you think you are, my lord*, she thought smugly to herself. Just so long as he did not fall into a ditch with her.

The snow was deepening by the minute, Decima realised, as the viscount turned and began to wade back through the drifts towards the horses. He was taking it slowly, placing his booted feet with care, which gave her the opportunity to experience this very strange experience to the full. It was the first time she had ever found herself in a man's arms, and it was doubtless the last, so, in tune with her New Year's resolution to live life positively, she might as well start here and absorb this new sensation.

The movement of his torso against her body was…disturbing. He was certainly strong and well-muscled. What did a gentleman do to get muscles like that? Charlton, at thirty-two, was already becoming soft around the midriff and she could have sworn he could not carry a toddler without puffing, let alone his beanpole of a sister. How old was Lord Weston? The same age as Charlton?

From within the shelter of her hood she studied what she

could see of him. That chin was even more determined in profile, and his nose matched it. The first traces of dark stubble were showing under the skin on his cheeks—it seemed his beard would be as dark a brown as the hair she could see under his hat. A very male face indeed, Decima decided, and then saw that his eyelashes were quite ridiculously long and thick. Longer and thicker than hers, she thought resentfully. How very unfair. They had snowflakes caught on their tips.

From the side it was difficult to see his eyes. As she was considering this, he turned his head to glance at her and she saw that they were more grey than she had recalled from that first glimpse. Perhaps it was some strange reflection from the snow, but they seemed almost to have silver lights dancing in them. She blinked away the snowflakes from her own lashes and found he was smiling at her. Without considering, she smiled back.

'Are you all right? Not much further now.'

'Yes, yes. I am perfectly all right. Thank you. My lord.' *Just prattling like an idiot,* she told herself. *For Heaven's sake, Decima, pull yourself together.* Why being carried like this should make her feel so hot and breathless she could not imagine. It surely wasn't embarrassment, not now it seemed certain he was not going to collapse under her weight.

She drew a deep breath and realised that to the list of new sensual impressions she could add scent. He smelt of some subtle citrus cologne, of leather and, faintly, of what she could only imagine was warm man.

Something was making her feel quite strange inside: melting and flustered. And then she realised that if she could catch the scent of him, so he could of her. That was a thoroughly unsettling thought for some reason. Not that there was anything more exotic for him to inhale than good Castile soap and a suitably refined jasmine toilet water. And there was no reason to think that he would find that remotely interesting or disturbing.

'Here we are.' He trampled a circle of snow, then set her on her feet, a few paces away from the groom who handed him the reins of two hunters with a grunt.

'Tied the carriage horses to that bush.' The man jerked his head in the direction of a pair of dark greys who seemed half lost already in the swirling whiteness as they turned their hindquarters to the prevailing wind.

His master did not appear to take either the curtness, or the scowl that accompanied it, amiss. 'Are our valises tied on, Bates?'

'Aye, sir.'

'Then go and fetch Miss Ross's maid. Here, you!' he shouted at the postilions, who were sitting hunched and miserable against the snow. 'Bring the valises from inside the coach.' Reluctantly, one of the men dismounted and trudged back passing the groom who, being considerably shorter in the leg than the viscount, was sensibly using his footsteps to make his way to the carriage.

'King Wenceslas,' Decima observed with a gurgle of laughter, and was answered with a deep chuckle.

'I cannot see Bates as anyone's attentive page, and I fear we are not going to be lit by the brightly shining moon tonight. No! I would not touch Fox—'

But Decima was already stroking the soft muzzle that was thrusting hopefully into her gloved palm. 'What a handsome fellow you are to be sure, and so good, standing here patiently in this horrid snow. What is the matter, my lord?' The viscount let out his breath in a hiss.

'Fox is reputed to eat stable boys.'

'I am not a stable boy.'

'No, and that horse is an arrant flirt. I'd never have thought it of him.' Lashes even longer than his master's were being batted at Decima as she continued to rub just the right spot on the chestnut's nose.

'Yes, you are beautiful,' she cooed, looking at the strongly arched neck and broad chest. 'Is he a stallion?' Without thinking, she bobbed down to look. He was, very obviously. 'So he is. He is very well made.'

Oh, no! As soon as the words were out of her mouth she realised what she had said, and to whom she had said it. That was not the sort of observation a lady was supposed to make, however much she knew about horses. Now, what did one say to a complete stranger after one had commented on his horse's…er…masculine attributes? The viscount had assumed an expression one could only describe as *stuffed*.

She was saved from floundering any further by an outraged shriek from the direction of the carriage. 'Put me down, you cork-brained jackanapes!' Pru's tirade was cut short on a gasp and Bates appeared through the swirling snow, the maid thrown over his shoulder. The effect as she wriggled was not unlike a man carrying a sack full of outraged piglets.

Their progress was slow. Decima watched with bated breath, not daring to look at Lord Weston. Bates was a slight man, if wiry. Pru, who stood a mere five foot two inches in her stockinged feet, more than made up for lack of vertical inches with a quite magnificent bosom and a rounded figure to match. At any minute the groom was going to sink into a snowdrift, of that she was sure.

The postilion with the valises overtook them with ease, depositing his burden at the viscount's feet. 'We'll be heading back to the Cock, sir. Where would you be wishful for us to call for the lady when the snow clears?'

'Um?' Lord Weston tore his gaze from the floundering figure of his groom and dug a card out of his pocket. 'Here. Anyone in Whissendine will give you directions. Mind you keep that baggage safe.' As this instruction was accompanied by the clink of coin, the man tugged his forelock respectfully and waded back, making some comment as he passed the labouring groom that provoked an even more violent wriggle from Pru.

'Stubble it, do, woman.' Bates arrived in front of them and set Pru on her feet with more haste than care. Red-faced and furious, she opened her mouth to berate him and succumbed to a paroxysm of coughing.

'Pru, are you all right?' Decima crunched through the snow to her side.

'Just a cold, that's all,' the maid assured her hoarsely, shooting a venomous glare in Bates's direction. 'Not helped by being hauled around like a sack of potatoes by that weasel-gutted looby.'

'If you are ready, I think we had better be getting on.' The viscount was dealing with this minor spat by the simple expedient of ignoring it. Decima envied him such a lofty disregard of his environment, or perhaps he was simply better at disciplining his subordinates than she was and did not look forward to an evening of being grumbled at.

'Bates, if those bags are secure, mount up and I'll lift your passenger up to you.'

Decima derived some amusement at the groom's face on being expected to ride with the fulminating Miss Staples and the coy expression that the prospect of being lifted up by his lordship produced on Pru's flushed countenance. It was certainly a welcome distraction from her own *faux pas* concerning Fox.

With Bates and Pru settled, the viscount turned and offered his cupped hands for Decima's foot. 'If I boost you up and then mount behind you, will you be all right?'

'Certainly.' Decima gathered the reins confidently and lifted her foot. As soon as she was in the saddle she began to have doubts. Riding sideways on a man's saddle would be manageable, for the pommel gave her enough purchase for her right knee, and the stirrup could be adjusted for her foot. But where would his lordship sit?

He swung up behind her, keeping his weight in the stirrups so he was virtually standing. Decima found herself lifted as he slid into the saddle beneath her and set her down again. Only this time she was sitting in his lap, her weight on his thighs.

'My lord!'

'Yes, Miss Ross?' He leaned over, took the reins of one of the greys from Bates, then turned Fox's head towards the right-hand arm of the crossroads. Under her she could feel the movement of muscles in his thighs, his arms were tight on either side of her and all she could do to avoid the painful pressure of the pommel on her own thigh was to lean into his body. It felt like leaning into a tree trunk.

'This is most…most…'

'Uncomfortable? I'm afraid it is, at least for you, but in those skirts I really do not think you could sit astride, and perching on Fox's rump is not going to be secure, not over this uneven surface.' As though to prove his point the big horse plunged into a depression, surging out of it again with a scramble. 'That must be the ditch.' He twisted in the saddle, giving Decima more unusual sensations to come to terms with as she balanced on moving muscle. 'Bates, keep to the right, I got too close to the edge just now.'

There was silence for a few moments, then the viscount commented, 'I imagine you ride very well, Miss Ross.'

'It is my chief enjoyment,' she confessed, pleased by the compliment. 'My father knew a great deal about horses and encouraged me to take an interest, too.'

'Did he breed his own?' Decima risked a glance at Lord Weston's face, but he was looking ahead, his eyes fixed on the road.

'Yes, and I helped him choose the bloodlines for the mare I have now.'

'Ah, I thought you knew your stuff.' There was the barest hint of amusement and Decima felt herself colouring. No, he hadn't forgotten her unmaidenly remark about the stallion.

'What makes you think I ride well?' Anything to move the conversation on to safer ground.

'You are riding me now, just as you would a horse, shifting your weight to respond to my movements.' He said it in a perfectly matter-of-fact tone, but to Decima's ears it sounded suggestively improper. It *felt* improper. She had never had more than a hand touched by a man who was not a close relative.

'I am sorry. Only I don't have anything to hold on to and I cannot keep my balance unless I shift my weight.' His thighs must be numb by now, she thought, new embarrassment seizing her.

'I see the problem.' His breathing seemed to be coming rather short—she could see the puffs of warm breath on the cold air. 'Look, if you undo my greatcoat and put your arms around me inside it, then my arms holding the reins will trap it around you. Just hang on and try and sit—still.' The final word came out as a gasp as Decima twisted to get at the big mother-of-pearl buttons. After a tussle she managed to open the coat and wriggle enough to wrap her arms around the viscount's body. The flaps of the coat closed with the pressure of his arms and she found herself in warm, man-scented semidarkness.

It was very odd. Sounds from outside were muffled, but her ear, pressed against his chest, could hear the sound of his heartbeat, out of rhythm with hers. Her palms curled against his sides with her fingers curving into his back—goodness, but he was large.

Certainly she didn't need to shift to keep her balance any longer, but things felt somehow different than before when she'd sat further forward. Decima settled more comfortably, then her mind caught up with what her body was feeling. *Oh, my heavens!* She suddenly became very still. No wonder he hadn't wanted her moving about. It seemed the cold had done nothing whatsoever to diminish his lordship's male reflexes.

Adam relaxed a little. Thank God she'd stopped wriggling. Now all he had to do was to breathe this blessedly freezing air deeply and think of completely unerotic things such as dying of exposure in a snowdrift or Fox breaking a leg in a concealed pothole and possibly, in about a week, his painful state of arousal might subside.

Why a befreckled beanpole of a young lady—not so very young, now he came to think about it—should have this effect upon him he had no idea. Possibly it was a reflex reaction to his sister's matchmaking; he felt immediately attracted to the first woman he saw who wasn't thrust into his path by a relative. And she was hardly a conventional lady at that. He recalled her knowledgeable assessment of Fox's attributes with a grin—Sal would faint dead away if she heard such a comment. Well, if one were to be marooned in a blizzard with a lady, then better an eccentric one than an hysterical young miss.

He snuggled his arms tighter to hold the greatcoat close around her and tucked his chin down on the top of her head. It was much easier to guide Fox with her in this position. And warmer, and altogether more…erotic, damn it. Her hands were clasped tightly around him and he could feel her heart beating, the swell of her breasts, even through the thickness of his coat. Despite her obvious embarrassment about her height, she wasn't particularly heavy as she rested on his thighs. He just hoped she hadn't noticed—or did not understand—what else she was resting on.

They rode in silence for what seemed like an hour. Adam twisted in the saddle as best he could and saw his groom was keeping up well. 'Are you all right, Bates?'

'Aye. I'd be doing better if I didn't have to manage this here fubsy bloss.' This observation was greeted by a hoot of outrage and the sound of a fist thumping against what Adam hoped was Bates's chest and not some vital part of his anatomy. It was followed by a flurry of sneezes and the groom's voice adding plaintively, 'And I'll have caught a streaming cold by the end of it, too.'

'What did he call her?' The voice was muffled under the greatcoat. Adam smiled.

'A fubsy bloss. I think he was implying that your maid is a well-endowed...I mean, plump young woman.'

There was a giggle. Really a very nice giggle. Adam was not normally taken by gigglers, but then usually they were batting their eyelashes at him on the dance floor and behaving as though his most banal remark was the acme of wit and intelligence. 'Pru's figure is usually much admired.'

'I imagine it is—but possibly her admirers have not had to get their arms around it while balanced on a horse in a snowstorm. I can see a fingerpost, thank heavens.' Provided it didn't prove he'd been riding round in circles all this time. He and Bates were fit and the horses were strong, but he wasn't sure how much more of this they could safely take. The snow was showing no signs of abating.

Bates forged ahead to read the signpost. 'We're on the right road,' he called back. 'This is Honeypot Hill—a mile down there and we take the lane on the right, then it's less than half a mile.'

Along a deep lane with high hedges. Either it was going to be protected and clear or it would be impassably deep in drifts. Adam kept his thoughts to himself and led the way down the hill, his hands automatically guiding and checking the horse as it slid and pecked, his mind working on ways round.

'It is getting worse, isn't it?' The voice from the region of his upper coat button jerked him back to the here and now. He could sense the edge of fear under Miss Ross's calm question, but she wasn't going to give way to it.

'Yes.' There was no point in lying to her, she only had to look for herself.

'You will manage.'

'You sound very confident.'

'I would not have come with you if I hadn't been,' Miss Ross said prosaically. 'I mean, I have had a lot of experience of men who are idiots, so it is quite easy to spot one who isn't.'

That was frank speaking indeed. 'I hope that was a compliment, Miss Ross.'

'Of course it was. Now my brother—or any of my numerous male cousins—would say that I should have stayed in the coach, so by now Pru and I would be well on our way to expiring of cold, my virtue indubitably protected. He would have prosed on for hours about the consequences of my having set forth on this journey at all without a male escort, so by now I would have strangled him and have ended up in the hands of the justices.'

'Why would you have strangled your brother?' They had reached the bottom of the hill now and the lane opened up, mercifully free of drifts. 'The lane looks clearer.'

'Good. Charlton? Oh, because he is patronising, authoritarian and insensitive, and he bullies my sister-in-law. He used to bully me, but not any more.' She sounded smugly satisfied.

Adam found himself grinning through cold-stiffened lips. 'As a magistrate myself, I can tell you that sounds like perfectly justifiable homicide. But why no more?'

'It's my New Year's resolution. One of them.'

Adam was conscious of a deep fellow-feeling for the unfortunate Charlton. Miss Ross sounded very resolved indeed. 'We're here.' He let out his breath with a *whoosh*, unaware until then just how tense he had become. It was one thing taking himself and Bates into danger, but risking two women was another matter altogether.

Miss Ross wriggled distractingly, and peered out from the shelter of his greatcoat. 'Are we? Where is it?'

'Up ahead. There are no lights showing; they must have given us up for the day and all be in the kitchen.'

The horses plodded up the driveway and round to the yard that served both stables and service areas. There was no light there, either. An unpleasant sinking feeling gripped Adam's insides. *What the hell?* It could only be just past four o'clock at the latest; anyways, no one with any sense would be out in this.

He edged Fox close to the porch that sheltered the kitchen door. 'Can you slide down?' He gripped Miss Ross round the waist, shifted her so that she was facing away from the horse, then let her slip. Under his hands layers of fabric shifted, slithered over each other and over skin. He felt a slender waist, the firmness of a ribcage confined in stays, the sudden, voluptuous, curve of the side of her breasts and then she was down. He had forgotten how tall she was.

Behind them there was the sound of a much-less easy transfer taking place, but all Adam was conscious of was a pair of very cool grey eyes regarding him.

'There does not appear to be anyone at home.' Decima stated it calmly, horribly aware that she seemed to have landed herself in exactly the sort of predicament that her female relations always warned her about. Men were beasts, that went without saying, they informed her, and they used every wile and pretext to lure innocent damsels to their ruin.

'And you think that this is the equivalent of me offering you a lift in my curricle and the traces breaking conveniently close to my love nest?' the viscount enquired with equal calm, swinging down out of the saddle and trapping her neatly between his bulk and the door.

Chapter Three

'**I** am just deciding *what* I think,' Decima replied honestly. If this was a snare and a lure and his lordship was intent upon ravishment, then he was both extremely opportunistic and pretty desperate to drag two women miles in the teeth of a blizzard. 'And I think I am prepared to believe that you are surprised as we to find the house apparently unoccupied.'

'Thank you, ma'am, for your good opinion.' He bowed.

'I must believe it. After all, my lord, if you prove to be a wicked seducer, then think how cast down I must be that my own initial judgement of your character was so at fault.'

That provoked a snort of laughter. 'Your own good opinion of your judgement must indeed be preserved at all costs, Miss Ross. Now, let me see if the door is unlocked.'

'Sir.' It was Bates. Decima turned to find him supporting the sagging figure of Pru, doubled up in a fit of coughing. 'The wench is in a fair poor state.'

'Pru, what is it?' Decima put an arm round the maid and touched her forehead. What had she done, dragging the poor girl out on this journey in the teeth of the threatening snow? 'She's burning up with fever. My lord, please, open up as quickly as possible, we must get her inside.'

She bundled Pru into an unlit, cold room, blinking impatiently at the gloom while Bates groped around for lights. At last one, then several lamps flickered into life, showing that they were in a kitchen. The range was dead, an apron neatly draped across the chair by its side.

'Mrs Chitty! Emily Jane?' Lord Weston threw open the inner door and shouted. 'No one. Bates, take the horses over to the stables, get them bedded down and check to see whether the gig is there—they must have gone into town shopping and been caught by the weather.' The groom stomped off and Decima lowered a shivering Pru into a chair.

'I must get her to bed at once. Which room shall I use, my lord?'

'On the first floor. They should all have fires laid and the beds made. The one at the end is mine, use any of the others. Here…' he lifted one of the spermaceti lamps '…I'll come with you.'

'I would rather you lit the range, my lord,' Decima said frankly, taking the lamp from him. Now was no time to stand on ceremony. The housekeeper would have known exactly what was needed—now she had no compunction about making the viscount as useful as he could be. 'I need hot bricks, hot drinks and hot food for her. Come along, Pru.'

'I'm sorry, Miss Dessy, don't know what's the matter with me,' Pru mumbled as Decima hoisted her to her feet and guided her out of the room.

'A fever, that's what. Lady Carmichael's maid had it over Christmas, don't you remember? I expect you caught it from her. Come along, we'll soon have you tucked up.' In a cold bed, in a cold house with two strange men for company and probably no chance of a doctor for days. Decima bit her lip and hoped that the absent Mrs Chitty was a prudent housekeeper and kept a well-stocked stillroom.

They made their unsteady way up the stairs and along a

corridor, Decima peering into each room in turn. What she wanted was a pair of bedchambers with an interconnecting door, She found them almost at the end of the passage: a spacious bedroom with an adjoining dressing room that had its own fireplace and small bed.

'Here we are, Pru. Here's a nice little room that will soon warm up.' Pru sank down in the chair without any persuasion and Decima set a taper to the fire and checked the bed. Cold, but not damp. 'Just you stop there a moment, I'll fetch our bags and we'll have you undressed and into bed in a trice.' Somehow she kept the anxiety out of her voice.

Decima ran downstairs to find their valises on the kitchen floor and his lordship, hands on hips, regarding the range— the still-cold range—with a scowl.

'You haven't lit it!' she accused.

'I'm trying to work it out,' he retorted. 'It's new. There are dampers and compartments and a bit with water in it and things to open and close. It'll probably blow up if I shut the wrong thing.'

'Oh for goodness' sake! Let me.' Five frustrating minutes later Decima admitted defeat, and retreated to glower at the viscount. 'Do something. You are a man.'

'Although undoubtedly true, that does not give me an affinity with…' he peered at the raised lettering on the cast-iron front plate '…Bodley's Patent Range. I'll open all the dampers, light it, stand well back and do not blame me if we find ourselves in the midst of smoking rubble.'

Decima looked up from her excavations in the valises. 'I thought a gentleman should be master of everything in his household,' she observed more mildly.

'The last person to try and master Mrs Chitty and her kingdom was the late—and note that, *late*—Mr Chitty. There. Let me carry those up for you, Dessy.'

'I can manage… *What* did you call me?'

'Dessy. That's what your maid called you, didn't she? Miss Dessy?'

'My name is Decima, my lord.'

'And what does Charlton call you?'

'Dessy.'

'And do you like it?'

'No.' She hated it, she realised. It made her sound five years old, or completely totty-headed. Or both.

'In that case I will call you Decima.'

Decima glared at him, but receiving no satisfaction beyond the undoubtedly admirable view of broad shoulders as he bent to light the range, she stalked out.

When she came back the viscount was hefting a large kettle onto the range. He gave the dampers a shove with the poker and rested one arm on the high mantelshelf, watching the fire. She stood silently in the doorway, studying her rescuer, glad of the opportunity while he was unaware of her scrutiny.

Tall, built to match, athletic-looking with an edge that made her think of racehorses in the peak of condition; everything about him seemed perfectly in proportion. Long legs: the recollection of those well-muscled thighs caused a distinct internal fluttering. Big hands with long fingers and one plain gold signet ring.

She raised her gaze to study his face in profile, lit by the flicker of the new fire. And a very good face it was, too, Decima decided. The strong jaw and nose gave him character, although he was no Adonis. His face was too characterful for any fatuous comparisons with Greek gods, however fashionable that type of look might be. Dark hair, ruffled so she could not tell whether its usual look was modish disorder or simple carelessness, those grey eyes now definitely more greenish in the lamp light. And the most sensual mouth she had ever seen.

Decima shut her own mouth with a snap and looked hastily away. Whatever had come over her? She had never in her life looked at a man's mouth and thought about how *sensual* it was, let alone felt the urge to ponder over the curve of the lips or the flexibility of the smile, the way it might feel on hers. She looked back and as she did she felt a *frisson* of fear run down her spine.

Not fear of the viscount. For some reason Decima didn't feel the slightest bit uncomfortable with this man. Why not? She should be feeling distinctly uneasy—after all, she was effectively trapped with a powerful, virile stranger in a house without any chaperonage.

No, the fear was of herself and the way she was reacting to him.

The strange, determined Decima who had rebelled that morning, decided to make up her own mind, think positively, live life—this Decima was experiencing the most wanton fancies. She *wanted* Lord Weston to kiss her, she wanted to feel the breadth of his shoulders under her palms again, not when she was shivering with cold, but now, when they were warm and safe inside. She wanted to touch his hair, run her fingers down the line of that determined jaw, know what it was like to have that expressive mouth covering hers.

This was dangerous folly, she knew it. However honourable a gentleman, it was asking too much of him to have an available female positively quivering with desire under his very nose.

Still, she thought, struggling to get her fantasies under control again, when he did look at her properly in good light at least there was the comfort that he knew the worst already and she would not have to see surprise be succeeded by pity or contempt in those grey eyes.

He was aware of her height, had carried her weight, and he had probably even noticed the freckles, the disastrous final straw as far as her looks were concerned, so he couldn't be too surprised. He'd had enough warning to manage to keep the reaction off his face at any rate.

There were two basic ways men looked at Decima. Depressed resignation if they were male relatives, or alarm if they were potential suitors lured into meeting her and finding themselves confronted with a befreckled, awkward beanpole. In return, she judged them simply on whether they were polite enough to cover their dismay for however long it took them to tactfully disengage themselves from the encounter.

Except for Sir Henry Freshford, of course. Henry came up to her eye level and quite cheerfully agreed with her that the last thing they wanted to do was get married to each other, not while they were perfectly good friends and could sympathise with each other over the matchmaking wiles of their respective relations. With the exception of Henry, she had felt hideously self-conscious with all unrelated men. Until now.

She came round from her reverie to find herself the subject of an equally thorough, silent, survey.

'Well, Decima? Do I pass muster?'

How long had she been silently studying him, and how long had he been aware of her doing just that? Decima smiled brightly. *Keep it light.* Apparently the words *wanton virgin seeks kisses* were not emblazoned across her forehead, or if they were he was well able to ignore them.

'You do. Provided you can keep that range in.'

'I've put bricks in the oven to heat and the kettle on the hob.'

'Oh, good. Nothing has exploded, then?' She sank down in one of the Windsor chairs and untied the strings of her cloak. 'Pru's gone to sleep. I've lit fires in all the rooms, including yours. I drew the curtains as well.'

One dark eyebrow rose, very slightly. 'You lit the fire in my bedchamber? Thank you, Decima.'

Decima felt herself flush at the fancied criticism. 'I do not see why you should go to a cold bed simply to save me from the shocking sight of a gentleman's chamber, my lord.'

'Indeed not, and with any luck Mrs Chitty had cleared away the scandalous prints, the empty brandy bottles and the more outrageous items of underwear. And my given name is Adam. Will you not use it?'

As he had no doubt hoped, the ridiculous nonsense provoked a smile from her before she could decide to be stuffy about first names. 'Very well, as I imagine we are going to be housekeeping together for several days. Adam.'

It was a good name, and it suited him. Decima let herself relax a little.

'Can you cook?'

'Oh…more or less,' she replied cheerfully, suppressing the ruthful answer that she couldn't boil water and they would almost certainly starve if it was up to her. Perhaps Bates could cook. 'Shall I have a look and see what food there is?' After all, how hard could cookery be?

She had just put her head around the door of the larder when the crash and the yell came. Adam was across the room, the back door banging, before she could wrap her cloak around her and snatch up the largest lamp. In its light she saw the sprawled figure of Bates in the middle of the patch of treacherous, glittering ice that spilt out from the base of the horse trough.

Even from that distance there was no mistaking the implication of the way Bates's lower right leg was twisted at an angle that was totally unnatural. The snow had ceased and everything sparkled with a hard cold.

Ducking back inside, Decima snatched up Pru's cloak and made her way gingerly across the glassy surface. 'Here.' She tucked it around the groom's shoulders. 'Have you hurt anything besides your leg?'

'No, and that's enough of a bl... No, miss, thank you.' He was white to the lips and, as Adam touched his leg, he recoiled convulsively. 'Hell and the devil! Leave it be, damn it!'

'Oh, yes,' Adam said sympathetically. 'I'll just leave you here, nice and comfy, to freeze to death, shall I? And watch your language while Miss Ross is within earshot.'

'Let him swear,' Decima urged, 'I'm sure it will help. We really ought to splint it before you move him,' she added.

'No time. It will hurt, but that's better than frostbite. Up you come, Bates.'

The resulting language as Adam hoisted the man up and carried him across the yard made Decima clap her hands to her ears, then cautiously remove them out of sheer curiosity. The groom did not seem to repeat himself once. She shut the door behind them and regarded Adam. 'Here on the kitchen table? It is warm and the light's good.'

'No, I'll take him upstairs. I don't want to have to move him once it's set. Which room did you light the fire in for him?'

'First on the right.' Decima ran on ahead up the stairs and cast a rapid glance around the room. The bed would have to move. She dragged it out from the wall, her muscles protesting, and shoved it back at right angles so there was access to it on either side. As Adam came in she pulled off the top bedclothes, then lit all the candles. 'There. Now, what do we need?'

'Go downstairs, please, Miss Ross.' Adam was bent over the bed, his gaze rueful as he met the groom's eyes. 'I do not think we are in for a very enjoyable quarter of an hour.'

Decima sighed. *Men.* Even this one, whom she had put down as sensible and non-patronising. She began to think out loud, counting off items on her fingers. 'A sharp knife to cut off the boot and his breeches. A nightshirt so we can get him into that first to save moving him later.' Bates sent her a look compounded of shock and outrage. 'Splints, bandages and laudanum. I'll go and see what I can find.'

When she returned Adam had got the groom out of his upper clothes and into his nightshirt, draped modestly to preserve everyone's blushes. She handed him the knife and began to pour laudanum into a glass. 'Miss Chitty has an admirable stillroom, thank goodness. Here, Bates, drink this, it will help. Do you think some brandy as well, my lord? I've brought a bottle.'

The groom swigged back the drug and Adam shrugged. 'Give him a stiff tot, it can't do any harm; he has a head like teak.'

'I've got the best straight kindling wood I could find for splints and I've torn up a sheet that was in the mending basket.'

'Thank you, Miss Ross, you are most resourceful.' Adam pulled off the boot from the uninjured leg, then fell to studying the other thoughtfully. 'Now go away, please.'

Decima turned to the door. She did not want to stay and see Bates suffering. She certainly did not want to see whatever removing that boot revealed and what would happen next. But it felt like cowardice to go meekly off downstairs like a good little woman when she could be helping.

She got as far as the landing before the sobbing intake of breath drove her back into the room and onto her knees next to the bed. 'Shove off, miss,' Bates snapped.

'You swear as much as you like,' she said encouragingly, hoping she wasn't as green in the face as he was. 'Just hold on to my hands and it will soon be over. And, no, my lord,' she said as Adam began to speak. 'I am not going to *shove off* downstairs, whatever either of you says.'

'Have you ever met a woman who wasn't as stubborn as a mule, Bates?' Adam remarked conversationally.

'Can't say as I have, my lord.'

'I have to say I am shocked at your language, Miss Ross: you must be mixing with the most uncouth men. Right, Bates, that's the boot. Now for the breeches. Are the horses all right, or am I going to have to drag over there after I've patched you up and sort them out?'

Decima half-turned indignantly, recalled Bates's state of undress and turned back in time to see him produce a twisted grin. 'They're all right and tight and rugged up, my lord.' Adam was talking to him to keep his mind off what was happening, she realised.

'Gig gone? Bates? Pay attention.' The groom, whose eyes had begun to roll up in his head, snapped back to consciousness.

'Yes. Gig's gone and the riding horse. Looks as though the lot of them went off for marketing and couldn't get— bloody hell!'

'Sorry. I needed to check if there's just the one break. Hmm. Skin isn't pierced at any rate. I'll set it now, there's no point in hanging around and letting the swelling get worse. You may faint any time you see fit, Bates.'

'Thank you. My lord.' Bates sounded anything but grateful. Decima shifted her position so that she blocked off as much of his line of vision as she could and smiled encouragingly. There was a minute of major unpleasantness while Bates went even whiter and she thought her fingers were going to be crushed in his calloused grip. Adam swore softly and continuously under his breath. Then Bates gasped and fell back, unconscious.

'He's fainted.' She was *not* going to be sick.

'Good. Look, I need another pair of hands. Can you grip his leg just above the knee and hang on while I pull to get the bones aligned?'

Don't think about it. Just do it. If it was a horse you'd do it. She fixed her eyes on the top of Adam's bent head, held on and prayed that Bates would stay oblivious.

'All right. You can let go now. Decima? Let go.'

'Oh. Of course.' She forced her fingers open and sat back on her heels. 'The splints and the bandages are…' Decima swallowed and got up. 'I'll go and get the hot bricks.'

She managed to get to the kitchen simply by talking to herself all the way down the stairs. 'Hot bricks for Bates and Pru. Might as well do all the beds while I'm at it. I must find something to wrap them in. Check the kettle, see the fire is all right in the range. We'll need something to keep the bed-clothes off that leg.'

The admirable Mrs Chitty kept a stack of neatly hemmed flannel squares in the stillroom. Decima wrapped four bricks and made her way unsteadily upstairs to meet Adam on the landing, a bolster under each arm. 'I can't find a stool the right size, but these should do to keep the weight off. You've got the bricks? Admirable woman. Here, give me one and you go and see to your maid.'

Pru was sleeping soundly and even Decima's touch on her hot forehead and the insertion of the brick at the foot of the bed did not rouse her. Decima hoped she would stay asleep until morning, but rather feared she would not. This could be a long night, and she only wished she did not feel quite so queasy.

She put a brick in her own bed, then opened Adam's door to tuck the remaining one between his sheets. From Bates's room came a gasp of anguish, cut off by the sound of Adam's voice. It was too much; to hear someone in so much pain clutched sickeningly at the pit of her stomach. Decima doubled up, retching feebly and unproductively over the lovely porcelain basin on the washstand.

'Decima? Where are you? Oh, my poor girl. Here, come and sit down and I'll fetch you something to drink.'

She clutched at the glass blindly and gulped, then choked as the fiery spirit burned down her throat. 'That's brandy!'

Chapter Four

'Brandy will do you good. Drink it all down.' It would probably make her drunk as a lord, given that none of them had eaten since breakfast, but anything was better than that pinched look around her mouth and those wide, shocked eyes. Adam took the glass from Decima's shaking hand and set it on the bedside stand. 'You were a heroine. I could not have managed without you.'

'It was just when I could feel the bone move—' She broke off and passed a hand over her face. 'I am better now. How is he?'

'He will be fine. I got another shot of laudanum down him and he went out like a snuffed candle. If I can keep him unconscious all night, it won't be so bad in the morning.'

'How do you know?' She looked at him with curiosity as she asked and he saw with concern the greenish tint of her skin. Otherwise it was very nice skin: smooth and pale and covered with those delicious freckles as though someone had dusted fine bran over her nose and cheeks. How long would it take to kiss each one? It would be like kissing the Milky Way. He found himself wondering if they appeared anywhere else on her body.

'I had the same bone break when I fell out of a tree when I was fifteen. I watched the doctor, while I wasn't yelling my head off, that is.'

Decima started to get up, then sat down again on the bed with a thump, eyes closed. 'My, I am dizzy. It must be the shock of it, I suppose.'

Adam smiled. She had had enough spirits on an empty stomach to knock her out for an hour or two. 'That'll be it. Now if you just lie back and close your eyes, you will feel better in a moment.' He eased her back onto the pillows, murmuring soothingly. With a sleepy mutter Decima curled up in the folds of the soft coverlet. 'There you are, just rest.' She was asleep.

Adam stood looking down at her, visited by a strange feeling of tenderness. She was hardly a fragile little bloom, but there was something very vulnerable about her, despite her height and age. Something vulnerable, yet she had plenty of courage to fight, too. He imagined any other single lady of his acquaintance undergoing what Decima Ross had that day without succumbing to hysterics, and failed. What she was doing unmarried he couldn't imagine. Her height was against her, of course, but with those unusual looks and lively mind, there must be scores of tall gentlemen who would have snapped her up.

Possibly there was a large and anxious fiancé somewhere who might be expected to call out Viscount Weston when he learned what had transpired. Not that anything would, of course, but just being alone with him was scandal enough. He was going to have to give some thought to that.

Meanwhile, what to do with a sleeping Miss Ross who was wiffling, gently, as she slumbered? She was not going to be very comfortable when she awoke to find she had slept in her shoes, let alone with her stays laced. The thought brought with it the recollection of her body as it had slipped through his hands to the ground in the yard.

With a grimace for his own over-active imagination, Adam flipped the other side of the coverlet over her and walked away.

He checked upstairs twice more as the evening wore on. The fires needed keeping in; he set water by the bedsides of the maid and Bates, both thankfully still unconscious, and made himself stay away from Decima. She did not need to wake up to find herself in a man's bed with the man himself in the room: that *would* be conducive of hysterics.

At one point he cut a wedge of cheese from a wheel of Stilton in the larder and fished some of Mrs Chitty's pickles out of the jar to go with it, but by seven o'clock Adam was thinking that he was going to have to forage for food or starve.

Then the kitchen door creaked and Decima was standing on the threshold, her face flushed with sleep, a shawl round her shoulders and her hair in tousled disarray. It just made him want to tousle it some more. Adam got hastily to his feet, then came to the conclusion that staying sitting with his legs carefully crossed would have been a better decision.

'I've been asleep,' she said accusingly. 'In your bed. Charlton would be outraged.'

'I imagine Charlton would be even more outraged if I had carried you off and put you in your bed. Do you think he will call me out?'

That provoked a deep chuckle as she came in, pulling her shawl snugly around her shoulders. 'What a wonderful image that conjures up. Charlton does not have the figure for duelling, let alone the temperament. Bates and Pru are still asleep and I am *starving*.'

'So am I. Now, you said you could cook, more or less.'

'I exaggerated…no, I lied.' Decima flushed and regarded her toes. 'I might as well be truthful about it. I haven't the first clue. Shall we look in the larder and see what there is?'

The meal they spread on the kitchen table—Decima

having put her head around the dining-room door and pronounced it fit only to act as an icehouse—owed nothing to
any culinary skill whatsoever.

Cold mutton, cheese, the heel of a loaf, butter and plum
cake were washed down with ale, or, in Decima's case, with
water. Adam could not recall enjoying a meal more.

For a start it was a pleasure to eat with a woman who showed
a hearty appetite and didn't starve herself and pick at her food
in an effort to appear ladylike. Then, Decima did not stand on
ceremony either: she forgot to take her elbows off the table
when they were in the middle of an argument about the Prince
Regent's taste in architecture, she waved her knife in the air to
make her point when she lectured him on horse breeding, and
she completely forgot herself and doubled up laughing when
he recounted a particularly wicked story about two of the
Patronesses of Almack's and the Duke of Wellington.

'No! They didn't? Not *both* of them,' she gasped, emerging
from her fit of the giggles, pink and glowing.

'I should not have told you that,' Adam confessed ruefully.
The trouble was, she seemed so at ease with him, and had
such an individual character, that it was like talking to one of
the dashing young matrons he was used to in London society.
Only Decima had a delicious innocence that none of those so-
phisticated ladies had shown for many a year.

'No, I don't expect you should,' she agreed with a twinkle.
'But I am glad you did. They were so beastly to me when I
came out, it is wonderful to be able to imagine them in such
an embarrassing fix.'

'Why were they beastly?' It was hard to imagine anyone
being unkind to Decima. 'Did you break one of those tedious
rules and waltz before you'd been approved or something
equally heinous?'

'Waltz?' She stared at him as if he was mad. 'Who on earth
would ask a girl five foot ten inches tall to waltz with them?'

'I would,' he replied simply. 'Do you mean you cannot waltz?'

'I can, I just never have for real. Charlton insisted I learn. *Poor* Signor Mazzetti. He did his best, but he came up to…' she coloured and waved a hand vaguely in the direction of her bosom '…up to there and I don't think he knew quite where to look. And I trod on his feet a lot because I was embarrassed. So it was a good thing I was never asked.'

'Well, I come to considerably higher up, I know exactly where to look and my feet are large enough for you to tread all over with impunity.' Adam found himself pushing back his plate and getting to his feet. *I must be mad.* 'Shall we?'

'What? Here?' She thought he was mad, too. 'There is no music and, besides, who's going to do the washing up?'

'Yes, here. I'll hum and I expect we will both do the washing up, eventually. Now then, this side of the table, I think, we don't want your skirts flying into the fire.'

Those wonderful grey eyes were wide and she was staring at him with a mixture of horror and mischief. Adam liked the mischief. 'Flying?'

'I am a very vigorous waltzer, Miss Ross. May I have this dance?'

There was that rich chuckle again. Decima got to her feet and made a neat curtsy. 'Thank you, my lord, although I fear I have not been approved by the Patronesses.'

Adam took her in his arms. *Oh, yes.* 'To hell with the Patronesses. Now. One, two, three…'

He was right: it was nothing like dancing with Signor Mazzetti at all And she *could* waltz, despite her sensible winter shoes and her heavy skirts, whirling between kitchen table and butter churn, dresser and flour bin, laughing, lending her voice to Adam's tuneful, humming dance rhythm, breathless, exhilarated, round and round in the circle of his arms until she stumbled and found herself caught and held safely, close against his chest.

'Oh, dear.' Her breath was coming in pants; part effort, part laughter, part a strange, fizzing excitement. 'That brandy—I must be tipsy.'

'You are dizzy. Rest a little.' Adam's eyes were on her, their colour that strange, unsettling silver grey that became green as they caught the candle flare. 'Just stand a moment.' He did not release her, one hand quite still at her waist, the other one lowering her own hand until it was at waist height.

Adam's breath was coming short, too—they must have been dancing more vigorously than she had thought. Decima felt herself leaning into him, towards that intent gaze, towards that sensuous mouth that so fascinated her.

Her lips parted instinctively. Why…what was she feeling? So breathless, so hot, so sensitised as though someone was drawing velvet over her bare skin. She should never have drunk that brandy; it was no wonder unmarried girls were forbidden spirits. 'I think…'

'Don't think.' His mouth was so close now, all she had to do was stand on tiptoe, just a little, lean just a little, raise her face. Her eyes closed. This was going to happen. Decima could not think any further forward than the next ten seconds. There was nothing beyond that. Nothing.

Warm breath feathering her lips. The scent of him, remembered from that cold ride: citrus, leather and now rather more of the exciting, disturbing muskiness of warm man. 'Decima.' The word was spoken so close to her lips that she felt, rather than heard, it.

'Mmm?'

The sound of a door banging upstairs. A faint voice. 'Miss Dessy?' Decima blinked, staggered backwards and caught a chair back in both groping hands.

'Pru. She must have woken up. I will just—I'll just go and see…' She fled.

Pru was standing unsteadily in the open doorway, blinking in the candlelight of the torchère that Adam had left on a table at the head of the stairs. Decima snatched it up and urged the maid back into the bedchamber. 'Get back into bed, Pru, you'll get chilled out here.'

'I need the privy, Miss Decima, and I can't find a chamberpot.'

That at least was one eminently practical problem to which she had an answer. 'There is a real indoor water closet, just along here at the end of this side corridor.'

The pair of them, both unsteady on their feet for very different reasons, gazed at this modern luxury, then Pru tottered inside and closed the door, leaving Decima with no excuse to think of anything but her behaviour in the kitchen. The exhilaration of the dance still fizzed in her veins but under it was a deep ache of unsatisfied longing. Adam had almost kissed her. She had wanted him to kiss her and her body was punishing her now for being left unsatisfied.

No one had ever kissed Decima other than family members. *How does my body know what it is missing?* she thought distractedly, passing her hands up and down her arms to try and rub away that strange shivery feeling. Her breasts felt heavier, too, her stays tighter, and lower down there was a hot, molten sensation that was very disturbing indeed.

How on earth am I going to face him again? He must think me some love-starved old maid desperate for caresses. A nagging little voice, the voice that she had thought she had left behind with Charlton and would form no part of her new, resolute self, hissed, *And so you are. A desperate virgin, throwing yourself at a handsome man.*

The rattle of the metal mechanism and the gush of water provided a fitting counterpoint to this unpleasant truth.

Decima forced herself to concentrate on the matter at hand; at least Pru could not be feeling too poorly if she could work out how to flush the unfamiliar closet.

The maid emerged and blinked confusedly up at Decima. 'Where are we, Miss Dessy? This isn't the Sun, is it?'

Oh, Lord! Decima made her voice as matter of fact as possible. 'No, Pru. This is Lord Weston's house. Don't you recall he rescued us from the snow?' She urged the unsteady figure back to her room.

'Snow? I don't remember any snow, Miss Dessy. Or any lord. Oh, my head…'

Decima smoothed the rumpled sheets, plumped up the pillows and tucked the maid back into bed. 'We are snowbound, Pru, and you are not at all well, but we're quite safe here.' She flinched inwardly at the lie. Pru might be safe, but her mistress was within an ame's ace of serious danger, mostly from herself. 'Now try and drink some water.' She really needed one of the drinks Decima could remember Cook producing during childhood illnesses. Barley water? Could that be one? 'Are you hungry?' That produced a grimace of rejection. 'How about a hot drink?'

'No, Miss Decima, I just want to sleep.'

The bed seemed warm enough now and the room was snug with the fire flickering behind its screen. There was probably something she should be doing, but goodness knew what. Biting her lip, Decima left the door ajar and went to look at Bates. He was sleeping soundly, snoring his head off, no doubt happily unconscious on laudanum and brandy. She made up his fire, then checked the fires in her room and Adam's before accepting that she was putting off the evil moment when she must go back downstairs.

Outside the kitchen door Decima stood breathing deeply, fighting to compose her face. She realised that her shoulders were hunching into the all-too-familiar defensive slouch that she used to use in a vain attempt to hide her height. It seemed that living life to the full meant taking responsibility for your own mistakes as well. *Come on, Decima.* She pulled back her shoulders and swept into the kitchen.

There was no sign of Adam but then she heard sounds from the scullery and peeped round the door, her embarrassment disappearing in a gurgle of laughter. His lordship was swathed in a vast white apron and had his hands in a bowl of hot water in which he was vigorously scrubbing a plate. 'What *are* you doing?'

'The washing up. The range had heated the water up very efficiently so I thought I would get it out of the way.'

'I am most impressed,' Decima admitted.

Adam regarded her seriously. 'This soda is vicious stuff. The maids' hands must get raw.'

'There should be some lanolin somewhere. That's what our cook uses.' Decima began to hunt. 'Look, here by the jar of soda crystals. Rinse your hands in clean water, dry them and rub some in.'

Adam fished out the last plate and did as she suggested, wrinkling his nose at the lanolin. 'It smells of sheep.'

'Now why haven't the apothecaries thought of that?' Decima mused, finding a cloth and beginning to dry the plates. 'Scented hand cream for the gentleman who does his own dishes. They could sell it with your crest on the jars—"Lord Weston's Special Washing-Up Hand Balm: By appointment. Every kitchen maid can have hands as soft as a viscount's."'

'Minx,' he observed appreciatively. She could feel his gaze on her as she stacked away the plates, then began to hunt along the shelves, but there was nothing of that sensual heat in his gaze now and she felt quite comfortable. She must have imagined that they had stood so close, imagined that his lips had almost been on hers. 'What are you looking for?'

'Something to feed Pru when she wakes up again. I must

tempt her appetite, she is feeling very poorly. And we'll need to feed Bates up; I am sure that helps knit bones. And then we will need breakfast, and meals tomorrow. Oh, yes, and I need barley water for Pru as well.'

'Try the stillroom,' he suggested. 'That's where I found the laudanum.'

Half an hour later there was a pile of notebooks at one end of the kitchen table and a row of small bottles at the other. Decima regarded them gratefully. 'Thank goodness for Mrs Chitty. There is cough syrup there, and a headache powder and lavender water and that red notebook is full of cures and recipes for medicines.'

Adam was thumbing through it. 'Here is the receipt for barley water. You'll need to put the barley into water to steep overnight.' He continued to read while Decima rummaged in the storage bins, emerging triumphant with a scoop full of barley and a bowl to soak it in. 'Warm water. Then in the morning, add lemon juice and sugar.'

'No lemons, but there is apple juice.' She came and leaned on the table next to him, reading over his shoulder. 'Stewed Quaker—what's that?'

'A sovereign remedy for colds, apparently. Burnt rum and butter. I must try it.'

'I think we will have to try baking before anything else,' Decima said ruefully, reaching over to pick up one of the cookery notebooks. 'There is one loaf left. And we cannot survive on cold meat for much longer, either.'

Adam twisted half-round in his chair to grin at her. 'I don't think we are going to be bored, Miss Ross.' Her heart gave a little flip at his nearness, but he looked away and began to turn the cookery book pages. 'To boil a turkey with oyster sauce—all we need is a score of oysters, a loaf and a lemon for this recipe. We have the loaf.'

'But no turkey or oysters,' Decima pointed out practically, squashing this flight of fancy. 'I just hope that Mrs Chitty does not think making bread too basic to put in her notebooks. Oh, my!' She broke off as a jaw-cracking yawn seized her. 'I must go to bed.'

Adam filled hot water cans and carried them up while Decima lit the way. 'I could make a reasonable hand at being a footman, don't you think?' He grounded one can on her washstand and paused by the door as she came in. 'Good night, Decima.' The kiss he dropped on her forehead was so swift that she was still blinking in shock as the bedchamber door closed behind him.

'Goodnight, Adam,' she said blankly to the expressionless panels of the door. That was not quite the kiss she had been fantasising about. With a little smile at her own foolishness, Decima turned back her bedcovers and began to undress.

Chapter Five

Decima managed two hours of sleep before sounds from the adjoining bedroom dragged her back to consciousness. She had expected it, leaving the interconnecting door wide open so she could hear Pru, but even so it seemed a bottomless pit that she had to haul herself out of before her eyes opened.

'I'm coming!' But Pru was not calling to her, simply talking loudly in her fever. Her forehead was burning hot as she tossed and turned, moaning and coughing. Decima worried that the fact she did not wake herself up meant her fever was very serious, but she had nothing to judge it against.

All she could do was sit by the bed, sponging Pru's burning face with cold water and talking soothingly to her. She vaguely recalled hearing that it was serious if the patient was not sweating, but as the memory contained nothing about how one could induce this, it left her anxious but no further forward.

Trying to support Pru's head in an attempt to get her to drink was fruitless, but eventually Decima hit on the idea of dipping a clean handkerchief in the water, then trickling it between the maid's parched lips. That seemed to help; Pru even sucked feebly at the moisture and, after several re-dippings, became quieter and calmer.

Out on the landing Decima could hear the sound of soft footsteps and the murmur of voices. His lordship was up and occupied with Bates. She hoped that did not mean the poor man was in too much pain, but it was reassuring to know that others were awake in the cold, still house.

She sat gazing into the fire, suddenly struck by how very lucky she was that Adam Grantham was the sort of man he was. An out-and-out rake, bent on seduction or worse, was one danger, of course, but she had never been in any real fear of that since the first moment she'd met those steady grey eyes with their intelligence and humour.

But she could never have hoped for a gentleman—a *nobleman*—who coped with unclouded good humour with housekeeping and sick nursing, or who could so cheerfully disregard his own comfort and convenience. Charlton might, if absolutely desperate, light a fire or scavenge in the larder for a snack for himself, but as for him happily consuming a makeshift meal or washing up afterwards, that was beyond her powers of imagination.

When the clock struck three the water was almost gone and the fire burned very low. Outside the door, all seemed quiet again. Decima stretched stiffly, went to make up the fire, then picked up the water jug. Best to refill it now while Pru was relatively quiet.

Opposite, Bates's door was open, the branch of candles within throwing strong bars of light across the shadowy passageway. She peeped in, but the groom was lying quietly, flat on his back, eyes closed. Of Adam there was no sign. Decima tiptoed to the landing and froze at the sound of approaching footsteps, then Adam appeared from what she was beginning to think of as the Privy Corridor, carrying an object discreetly shrouded in a towel.

He smiled at the sight of her, his teeth white in the half-light. 'Good morning, Decima.' She averted her gaze from the disguised chamberpot, instead taking in the full glory of the quite splendid brocade dressing gown Adam was wearing. It must be Oriental silk, she realised; dramatic black dragons writhed across a background of scarlet, jets of gold issuing from their mouths. It was luxurious, exotic and masculine in the extreme.

'How magnificent!'

'Why, thank you, Miss Ross.' Adam's smile was quite blatantly flirtatious.

'I meant your dressing gown,' Decima retorted repressively, managing not to stare at his bare feet. Why the sight of a man's bare feet should be quite so disturbing she could not imagine. And in any case, they'd be very cold and in bed that would be— She caught herself in this utterly improper thought and dropped her eyes, only to realise with horror that she had not stopped to put on her dressing gown and the only thing between her and the viscount's interested gaze was a thin nightgown.

'How magnificent,' he echoed, his voice an appreciative purr. 'You know, under normal circumstances the bedroom corridors of a country house at night would be busy with the guests swapping rooms on some amorous errand or another and here we are, each laden with an article of domestic chinaware, with nothing on our minds but sickroom nursing.'

From the glint in his eyes his mind was on almost anything *but* the sickroom. Decima felt her colour rising and realised in horror that her nipples were peaking under the thin cotton. It must be the cold, nothing else would make them react like that, but she was sure Adam had noticed.

'I must get some more water,' she squeaked, scuttling downstairs with more haste than dignity.

'Could you put the kettle on?' he called as she reached the hall. 'I'll come down for it in a minute.'

'All right,' she called back.

She filled her jug, dealt with the kettle, and stood for a moment, bathing in the heat from the range. Her nipples were still showing no sign of calming down, however warm she got. It was baffling.

Upstairs there was, thankfully, no sign of Adam. She pulled on her dressing gown, although it felt poor protection, for it was a thin cotton garment she had selected specifically to take up as little room as possible in her valise.

Pru sucked thirstily at the freshly wetted handkerchief and this time cooperated when Decima pressed a cup to her lips. Encouraged, she stirred a little of the headache powder into the water, then, when Pru would take no more, settled down to soothe her brow with lavender water.

Behind her the door opened and, before she could turn, the soft, heavy mass of a silk brocade dressing gown settled gently around her shoulders.

'What...?'

'Shh.' It was Adam, leaning over to set a cup of tea on the bedside table. 'I have two, use this one. Look, if you just slip your arms into the sleeves, I am sure we can roll them up.'

He showed every sign of helping her do it, so Decima got to her feet and shrugged on the garment, its heavy amber silk decorated in a dizzying pattern of orchids and lilies in ivory, gold and browns. 'It is lovely,' she breathed. The robe pooled around her feet and her hands vanished into the deep sleeves.

'Let me.' Adam's hands were reassuringly brisk as he folded back the sleeves until her hands appeared again. 'There. Now, if we just do up the sash...Where has that vanished to?' And then things were not so reassuring after all. His hands went round her waist, searching for the dangling sash ends, and Decima was suddenly close against his chest, silk-covered breasts brushing against him in a manner that sent quivers of awareness through her body. And this time she was left in no doubt at all what was making her nipples hard.

'I'll do it!' She snatched the ends from his hands and fumbled them into a bow. 'Thank you!' Beside her Pru stirred uneasily and Decima turned to her, thankful for the excuse. Adam was suddenly too close, too big, too warm and far too male, and she wanted to be left alone to come to terms with all the disturbing new reactions her body was producing in response to him.

She soothed the invalid's forehead with lavender water, glancing back over her shoulder with an uneasy smile that she hoped combined gratitude with dismissal. 'I should not have been talking,' she whispered, 'I think it disturbs her.'

Adam merely smiled, a glint in his grey eyes that told her he knew that it was not Pru who was disturbed by his presence. Decima looked away and after a moment the door shut softly behind him.

'Oh dear, Pru,' she murmured, settling down again by the bedside. 'This experiencing life is all very well, but I wish I knew what I was going to feel next. And what to do about it.' She snuggled into the soft warmth of the dressing gown, took Pru's hot, dry hand in hers and closed her eyes.

As the clock struck six Adam blinked and straightened up in the chair, wincing as his cramped muscles protested. Bates had finally succumbed to exhaustion and a quantity of brandy guaranteed to give him a headache that would take his mind off his broken leg in the morning. Now he was fast asleep, the air resounding with his snores.

Adam groped for the candle and made his way to the still-glowing fire to rekindle it, then reached for the cup of tea that had gone cold and gulped it down with a baleful glare at the clock. Was it worth going back to his own bed and snatching another hour's sleep?

There were four horses to tend to, logs and coal to bring in, fires to make up and food to be found on top of whatever assistance Bates was going to need. He wrestled with unfamiliar priorities and decided on fuel first, then stables. And at some point during the morning, he promised himself, a hot bath. A deep hot bath. With fine milled soap. And the back brush. And a pile of Turkey towels that had been warming in front of the fire.

And who, he asked himself, through a jaw-cracking yawn, *is going to lug up the cans of water, find the towels, empty the bathwater…?* How much was he paying his staff? Not enough, obviously, if his experiences of domestic duties so far were anything to go by. And Mrs Chitty deserved a salary at least equivalent to that of a circuit-court judge.

He stretched, warming himself up with the thought of that imagined bath and Decima scrubbing his back, rasping the bristles across his shoulders in a mass of foam, running her— *Stop it.* He was certainly awake now. What was the matter with him? Adam grinned ruefully. It was no mystery what ailed him, only why, when it was but a few days since he had left the bed of his delightful and highly skilled mistress, that he should be lusting after a leggy spinster.

He padded across the landing and applied an ear to the door panels. Silence. He eased the door open and found Decima sleeping uncomfortably in the chair, her upper body slumped onto the bed beside Pru. He edged round and laid the back of his hand on the maid's forehead. It was warm but damp, and she was sleeping heavily with none of the restlessness of the night. The fever had broken.

He stood for a long moment, staring down at Decima, surprised by the sudden wave of protectiveness that swept over him in place of the erotic thoughts that had been occupying his mind. She should have looked ridiculous, cramped and hunched, her face pressed against the counterpane, one tendril of hair straggling across her face where it blew slightly with every breath, her face shiny with sleep. Instead she looked adorable.

Cautiously, he bent and straightened her up, then scooped her into his arms and walked through to her bedchamber. The bedclothes were turned back from when she had got up to Pru and he laid Decima down into the dent her body had left. He straightened the dressing gown over her legs, eased off her kid slippers and drew the bedclothes back over her body. She did not stir.

Adam found that he was breathing as though he had carried her for a mile uphill and that he was uncomfortably hard. Damn it! One did not trifle with virgins, one did not take advantage of gentlewomen seeking sanctuary under your roof and one certainly did not stand there in a lady's bedchamber, recalling with intense erotic detail the sensation of her long, strong legs flexing and balancing on your thighs as you rode with her through the snow. Not if one hoped for any relief at all from mental and physical torment.

It wasn't even as though she had the slightest idea about flirtation, he thought. She had been taken utterly unaware when their impromptu waltz almost ended in a kiss and on the landing during the night she had been adorably, and very innocently, flustered by his teasing.

What on earth was wrong with the men she had met? Why wasn't she married? It was obvious that she had this ridiculous self-consciousness about her height, but why? He had never come across a woman as tall as she, but society was full of tall gentlemen who would be as entranced as he was by her grace and beauty and original charm.

Brooding, Adam pulled himself away from her bedside and went to make up the fire, placing pieces of wood as delicately as though he were playing spillikins. No money, perhaps? A complete lack of dowry would be an impediment to the most handsome woman, but her style of dress, the quality of her hired coach and the presence of two postilions rebutted that theory.

With a lingering glance at the figure in the bed, Adam went

to make up the other fires, then washed with haste in the cold water in his bedroom, dressed and went downstairs to face the waiting chores.

Decima woke slowly, more than a little inclined to snuggle back down into the warmth of the soft bed, into the caress of the wonderful silk sheets. *Silk sheets?* Her eyes opened with a snap. No, not silk sheets, her feet were tangled in the weighty luxury of an Oriental dressing gown.

'How on earth did I get back to bed?' Decima sat up and regarded the room in the clear, chilly morning light. The blankets were tucked in, which she could never have managed for herself, her slippers were neatly together in front of the fire and the fire itself was crackling cheerfully behind the screen. 'Oh, heavens. He put me to bed.'

Decima gulped and threw back the covers. She was still decently tied up in the dressing gown, its skirts and those of her night rail gathered modestly around her calves. But that was not reassuring; Decima's imagination produced a vivid mental picture of Adam's tall figure bending over the bed, smoothing the clothing down, his fingers brushing against her ankles.

That strange, hot, molten feeling inside her came back. She felt restless. Tense. Surely she couldn't be coming down with Pru's fever?

Lord! Pru. She should not be idling in bed, wrestling with an utterly inappropriate and unmaidenly attraction to Adam Grantham, she should be nursing her poor maid. Decima scrambled out of bed and hurried to check on her.

'Pru? Are you awake?'

'Mmm? Miss Dessy? Ooh, my head.' Anxiously Decima touched her forehead, deeply relieved to find it hot but damp. The confused expression of the night before had gone.

'Lie still, Pru, you've got a nasty fever. Would you like a cup of tea?'

'Yes, please, Miss Dessy.' She struggled to sit and Decima helped her up against the pillows. 'But you shouldn't be waiting on me, where's the maid?'

'There are no staff here, Pru. Here, let me put this shawl around your shoulders. We're snowed in with Lord Weston and his groom, who has broken his leg.' Pru blinked in surprise, but seemed to be understanding what she was being told. 'I'll find you some breakfast and then you can have a nice wash and a fresh nightgown.'

Downstairs there was no sign of Adam, but a glance across the yard showed the stable door open and a wheelbarrow full of soiled straw steamed in the cold air. Inside, the range was glowing and beside the door was a stack of damp logs.

Twenty minutes later she climbed the stairs with a tray, pleased with her efforts. She had found milk, still fresh-tasting thanks to the cold, and had warmed it on the fire, adding torn-up bread, sugar and a little cinnamon. Surely Pru's poor throat could manage that?

Pru spooned it down eagerly and drank the tea, as well. Decima began to feel quite encouraged, but, after a slow trip along the landing to the water closet, the maid suddenly seemed to fail again, and Decima had to virtually lift her into bed. She was asleep before she could finish tucking her in.

It was only to be expected, she told herself, and the more sleep she got the better; a wash could wait. Bates was still snoring away, so she went back to her room, pulled on her heavy shoes, wrapped a thick shawl around her shoulders and ran downstairs. Time to face his lordship again.

Adam dragged a shirtsleeve over his sweating brow and started grooming the second carriage horse. He had mucked out the four stalls, fed and watered the animals and was now working his way along the line, grooming and checking for any injury sustained in the journey through the snow. Bates would have checked yesterday evening, but a strain might have made itself felt overnight.

His greatcoat hung on a bridle peg with the coat he'd discarded after five minutes and the waistcoat he'd stripped off after that. The hard physical work felt good. In the crisp air the heat and the honest smell of the horses were invigorating and the practical tasks kept his mind off concerns about what to do with an unchaperoned lady he wanted to take to his bed, and the singular lack of anyone to cook for them.

The door creaked behind him and a welcome pungent smell wreathed around his nostrils. 'Coffee?' Decima enquired, coming in to set a sturdy earthenware mug on the edge of the manger. 'I have left it black, with sugar, but I can bring some more if that is not right.'

Adam ducked under the horse's neck to reach the mug, realising as he did so that he was avoiding looking at Decima or getting too close to her. 'Just right, thank you. Good morning. Did you sleep well?'

'Yes, I did. Thank you for putting me to bed.' No beating about the bush then! She sounded quite composed, if a trifle cool.

'You looked uncomfortable. I thought you would sleep better and your maid seemed quiet.'

'She managed some bread and milk this morning, although she is as weak as a kitten.' Decima's voice seemed to be coming from further away. Adam ducked back under the grey's neck and found her gone. 'Good morning, beautiful! Yes, you are a handsome fellow now I can see you properly. And how did you know I've got sugar in my pocket, might I ask?'

She was in Fox's stall. With a muffled oath Adam followed her, expecting to find her cornered by the stallion's snapping teeth. Instead she was feeding him titbits with one hand and scratching him gently behind one ear with the other. The great horse had an expression of sleepy contentment, although at Adam's arrival he rolled an eye in his direction.

'You might well look bashful, you old fraud,' Adam scolded. 'He has the most shocking reputation for biting, but just look at him,' he added to Decima.

'That's enough,' she said firmly, dusting off her palms. 'You'll get fat. He is a pussy cat really, it just needs confidence. He does not bite *you*, I imagine.'

'No.' Adam regarded her warily. She was wearing a plain brown dress with a large wool shawl wrapped over her shoulders, then crossed to tie behind her waist. Her hair was pulled back by a ribbon into a long tail down her back and her hands were ungloved. Her nose was pink with the cold, tendrils of hair were escaping to curl around her cheeks and Adam thought she looked utterly enchanting. Why? Her dress was utilitarian, her coiffure non-existent, she wasn't jewelled or powdered or perfumed. In fact, with smudges of tiredness under her eyes and Fox's affectionate slobber on her sleeve, she looked completely unladylike. And original. And beddable.

'What is wrong?' She was regarding him with anxious eyes. 'You are frowning so.'

'I am sorry. Fox has slobbered all over your sleeve.' Adam gulped hot coffee. 'Don't stay out here, you will get cold.'

'Not if I do some work.' She reached up, took the dandy brush and curry comb off the beam above the manger and slapped Fox on the shoulder. 'Get over now.'

'You cannot groom my horses!'

'Why ever not? Papa always insisted I groomed mine at least once a week, otherwise you do not know all about them, however good your grooms are. I still do it.' She was passing the brush over Fox's neck in long, hard sweeps, dragging it across the teeth of the curry comb after each stroke. Adam watched, mesmerised. She was strong; those were no mere pats with the brush, but good firm strokes, massaging the skin and muscles beneath it. With her height she had all the reach she needed, except to brush Fox's poll, and there she simply grabbed his forelock and pulled until the big horse obediently lowered his head for her.

Strong, confident, tall—she should have seemed unfeminine, but instead Adam thought her like some goddess, or an Amazon, magnificently female with her long limbs and her mane of hair.

'His legs are cool.' She looked up from her bent position, running her hands down Fox's legs. 'He doesn't seem to have strained anything yesterday.'

'Good.' Adam did not seem to be able to find anything else to say. All the words that occurred to him were either banal or would get his face slapped. Instead, he leaned on the half-door and watched.

'Have you finished the others? Only I want my breakfast.' It was not a complaint, he realised, just a cheerful observation. Decima would quite obviously work away until the horses were looked after, however hungry she was.

'No, a horse and a half left to go.' He strode back to finish the grey and found the hoof pick, praying that by some miracle Mrs Chitty would appear out of the snow-drifts before he found something else about Decima to attract him.

'I will race you,' she called. 'What is your other hunter called?'

'Ajax.'

'First one to Ajax's tail gets the egg, then.'

'Which egg?'

'The one and only hen's egg left in the larder!'

Laughing, Adam pressed on. They met at the door into Ajax's stall, Decima diving in first to seize the brushes so he was forced to rummage for those in the stall next door.

'Cheat,' he grumbled. 'Look, you've left me with all of his mane.'

'I will do his face.' She sounded breathless now, half with effort, half with laughter at this ridiculous race. 'Loser gets the tail.'

'Where's the leather?'

'What leather?' For a moment he was deceived, but only for a moment. He was getting to know Decima.

'The one you are hiding.' He ducked right under the hunter's belly, surprising her so that she jumped back with a squeak, but not before he saw the yellow chamois leather flick behind her. 'Come on, you've finished with it.'

'Find your own.' She was laughing at him, her generous mouth wide to show even white teeth.

'No, you've got what I want,' and he lunged for it.

Decima found herself pressed against Ajax's shoulder, the solid bulk of the horse unyielding at her back. Adam was right in front of her, a laughing challenge in his eyes. 'Come on, hand it over.'

His shirt was open at the neck, showing a tantalising glimpse of dark hair, the sleeves were rolled up, exposing strong forearms with elegantly long muscles, his hands were raised in mock menace and he was smiling with absolute confidence that she would yield. His body heat seemed to wash over her, bringing the startlingly arousing scent of fresh sweat, hot man and leather.

Decima thought wildly that she had never seen anything more male in her life, and that included the stallion in the next stall. Suddenly she knew she could not deal with this; she was out of her depth, playing with forces she did not understand, and whatever happened next she was about to make an utter fool of herself.

'Here.' She thrust the leather into his hands and slid down, under the horse and up the other side where, thank God, it seemed possible to breathe. 'You win. I'll go and cook breakfast.' Her exit from the stables was, she was certain, anything but dignified.

Chapter Six

Any fool could cook bacon and eggs, surely? Even a fool who let herself be entranced by a virile man who had nothing else on his mind other than passing a few days' isolation by flirting with an old maid. Decima peered miserably into the mirror that hung in the scullery above the small basin where she was scrubbing her hands.

'Look at you,' she muttered angrily. Her nose was pink, her cheeks flushed. The beastly freckles stood out as though each one had been individually touched in with sepia ink. Her hair was all over the place and she looked positively haggard from lack of sleep. In fact, she looked every one of her twenty-seven years, if not more. She pulled a face at herself, then winced at the way it widened her mouth. Her wide mouth was not the worst of her faults, she had been given to understand, just one of many, but it did not help. *Fishy lips*, her unkind young cousins had called her when they were children.

She realised that she was having to stoop in order to look in the mirror that the housekeeper and the maid used every day. Doubtless they were normal-sized women, not fairground oddities.

Fool, fool, fool. How did she think she could turn herself from the passive, quiet freak of an unmarried sister into an independent, assured woman who experienced life on her own terms? Possibly it was achievable, but not in the space of a day and a night, not in the company of an experienced man of the world who was just too much of a gentleman to laugh at her.

He laughs with *me,* the pathetic little inner voice mumbled, *he finds me amusing.* The old, cynical destructive voice snapped back, *Just like you'd find a child aping its elders amusing, no doubt.* It hadn't needed that brandy last night to turn her head, she had been drunk on freedom and excitement and the edge of danger and she had behaved like…like a *fool.* Why search for another word when that one summed it up so neatly?

Decima scrubbed her hands viciously on a towel, threw off her shawl and found an apron. Bacon, bread, the one egg. Enough for three, for Bates must surely be awake and hungry by now.

Knife, bread board, toasting fork. What do you cook bacon in? A frying pan, presumably. Fat.

She moved around the larder, gathering things up, forcing herself to work out timings to keep the apprehension at bay. He would be back in a minute, wondering why she had fled in that idiotic way.

In the event there was a pile of only slightly charred toast on the table and the bacon was sizzling nicely—provided one had a fancy for it crispy—by the time the back door opened.

Decima kept her back to the door, busying herself pouring hot water over the coffee grounds.

'All done,' Adam said cheerfully, as though she had not just fled in disarray from a game she had initiated. 'That bacon smells good.'

Hastily, Decima flipped it onto a platter before it went any blacker. How did one fry eggs? Tentatively, she cracked it on the edge of the frying pan, then leapt backwards as the contents landed on the fat in an explosion of spitting droplets.

'Too hot.' Adam leaned across her and lifted the pan off the heat while the egg spluttered and went white with an uneven frill of brown around the edges.

'It's spoilt,' Decima said, alarmed to find that her voice trembled.

'No, it's not.' Adam slid it out onto the platter where it sat, the yolk looking decidedly underdone in its hard brown-and-white ruff. 'I'll wash and then take Bates's food up. I will not be a minute.'

Decima buttered toast and put it with bacon, a pot of jam and a mug of coffee onto a tray, pushing it across the table to Adam as he emerged from the scullery. 'I hope he feels better this morning and his leg is not paining him too much.'

'More likely his head.' Adam grinned and lifted the tray. 'I'll check on Pru while I'm up there.'

Automatically Decima set the table, buttered the rest of the toast, put out the jam and the platter of bacon. It looked decidedly overcooked, but somehow, against all the odds, the kitchen table seemed homely and charming with the fragrant bacon and the chairs close to the warmth of the range. Why that should so overset her she had no idea, but her eyes filled with tears, a sob caught in her throat and before she knew what she was doing she was sitting down, her face in the apron, weeping.

'Hey! What's this? Decima?' Adam was on his knees by her side, gently prising the apron from her face. 'Have you burnt yourself?'

'No, I am sorry, this is ridiculous, I'm not crying, I never cry.' She tried to hide her face again and was firmly prevented. Adam pressed a large white handkerchief into her hands.

'Never?'

'Never.' Her voice wavered. This was *dreadful*. Her nose would be red, her eyes red, her face blotchy.

'Oh well, then, if you aren't crying,' Adam said briskly, 'you are sick of the mulligrubs. That is easily cured.'

'The what?' Decima emerged cautiously from the shelter of the white linen.

'Mulligrubs. Look, come and eat something, that's the best thing to cure them. It ought to be cake, or sweets—the stickier the better—but bacon will do.' He heaped a plate and pushed it towards her. 'Go on.' This had to be some kind of dream. A viscount, sitting in his breeches and shirtsleeves at a kitchen table, eating her burnt offerings and discussing mulligrubs.

'But what *are* mulligrubs?' The bacon smelled delicious. Decima took a forkful, chewed, followed it with a bite of toast and the wobbly feeling inside subsided.

'I am not sure exactly.' Adam was gingerly cutting into the egg. 'It's what my old nurse used to call it when I was a little boy and was cast down or in the dumps for no good reason. But food always works.'

'Do you…do you get the mulligrubs often now?' she enquired. He ate the egg without any expression of revulsion; perhaps her cooking was not that bad.

'I haven't had them for years. I suspect they go away if there isn't anyone around to cure them with a dose of toffee. Bates is awake and appreciating your bacon, too. He says that his blanking leg is hurting like blank, if his lordship will excuse him saying so, and he'd have done a better job himself on a dog, but he is sure his lordship did his best considering he hasn't had much practice. Pru fortunately slept through that expression of gratitude for our efforts.'

'Is he always that outspoken?' Decima blew her nose and stuffed the handkerchief away.

'Usually he just grunts. It was one of the longest speeches I have ever heard him make, other than that tirade when I carried him in last night. I inherited him from my father, another man of very few words, who took him on as a half-starved brat. I think they suited each other. He's tough, loyal, damn good at his job—all qualities I would put before obsequiousness or a tendency to chatter.'

'Indeed, yes.' Decima pushed away her greasy plate and reached for the preserve jar. The memory of breakfast the day before and her sudden resolution came back to her. 'Do you know, it is New Year's Day tomorrow?'

'So it is. We must do something to celebrate.' Adam took the jar and began to heap gooseberry jam lavishly onto his toast. 'We could bake a cake.'

'No eggs. Even I know you need eggs for a cake.'

'True. Then we will play in the snow.'

'In the snow? But what can we do?'

'I will think of something. Now, you are going back to bed.' Adam poured another cup of coffee and pressed it into her hands. 'Off you go.'

'But I have only just got up! It is nine o'clock and there is goodness knows what to do.'

'Such as?' He began to push her gently towards the door. 'Bates will be scandalised if you try and nurse him, Pru's asleep, the horses are fine until this evening. If Pru needs you, I will wake you.'

'But…' Decima dug her toes in on the threshold and waved a hand at the kitchen table.

'A few plates and some knives and forks are not going to exhaust me. They may ruin my lily-white hands, of course, if the lanolin runs out. Now go on. You are tired out.'

'But—'

'If you say that once more I will carry you. Do you want me to put you to bed?' That was not said with the slightest edge of flirtation. That was a threat. Decima turned tail and did as she was told.

* * *

She woke when the clock struck one, although she had slept through the twelve-o'clock chimes like someone drugged. There were sounds from the adjoining room, interrupted by a fit of coughing.

Decima scrambled out of bed, dragged her stay laces to and buttoned her gown. 'Pru? Are you awake?'

She was, bleary-eyed and very pale, but propped up in bed with a tray by her side bearing a jug of cloudy white liquid, a spoon, a bottle of Mrs Chitty's cough linctus and the remains of what looked like a bowl of soup.

'Hello, Miss Dessy. Did I wake you?'

'No, not at all. Pru, I'm so sorry to have been asleep when you woke up.' Decima perched on the edge of the bed, disturbing a pile of journals. 'How do you feel?'

'Weak as a baby.' Pru grimaced. 'But the fever seems to have burned itself out; there's just this pesky cough left. That medicine's good, though. His lordship brought it up, and the barley water, and some soup at luncheon time.'

'Where on earth did he get soup?'

Pru shrugged, then coloured. 'Don't know, but honestly, Miss Dessy, I didn't know where to look. I was dying for the you-know-what, but I wasn't sure if I could walk there all by myself and he said, bold as brass, "Would you be wishing to visit the other end of the corridor, Miss Prudence?" Well, I didn't know where to look, but do you know, he carried me, set me down outside and strolled off, all tactful like, until I opened the door again. He's a real gentleman, even if he is a viscount.'

Perplexed, Decima tried to work that one out. 'But, Pru, if he is a viscount, you would expect him to be a gentleman.'

'Doesn't follow,' the maid said darkly. 'Most of them are out-and-out rakes from all one hears. No woman is safe with the likes of them.'

This conjured up an image of Adam, grinning lecherously

and chasing Pru's buxom figure and Decima's lanky one round and round the kitchen table. Decima bit her lip and said merely, 'I think we are safe with this particular viscount.' She was not entirely sure whether she was glad about that. Or even whether it was entirely true. 'Now, don't you think you should lie down and rest again?'

'I keep nodding off. Miss Dessy—you aren't going downstairs looking like that, are you?'

'Like what?'

'Your hair is a mess, and that gown's all crumpled and I don't reckon you've laced your stays up tight, either.' She levelled a disapproving look at Decima's bust line.

'I will do my hair, but I am not going to try and lace myself up tightly. I'd need to be a contortionist to do that!'

'Let me,' Pru nagged. 'You want to look your best.' Decima merely gave her speaking look over her shoulder as she went to find her hairbrush. 'You never know,' Pru retorted mysteriously. 'I'll fret if you don't come here and let me do it.' She managed a pathetic cough to underscore her point. 'Men notice these things.'

Brushed, laced and uncrumpled, Decima made her way downstairs. There was silence from the kitchen, but an appetising aroma wreathed through the air.

'Miss Ross.' Adam emerged from one of the front rooms and sketched a bow. 'If you would care to go into the dining room, I will bring you your luncheon.'

Decima swallowed. She had been expecting an afternoon spent in the kitchen and running up and down the stairs looking after Pru and Bates. That was safe, practical and distanced her completely from being Miss Ross, who had to make polite social conversation with a gentleman.

This particular gentleman had transformed himself from a good imitation of a groom into the perfect image of the Englishman at home in his country retreat—elegant withou trying too hard just about summed it up. And heart-thump ingly attractive without trying at all. Decima remembere Pru's approving words. No, he might not be a rake, but tha did not make him any safer.

Adam observed the flicker of surprise, swiftly followed b a flash of some other emotion. Was it mischief? Laughter Then Decima had her face perfectly under control. Now, wha had provoked that?

'Thank you,' she said, 'but you should let me help.'

'Not at all.' Adam opened the dining room door for her an smiled at her exclamation of surprise. The fire was lit, th room warm, candles flickered and he had laid the table. decided that we had had enough of playing at Below Stair so I have lit fires here and in the small salon and, althoug we might have to slip back into our roles of groom, cook housemaid and sick nurse at regular intervals, at least we ca come here afterwards. Now, if you will excuse me, Mis Ross, I will become the butler for one moment.'

She meekly took the chair he pulled out for her and shoo out her napkin. Adam retreated to the kitchen, admitting t himself that he was a trifle apprehensive about her reactio to his morning efforts in the kitchen. It was an interestin novelty to be attempting to please a woman in an area wher one was a complete beginner. He grinned to himself; the las time he'd been in that position he had been—what? Just sev enteen? And the field of expertise to be acquired wa somewhat different. Learning to cook seemed unlikely to b as fascinating, but was probably much safer.

'Soup, ma'am.' He set the tureen in front of her.

'My goodness.' Decima lifted the lid and sniffed. 'It smell wonderful. And what is that?'

'Ah.' She was eyeing with cautious interest the dark brow

lump he was attempting to slice. 'Bread. I do not think it is supposed to be quite like this.'

'I am sure it will be delicious,' she said politely as a slice thumped onto her plate. 'A local recipe, no doubt.' She was teasing him, he was convinced of it. Yes, there was that wicked sparkle again. 'Possibly it requires lemons?'

'That's the Leicestershire version,' he retorted. 'The Rutland receipt should really have walnuts. Tell me, Decima, what made you look so amused when you came downstairs just now?'

She paused in ladling out the soup and coloured slightly. Adam discovered that he enjoyed the fact that he could make her blush like that. The colour ebbed and flowed rapidly under her fine skin—the skin that was becoming an obsession with him. It was those damned freckles.

'I could not possibly say.' She passed him his soup and began to ladle out hers. Now, most women would have enquired archly what he meant, would have fluttered their eyelashes and would probably have giggled at him.

'Why not?' He pushed the butter towards her. The so-called bread would need all the help it could get.

She shook her head. 'No, I couldn't possibly. It is most improper. My goodness, this is excellent soup. What is it?'

Improper? Adam realised that he had not the slightest objection to provoking improper thoughts in Miss Ross. Quite the contrary. Although he had not expected her to admit to them quite so frankly.

'There is probably a word for it in French, but I call it The Complete Larder soup—in other words, I threw in a bit of anything I could find. Now, Decima, you are going to have to tell me about your improper thoughts or I will be imagining the most lurid things.'

Not that he would be able to act upon any of them if he ate any more of this bread. God, it was like chewing tree bark.

'Well…' She stirred her soup and gazed thoughtfully into

the bowl, then shot him an assessing glance from under her lashes. 'I was thinking how much the gentleman you looked, and Pru had just observed that, despite you being a viscount, you obviously *were* a gentleman.' She laughed at his expression. 'I know, it puzzled me, too, but she maintains that you cannot trust the aristocracy, and all noblemen are rakes.'

'Except me?'

'Apparently.' Decima chuckled. 'You look as though you do not know whether you have been complimented or insulted.'

This was exactly what he was thinking. 'Do you believe me to be a rake?'

'Certainly not, otherwise I would not have dreamt of coming with you. You are too large, in any case.' She chewed gamely on her bread.

'Large?'

'I have always pictured rakes as being thin and sinuous somehow. Insinuating, possibly. Not that I really have any idea what constitutes a rake, other than presumably they go about seducing innocent damsels as a matter of routine.'

'That certainly. I believe it to be a prerequisite,' Adam agreed gravely. 'Along with a ruinously bad gaming habit, a tendency to stay up all night carousing, and frequenting the haunts of low company and loose women. Patronising actresses and opera dancers and, of course, maintaining a string of expensive mistresses are also essentials.'

'Oh.' He was coming to love the way she listened, thought about what he said and then came out with the most outrageously unexpected responses. What was she going to say to that?

'Do *you* have a string of mistresses?'

Adam choked on a piece of carrot. 'Certainly not! Just the one.' *Oh Lord, now what have I said?*

'Is she nice?' Decima enquired.

'Obviously, or I wouldn't keep her,' he retorted.

'Well, you might if she was exceptionally beautiful, or…er…talented,' Decima observed thoughtfully. 'Are mistresses very expensive?'

'Yes,' he replied with feeling. 'The *er…talented* ones are, if you keep them in style and look after them decently once the affair is over.' Now why was he thinking about ending the affair? This time yesterday he had not the slightest intention of parting with Julia.

'I do hope Charlton hasn't got one. I am very fond of my sister-in-law and, although I am sure he could afford one, Hermione would not like it at all.'

'I doubt if he has,' Adam said encouragingly. 'Charlton sounds far too respectable and somewhat stodgy. I am sure your sister-in-law enjoys his complete devotion.'

'So, only stodgy husbands are devoted? Hmm.' Decima regarded him quizzically. 'It follows, then, that if one is to marry one must choose between stodgy devotion and interesting infidelity.'

'Is that why you never married?' he asked impetuously, and was punished by the instant extinguishing of the mischief in her grey eyes.

'No,' she said baldly.

Damnation. Adam found himself lost for a response: an unusual sensation.

She smiled and took pity on him. 'This bread is really very good for a first attempt. What do you think we should have for dinner? If either of us has room for dinner, that is.' She regarded the leaden lump on her side plate dubiously.

'Pigeon, if I can shoot any.'

'Then I will clear up and look after Pru and Bates. Could you carry me up some hot water? I promised her a bath.'

Half an hour later Adam let himself out of the back door, his shotgun cradled in the crook of his arm, his shot belt looped over his shoulder. He paused at the sound of running feet in the hall and Decima looked round the kitchen door. 'You will wrap up, won't you?' She took in his greatcoat and muffler, nodded approvingly and vanished as quickly as she had appeared.

From one of his sisters that would have produced a growl of irritation. From Decima the solicitude left a small glow of warmth that she was concerned about him. Adam was halfway across the yard before the novelty of that response dawned on him. He frowned fiercely; he was going to have to get their relationship back onto a firm basis of stranded gentlewoman and accidental host before she got under his skin any further.

In twenty-four hours this Long Meg of a spinster had made him want to throw all tenets of gentlemanly behaviour to the winds and ravish her; had made him enjoy—most of the time—acting as his own footman, cook and groom; had created doubts in his mind about the desirability of keeping a mistress and now had reduced him to a state where he enjoyed being fussed over. With a scowl that boded ill for any passing pigeons, Adam crunched through the snow towards the copse.

Chapter Seven

Decima yawned, stretched and lay in bed watching the cold, clear light on her bedroom ceiling with a feeling of deep contentment. There had been no thaw in the night. Today was the first of January and she was still snowed in. With Adam.

With Pru as well, of course, and with Bates, but there was no need to feel guilty about them being out of reach of a doctor, for they were both doing well. Pru had even spent two hours sitting by the bedroom fire yesterday afternoon after her bath.

Decima sat up, reached for her shawl and listened to the regular sound of Pru's breathing.

Yet there was a creeping unease as she thought about Adam. Last night, when all the chores were done and they had sat either side of the fire in the drawing room, he had seemed strangely distant, almost formal, as though she was a chance acquaintance he was having to entertain.

They had spoken of commonplace matters, quite easily and pleasantly. At the time, tired and warm, nothing had struck her as different. Now, thinking back, it seemed that the spark of intimacy between them had gone. She had lost the feeling that she could tell him anything, and he no longer gave back to her the warm feeling that her company amused and stimulated him.

Shaking her head at herself for being fanciful, Decima got out of bed and lifted the can of water she had left in the hearth. It was still warm and she washed and dressed quietly. But not quietly enough.

'Miss Dessy! Let me lace your stays properly—like any respectable lady should be laced!'

Pru insisted on getting up to sit in the armchair once she had had her wash and Decima had helped her braid her long mousy brown plait. 'Are there any more journals, Miss Dessy?' she asked. 'Some general ones, not just the ladies' fashion journals?'

'I'll see what I can find,' Decima promised. 'His lordship obviously keeps a good supply of reading matter for his guests.'

When she opened the door she could hear Adam arguing with Bates from across the landing. 'Wait a minute and let me shave you or else grow a beard, man! You'll cut your own throat at this rate.' There was a grumble from the groom.

'Happy New Year,' she called through the crack where the door stood ajar and jumped as it swung open to reveal Adam in his shirt- sleeves, an open razor in one hand and a towel in the other. He was half shaven, one side of his chin still a mass of soapy foam. Behind him she could see Bates, looking mulish, sitting up in bed with blood-flecked foam on his face.

'And to you,' Adam rejoined. 'If I succeed in getting the pair of us clean shaven to greet the new year, I will join you in the kitchen shortly.'

Decima found she was blushing, yet her feet did not want to move. She had never seen a man shaving before. It was curiously intimate and Adam was dressed only in breeches and his shirt, his stockinged feet shoeless.

'Yes, of course,' she mumbled. 'I'll put the kettle on.'

Oh, this really will not do, she chided herself as she began to assemble breakfast, bustling around with unnecessary briskness. Adam had made it quite clear last night that he wanted to maintain a decent distance and formality. *Then why open the bedroom door half dressed?* Whatever he felt and whatever his motives, she had to remember that he was an experienced man of the world and she, despite her age, was a singularly sheltered virgin.

But she was certainly garnering a wide variety of experiences and sensations with which to begin her new, independent life. Perhaps she might even have the confidence to venture up to London for a week or two this Season. That *would* scandalise Charlton.

'A penny for them.' Adam had come into the kitchen and was regarding her quizzically. 'You are standing in the middle of the room, a platter of bacon in your hands and a decided smirk on your lips.'

'What a horrible word. I never smirk.' Decima put down the bacon and went to find the frying pan. 'I have just thought of something I would like to do, which will scandalise Charlton.'

'What, more than the discovery that you have spent several nights unchaperoned with a man? Poor Charlton, I am beginning to have considerable fellow feeling for him.'

Decima stared at him. 'I have not the slightest intention of telling Charlton about this. Good Heavens, the fuss he would make! He would be on your doorstep demanding you marry me or some such dreadful nonsense.'

'Very right and proper,' Adam observed coolly. 'That is exactly what an outraged brother should do. It is what I would do if it happened to one of my sisters when they were unmarried.'

'But nothing has happened.' Decima shook her head in bafflement at his obtuseness. 'And Charlton won't know about it. When I get home I will write and say I had a difficult journey because of the snow, which will make him feel superior because he warned me not to start out in the first place, and Augusta does not know when to expect me so she won't be worrying, either.'

Adam took the platter from her and began to lay rashers in the frying pan. 'Should you be telling me this? Perhaps the only reason you are safe with me is that I am expecting your brother to come in search of you at any moment.'

'Now I have shocked you and so you are trying to frighten me for my own good,' Decima said with a sigh. 'You notice I did not say anything when we first met about who was expecting me and when—I am not completely naïve. Now I know I can trust you, so it does not matter.'

'And if my sense of honour demands I go and confess all?' Adam shook the pan over the heat and set it down again.

'You wouldn't.' Surely he was teasing her? But the grey-green eyes were serious and steady. 'That would be *dreadful*.' To have avoided all those reluctant, horrified suitors only to find the one man she had ever found who she liked forced to offer for her—that was the stuff of nightmares. 'I don't want to marry you, and you certainly do not want to marry me. Promise me you will not tell Charlton.' He shrugged and Decima came round the table hastily to grasp his wrist. 'Please, promise, Adam.'

His other hand closed over hers. Under her fingers she could feel the beat of his pulse, hard and steady like his eyes. Then he smiled. 'I was teasing you, Decima. I promise.'

Furious with him, she shook off his hand and whisked round the table, banging plates down to emphasise her irritation. But it was not all anger; part of it was the humiliating awareness that she had lied and would like nothing more than to be married to Adam Grantham. But only if that was what he wanted, too.

She tried to maintain a lofty silence, marching off to take the invalids their breakfast, then settling down in an affronted flounce of skirts to eat her own. After a minute she realised that Adam was watching her with a decidedly satirical twinkle in his eyes.

'What?' she demanded inelegantly. 'Why are you looking at me like that?'

'You are a very bad sulker, Decima; I can only conclude you do it rarely. My sisters are all champions at it, so I am a good judge.'

'No, I suppose I don't. Truth be told, I always used to spinelessly do what was required of me or just pretend horrid things were not happening. I never did anything as positive as sulking. Is it effective?'

'It's a game,' Adam admitted with a grin. 'Emily and Sally would sulk and pout and wheedle and I would pretend to be hard and uncaring and then, nine times out of ten, I would give them what they wanted. They were only practising the tricks they now play on their husbands.'

Decima chewed thoughtfully. 'Without wanting to criticise your sisters, that seems rather…unsatisfactory. I don't think I would want a relationship where I had to pout and wheedle to get things. I would rather discuss it and argue my case.'

'As you do with Charlton?' he enquired.

Decima felt herself flush. 'As I intend to do in future, yes.'

'Leave the dishes,' Adam said as she began to gather them up. 'No housework on New Year's Day. Wrap up, and we'll go and look at the horses.'

It was all right for men, Decima thought wryly as she went to put on her thick shawl and check on Pru. They just issued orders and the women and servants did as they were told. For a moment she was tempted to announce that she intended to sit by the fire with Pru reading all day, then she remembered what Adam had said about playing in the snow.

'Pru, I'll be outside if you need me,' she called, seizing her gloves and running downstairs in her heaviest boots.

Adam was already in the stables as she made her away

across the yard. She began to skirt the treacherous slick of ice where Bates had fallen, then looked at it with new eyes. Every year she and Augusta skated on the frozen mere half a mile from the house; how was this any different?

She took a run up and slid a full twelve feet, arms waving until she caught her balance. Laughing, she went into the stables to join Adam.

The clear ripple of amusement brought him to look over the door of the stall where he was forking fresh straw. It was even more charming than her giggle. Damn it. Why couldn't the woman do something to give him a disgust of her? Last evening, respectable and staid as it had been, had done nothing to put his unruly feelings back on track.

At first it had seemed to work just as he had hoped: formality, social chitchat and unexceptional subject matter had reduced Decima to a shadow of her vibrant self.

She had agreed politely with everything he'd said, followed all his conversational leads, never ventured a single opinion of her own and had sat, hands folded, feet together by the hearth. If it were possible for a tall, attractive woman to become invisible, she had almost managed it. It should have made him feel safe. Instead, he hated it. It was as though someone had snuffed a candle, leaving him alone in the darkness.

He pushed away the enormity of what that implied. 'What is so amusing?'

Decima twinkled at him as she went towards Fox's stall. 'I'll show you when we go outside. Hello, handsome!'

Fox put his head over the half-door, pushing expectantly at her caressing hand. 'Yes, I have sugar. This is outrageous cupboard love, you wretch.' She turned to Adam, still rubbing the one spot on the big stallion's nose that seemed to reduce him to a blissful trance. He found himself watching her hands.

'I have been thinking of breeding from my mare, Spindrift. You wouldn't consider putting Fox to her?'

She said it so practically, without the trace of a blush. Adam swallowed. 'He is a big horse—seventeen hands.' Now how, exactly, did one put this without becoming coarse?

'You think the foal would be too large for her?' Decima regarded Fox, head on one side. 'She is sixteen hands, I am sure that would not be a problem. Of course, we would have to draw up a proper agreement and I would naturally pay the correct fee for a successful foal.'

'She's a large mare.' It was all he could think of saying.

'She needs to be,' Decima countered with a grimace. 'What do you think? Obviously you want to be careful about bloodlines, but I can let you see Spindrift's. She's one-quarter Arab.'

'Yes. I don't see why not. We'll discuss it.' It was a feeble answer, but Adam turned back abruptly to his task. The thought of putting his stallion to her mare produced such a flood of primitive emotions in him that he didn't think he could face her. Decima appeared to have not the slightest idea of her own effect on him, of the earthy sensuality she exuded when she was not being the prim and proper spinster miss. Even when she *was* being prim and proper, come to that. Surely men had made overtures to her before, surely she was aware of the effect she had?

They finished in the stables and went outside. 'Now, tell me, what made you laugh?' Anything to stop thinking about her, tall, slender, lithe and naked in his arms.

'This.' Decima took a few running steps, then slid elegantly across the ice slick, arms out for seemingly effortless balance. He froze, terrified that she would fall. She turned and slid back, laughing at his expression. 'Can't you skate?'

'No, I've never tried. Stop it, you'll fall and break something.'

Decima came to a controlled halt a few feet away. 'I will not! I am an excellent skater, watch.' And to his horror she took a gliding step and spun round, full circle. 'See?'

'Come off the ice. Now.' Adam felt his voice catch in his throat. He did not know what it was: the sudden vision of her lying injured on the treacherous surface or the reality of her, her hair flying out behind her, her cheeks pink, her bosom rising and falling with her breathing.

Something must have shown in his face because she stopped and slid carefully towards him. 'Very well, if you insist.' Her voice was meek, but rebellion flared in her eyes and Adam realised he didn't trust her an inch not to pirouette away at the last moment. As she came within reach he seized her arm and spun her off the ice onto the trodden snow. 'I don't believe you,' he stated harshly.

Decima gasped as she was jerked against Adam, her arm held in a grip that left her in no doubt that it could close like a vice around her wrist if he so chose. 'Let me go.' There was heat in those grey-green eyes, a spark as though flint had struck iron. 'Don't be so dictatorial, Adam—you are as bad as Charlton.'

But that was not true; being reproved by her half-brother felt nothing like this. That provoked resentment and embarrassment, but not a flare of temper to match his, not a pounding of her heart as though she had been running. And she would not be racked with the shameful desire that he would drag her closer, fix those hard arms round her until she could not struggle and could only yield to him.

Adam's anger—if that was what it was—flickered and was gone, replaced by rueful amusement. 'To be compared to Charlton is an insult indeed. Just promise me you will not slide on the ice again. I don't want to have to set *your* broken leg.'

'I promise.' She looked up at him, struck yet again by the

novelty of a man she could look in the face without having to stoop. 'I am a very good skater, though.'

'I am sure you are, and if you had proper skates and a doctor within five miles I would not turn a hair. And don't pout at me.' He let her go abruptly and walked away towards a wide stretch of virgin snow.

'I wasn't,' Decima protested, stamping after him through the crunching whiteness. 'And if I was, why shouldn't I?'

Adam turned, his eyes on her mouth. 'Because it makes me want to nibble your lower lip, if you must know.' He carried on walking.

'Oh!' Decima stared at his retreating back. *Nibble?* He did not sound very pleased at the prospect, more like someone warning a child that if they did not stop doing something naughty they would have to be spanked. There didn't seem to be anything to say to that, or anything to do, other than to retreat inside, all injured dignity, or pretend she had not heard him. Nibble? Would that be pleasant? Was it even normal? Now what was he doing? Adam had stopped and, crouching, began to roll a snowball in the snow. It got bigger and bigger, leaving a clear track of muddy green where it had passed. At last, apparently satisfied, he stopped and began the whole process over again.

'What are you doing?' Decima approached cautiously.

'Building a snowman. You do a smaller ball for his head.'

'But I haven't built a snowman since I was—' She broke off, racking her brains. 'Eight. I must have been eight.'

'I don't think I have, either.' Adam lifted the snowman's torso up with a grunt and settled it on the base. 'But as we do not have any eight-year-olds to hand, and all this good snow is going to waste, it seems a pity not to take advantage.'

Decima looked from the half-built snow figure to Adam and then hastily back again. The sudden dark mood by the ice patch had vanished; he was quite obviously intending to play.

His eyes sparkled, his grin was infectious—but there was nothing in the least childlike about the breadth of his shoulders or the length of leg where the muscles rippled as he bent and lifted.

Decima had always considered that she and Augusta had enjoyed themselves quite light-heartedly whenever the mood took them. Skating in the winter, picnics in the summer, riding and shopping and socialising with neighbours all the year round. But it had never occurred to her to do something so spontaneous, so undignified, so unladylike, as to play in the snow.

She bent and gathered up a handful of snow, shaped it into a ball and began to push it along, patting and shaping as it grew. When it seemed big enough she lifted it and set it in place, only to find Adam had vanished. The snowman appeared well built, but somewhat lacking in features. Decima went and picked up broken branches from under a tree and set them in as arms, then had another idea and ran to the coal shed, returning with enough small pieces for eyes, buttons and a row of black teeth.

She was just standing back to view the effect when Adam reappeared from the stables, his arms full.

'There.' He set a battered tricorne on the figure's head, fashioned a scarf out of sacking and added one of the bruised carrots that were used in the horses' feed for a nose.

They backed off to admire their work. Decima found she was taking the most ridiculous amount of pleasure from the crude figure and turned, laughing, to look at Adam. He was regarding it with an expression of smug satisfaction that struck her as so typically male that she gathered up a handful of snow and threw it, hitting him neatly in mid chest.

'Why, you little…'

Decima took to her heels, but not before a snowball broke against her backside with a resounding thump. She whirled round, convinced that was no random shot, and saw from the wicked grin that he had struck her exactly where he had intended.

Grabbing snow, she retaliated with a throw that hit Adam in the top vee of his coat. 'This is cheating,' he said, frantically shaking snow out before it melted. 'Girls are not supposed to be able to throw, let alone hit anything.'

Laughing, Decima began shaping another missile, only to back away hastily as Adam scooped up a double handful of loose snow and began to run towards her. 'No! You wouldn't! You beast…'

Breathless and gasping with laughter, she found herself backed up against the stables wall with no escape. 'No, Adam, you wouldn't…please…'

With a teasing grin he lifted his hands, then opened them, letting the snow shower harmlessly down between their bodies. Suddenly they were very close indeed, their breath mingling as steam on the cold air.

Decima's heart was tight in her chest, her breathing jerking as though she had raced the length of the stable yard. Adam's eyes were on her mouth and she remembered his words. She wasn't pouting, was she? Her lips parted, the tip of her tongue running nervously between them. He was going to kiss her. *Oh, please…please…*

Chapter Eight

Right overhead the stable-yard clock struck one like a blow from her conscience. Decima blinked and slipped sideways away from Adam. 'Goodness, look at the time. Poor Pru and Bates will be wanting their luncheon.'

Without looking back, she walked briskly to the kitchen door, untying her shawl as she went. She could hear his footsteps following her. 'There is some soup left, and cheese and pickles,' she called from the scullery where she was washing her hands.

Adam was making up the fire. He turned at the sound of her coming out again, his face betraying nothing but agreement with what she was saying. She must have misunderstood his intentions, or more likely it was her own overheated imagination and longings that were behind her discomfort. Probably he had had some secreted snow still in his hand to drop on her head and had not the slightest intention of kissing her. She must have misheard, or misunderstood, that remark about her lips.

They climbed the stairs together with loaded trays, only to stop on the landing at the sound of voices. Adam raised an eyebrow and edged forward to look round the door of Bates's room.

The groom was sitting up in bed, his leg still protected by the tented bedclothes. Beside him in an armchair Pru was curled up, a pile of journals by her side and one clasped in her hands.

'That's just plain foolishness,' Bates was saying. 'Why did they go to the castle in the middle of the night when everyone had warned them about it? Young idiots.'

'But don't you recall, in the last episode they discovered that their wicked guardian had secreted the papers proving Adelbert's inheritance in the vaults of Castle Grim,' Pru explained earnestly. 'How else could they retrieve them and prove he was the rightful heir?'

'Well, he's a mutton-headed brat is all I can say,' the groom grumbled. 'Fancy dragging that Mirabelle along with him; a pretty little thing like that should be at home safe.'

'She's his sister, and ready to undergo any trials for his sake and that of the family's honour. I think it's lovely.' Pru's voice shook with emotion. 'Oh, my lord, Miss Dessy, I didn't see you there.'

Bates had gone a deep and unlovely crimson, not helped by the expression of unholy glee on Adam's face as he took in the mass of reading matter strewn across the floor.

'A change from your usual sporting news, Bates,' Adam observed with every appearance of interest. 'How kind of Miss Prudence to keep you entertained. You must explain the plot to me later, possibly I would enjoy it, too.'

'It's the most chuckle-headed load of whipped syllabub I've heard in my whole life,' Bates muttered defensively.

'And you are on episode eight.' Decima picked up the discarded journal. 'How patient of you to listen to all that, Bates, just for Pru's amusement.'

Adam finally took pity on the fulminating groom. 'I think

you ladies had better excuse us.' Decima helped Pru to her feet and tactfully removed her from the room with a hissed word in her ear.

'Well, why wouldn't he say so?' Pru hissed back on the landing. 'It isn't as though I haven't taken gentlemen their chamber pots, time out of mind.'

'I doubt Bates is used to receiving such attention, though. Come along, I have brought your luncheon and then you should have a lie down.'

Decima went out to retrieve the tray, unashamedly pausing for a moment to listen to what the men were saying.

'...butter wouldn't melt in her mouth,' Adam said. 'You old fool—what are you carrying on so for?'

'Aye, and cheese wouldn't choke her, either!' Bates retorted. 'Didn't know where to look when she marched in with her journals, me in my nightshirt and stuck in bed...'

'She obviously feels quite safe with you,' Adam said consolingly. 'A mature, respectable man like yourself.' Could Bates hear that betraying thread of laughter? No, he was still indignantly trying to cover up being caught listening, enthralled, to a Gothic novel.

They were both still chuckling when they went downstairs to prepare their own meal. 'It seems Pru has forgiven Bates for manhandling her,' Adam remarked, cutting wedges out of the Stilton.

'More likely they are both so bored they have arrived at a truce,' Decima countered. 'Pru is normally of the opinion that all males are a lesser life form and barely to be tolerated beyond normal politeness to her employers.'

'Of course, you have told me her thinking on noblemen. What is your opinion of men, Decima?'

She pushed the jar of pickles across the table while she thought. 'I think it would be easier to accept the male sex's valuation of itself as lords of creation if so many of them were not arrogant, ineffectual, blustering bullies.'

There was a pause. 'I was waiting for you to say, "Present company excluded, of course,"' he remarked.

Decima smiled. Adam wasn't looking exactly offended, but he had put on the expression she thought of as *gentleman on his dignity*. It appeared to be a universal male expression. 'I acquit you of all of those, although I must tell you that you do a very good impression of being a lord of creation on occasion.'

'Mmm.' Very sensibly he was not going to pursue that. 'And is your poor opinion of men the reason you are still unmarried?' Decima stared at him. Was he serious? Didn't one good look at her tell him why she was unwed? For some strange reason he seemed inclined to flirt with her, so he obviously did not find her entirely repulsive, but on the other hand flirting was probably an almost automatic reaction to being alone with a female, especially if one was an active male cooped up with little diversion.

She thought of giving him an honest answer, but then common sense took over. If she listed her faults, a man with his good manners would feel bound to disagree with her and she couldn't face getting into an argument over such a sensitive topic.

'Of course. I am afraid life with Charlton has not given me a high opinion of the male sex or of the married state.' She delved in the jar of water biscuits and pulled one out. 'And I have a perfectly satisfactory—and very independent—life, which I am certain I could not live if I had a husband to comply with.'

'Is there nothing about marriage you might be missing?'

'Children, you mean? Well, of course. But…'

He was regarding her with a wicked twinkle. 'But what if they turned out like their father? Is that what you were going to say? Poor little things.'

'Yes, but I wouldn't marry the sort of man whose children might be like that—' She broke off, chuckling. 'Now you have got me in a muddle. I am a tolerably good aunt, I believe, and the benefit of that is that one can hand them back the moment they become tiresome.' She felt her lips curve reminiscently at the thought of her cousin's three youngest. 'Some of them, I must admit, are enchanting, if a complete handful. What is it?'

Adam was gazing into the pickle jar, his forehead creased slightly in thought. 'I am just trying to recall where I left something. Talking of children reminded me.' His brow cleared. 'Of course. Come on, leave the dishes, let's go back outside while the sunshine lasts.'

'I will just check upstairs.' She ran up, halting at the landing at the sound of Pru's voice from Bates's room again. Well, the two of them were obviously determined to finish their Gothic tale; she did not want to embarrass the groom by catching him intent upon it for a second time.

When she reached the yard Adam was emerging triumphantly from a cobwebby wood shed, towing something behind him. 'A sledge!'

'The local carpenter built it two winters ago for my nephews. If it will seat four boys, it ought to carry us.' He looked a boy himself, hat discarded, hair rumpled, his eyes alight with fun.

'Us?' It was tempting, but while ice skating was a perfectly ladylike thing to do, hurtling down hillsides on a sledge was quite another matter. 'Charlton would be scandalised.'

'We must definitely do it then. I thought your New Year's resolution was to scandalise Charlton.'

'That was not quite how I put it,' she objected. The prospect was wickedly enticing, though. 'Where will we find a hill?'

'Just the other side of this copse.' Adam set off, dragging

the sledge, and Decima ran after him, through the narrow copse and out into the open field, which sloped up, temptingly white and crisp. Tracks criss-crossed it: birds' feet, the marks where a hare had run, and after it the paw prints of a fox, and now Adam's booted feet with the runner tracks following.

He halted halfway up, straddled the seat, sat down and pushed off. The sledge sailed down the hill, coming to a halt in a flurry of snow almost at Decima's feet. 'Dare you try?'

'Yes!' She felt utterly reckless. If he had suggested they try to fly, she would have agreed. This time she followed him up the hill to the same spot and climbed onto the sledge, putting her feet on the front bar and tucking her skirts tight around her legs. Adam got on behind her, his arms either side on the ropes feeling as they had on the horse when he had rescued her: secure, protective, hard.

With a double kick of his feet they were off, swooping down the slope, the cold air rushing past her face, the heat of Adam's body secure at her back. All too soon they were at the bottom. 'Can we go higher this time?' she demanded, panting as they climbed back up.

'All right.' Still they were not at the summit, but Decima had to be content; Adam seemed unwilling to risk her on a very long run.

They slid down, trudged back, and slid down again so many times that Decima lost count. All she was aware of was the hot blood pounding in her veins, the sharpness of the cold air as she breathed, of Adam's open delight at the sport, her own tingling awareness of his closeness.

'This must be the last run.' Adam tightened his grip on the ropes and began to climb again. 'Look how the shadows are lengthening.'

'Right from the very top this time,' she pleaded, tugging at his arm. 'Please.'

'Very well, right from the very top.'

Decima was breathless by the time they reached the crest, staring round her with eyes watering from the keen breeze on the unprotected hilltop. 'Brrr. We must cook something especially hot and filling tonight.'

She settled herself on the sledge, suddenly apprehensive at the sight of the long slope in front of her—it was more than twice the distance they had covered before. 'Too high?' Adam was watching her face.

'No—just scary enough to be exciting.' And once he settled behind her, his arms tight at her sides, the fear vanished into an exhilaration that only built and built as the sledge gathered speed, swooping down the long hillside. Decima heard herself shrieking with excitement as they went and Adam's chuckle of amusement almost in her ear.

What went wrong she had no idea. Suddenly the sledge bucked, jumped, then Adam's feet were out at the sides, digging in to turn it back on course, but it tipped and she was in the snow, rolling over and over down the hill.

After one startled scream Decima realised she was quite safe. The deep snow was cushioning her from anything hard on the ground below. Over and over she went until she reached the bottom and lay still, gasping for breath and more than half inclined to burst out laughing from sheer shock and excitement.

Then she was hit by a solid weight and threw out her arms, only to find them clasped hard around as much of Adam's body as they would reach. 'Ooof!'

'Decima? Are you all right?' He was lying on top of her, his elbows jammed into the snow on either side in an effort to keep from crushing her.

'Yes…get off…oh…' She realised why he was covering her when the sledge finally caught up with them, hit Adam solidly on the shoulder and juddered to a halt.

He swore under his breath, shoved it away, then pushed her tumbled hair out of her face. 'Decima?'

'I am quite all right, honestly…' Her voice trailed off as she saw how he was looking at her. Looking at her mouth. Then she could not see his expression any more and his mouth was covering hers, angling to capture her lips with his.

His lips were cold, then startlingly his tongue touched her, hot, insinuating, and she gasped, parting her own mouth for him. He tasted delicious: slightly of mint, slightly of ale. Then she lost the ability to think analytically of taste and smell and touch as individual things. It all became a blur of sensation. His weight on her should have been frightening, but all she felt was a primitive thrill at his strength, at the easy way he was mastering her body.

His tongue, his lips were plundering her mouth and all she could do—all she wanted to do—was to let him. She heard a little moan, deep in her own throat and he shifted at the sound, his hands grasping and tangling in her hair on either side of her face, holding her still while he explored her at his leisure.

When he lifted his head for a moment she stirred, distressed by the loss of his touch, then she froze as he began to nip gently at the fullness of her swollen lower lip. The tiny, nibbling bites sent shudders through her. Instinctively she arched towards him, her breasts under their thick covering straining against his chest, but the relief she was seeking eluded her. Inside everything was turning hot, heavy, aching. Her legs shifted restlessly under him and were trapped by the pressure of his thighs.

Adam released her mouth, his own trailing hot kisses down her cold cheek, down to where her neck rose from the folds of her shawl. Decima whimpered as his tongue licked, tasted, then found the tight whorls of her ear, flickering against the sensitive flesh until she was gasping.

Her hands clenched hard on his back, urging him closer to her and she felt, rather than heard, him groan, deep in his throat. 'I want you, Decima.' She shuddered and he went still. For a long moment he stayed there, his long body tight against hers from breast bone to thigh, then he straightened his arms, levering himself off her.

'Adam?' She was cold now that his heat had left her, cold and dizzy and full of the new, surging emotions and feelings that were rioting through her.

'Decima, I am sorry, you must be frozen.' He lifted her, despite her half-hearted struggles, and began to carry her back to the house. 'You are soaked. Poor sweetheart, I did not mean this to happen.' His breath was coming hard and she recognised it for what it was, despite her innocence. He was struggling with arousal and desire and holding himself in check with an effort that shook his body.

'I will be fine, just let me walk,' she protested, her face buried against the front of his greatcoat, too shy to raise it and look at him. Was it the realisation of where they were that had stopped him, or had she done something wrong, something that revealed her complete lack of experience?

He ignored her protests, shouldering open the kitchen door and setting her on her feet by the range. She stood there, head down, shivering with embarrassment and cold as he tugged off her shawl, unbuttoned her pelisse and freed her of her soaking outer clothing. 'Sit down.' She found herself pressed back into the big Windsor chair and he knelt, unlacing her boots, drawing her cold feet free. 'Poor darling.' He lifted both her feet and began to rub them between his broad palms. 'You need a hot bath.'

'Yes, yes, that is all. I will be fine then.' Decima felt herself gripping the arms of the chair in an effort not to reach out and catch his damp, dark head in both hands and pull him to her. 'I'll just take some water…'

Adam stood up, pulling her to her feet and she saw his face properly for the first time since he had kissed her. His mouth was set hard, a muscle throbbed in one cheek. Oh God, he was angry with himself for kissing her, with her for being such a gauche, awkward old maid. Then she saw his eyes and the breath caught in her throat. They were silver, intense, and as they met hers they held such a look of tenderness and desire her hands flew to her mouth, holding back the plea to kiss her again, to take her, here and now, on the old rag rug in front of the range.

'I will bring you water. Go into my dressing room, there is a big tub permanently in there.' She hesitated and he snapped, 'Go,' his eyes turning fierce.

Decima fled upstairs, whisking past Bates's half-open door on soft feet. The murmur of voices reached her, then was gone as she entered Adam's bedroom. She should not be doing this, should not be in this masculine room that smelt of his cologne and of leather and of him. Her hands trembling, she opened the door in the corner and found herself in a spacious dressing room. As might be expected, it had a washstand and shaving mirror, a screen across one corner of the room, a rack of thick towels, but it also had, in pride of place, a handsome tub. The sides were painted in imitation of green marble, it stood on ball-and-claw feet and a spigot hung over the side against the wall. Decima tried it cautiously: cold running water. Such luxury.

She heard footsteps in the bedchamber and stepped behind the screen.

'Decima?' She tried to reply, but only managed a squeak of acknowledgment. Quantities of water were poured into the tub. 'This will take a few more journeys. Get out of those wet clothes as quickly as possible.'

Decima took a deep breath and tried to pull herself together. He had kissed her, that was all. It was nothing to get into such a state about. She had wanted it, for goodness' sake. It had been wonderful. She wanted him to do it again—and she was terrified that he would.

She untied her garters and rolled down her stockings, then reached behind her and unhooked her gown, even managing the final tricky button that needed her to reach back over her own shoulder. Her petticoats came off easily, clinging to her calves with chill dampness around the hem as they fell away. That left only her stays over her chemise.

Decima stilled, her fingers on the stay laces as another torrent of water poured into the bath. 'One more journey,' Adam said. His voice sounded perfectly normal. Decima wondered if she could ever open her mouth and say a coherent word again.

The door closed behind him and she began to tug at the laces. They were wet where the melted snow had soaked through the back of her clothes and cut unpleasantly into her fingers as she fought with them. They would not untie, she realised. They had swollen with the wet and now were set into hard knots. Decima winced as a fingernail broke, but she struggled on. No, it was hopeless.

The door opened again. 'There you are, full now.' Adam's voice rose over the splashing water. 'Use the spigot on the wall if you need to cool it down a little. I'll go and start dinner.'

Decima hesitated, racked with indecision. She should wait until he was gone, then creep out and call Pru. But if she did that she would have to explain how she came to be soaked through, so wet that her hair was sodden.

'Adam!'

'Yes?' She could hear him come back into the room.

'May I have some scissors, please?'

'Of course, but for heaven's sake, don't hang around getting chilled cutting your fingernails, have your bath first.'

'I can't...I cannot untie my stay laces.'

Silence. Did he think that was amusing? Or perhaps she had embarrassed him. No, of course not. This was an experienced man of the world; he had probably untied more sets of stay laces in his time than she had.

The screen moved. 'No! Just give them to me.'

'And have you stab yourself in the back? Let me see, Decima, I might be able to untie them.'

Crimson with embarrassment, she turned her back and mumbled, 'All right.'

The screen panel shifted and she could feel the heat of his body right behind her. There was the brush of linen against her shoulder. He must have shed his coat before carrying the water. Decima shut her eyes as the image of Adam standing there in shirtsleeves and breeches filled her mind.

His fingers caught in the laces, pulling and twisting. 'You had better cut them,' she muttered.

'No, almost…almost got it. There.' The knot gave with an immediate lessening of the pressure, but not content with that he began to loosen each of the criss-crossing strands. Then he stopped, his hands resting either side of her ribs. 'They do go all the way down,' he murmured.

'What?' Decima gasped. *If he didn't take his hands away in one second, she was going to turn round and…*

'Your freckles. I wondered if they went all the way down and they do. Here.' His fingertip touched lightly across her shoulders, across the nape of her neck, trailed lightly down the dip of her spine.

Decima shuddered at the touch, her mind reeling at his words. *Her freckles? He found those disfiguring brown marks attractive?*

Then his lips replaced his hands and she was pulled back against him, his hard thighs supporting her, his mouth trailing tiny kisses across the soft skin of her shoulders. His aroused body was branding her buttocks with heat through her flimsy chemise and she gasped at the feel of him and the primitive urge that coursed through her to press herself back, rub herself like a cat against the evidence of his arousal.

His hands lifted to cup her breasts gently, his palms

cradling the soft weight, while his thumbs touched the hard peaks of her nipples, which were thrusting shamelessly through the fine fabric.

'Decima.' His face was buried in the curve of her shoulder, his voice harsh and muffled against her neck. 'One of us is going to have to step away from this. Now.'

'I know,' she murmured, her voice shaking. 'I know, and I do not think I know how to.'

Chapter Nine

Adam drew in a deep breath. He had never had a problem with self-control before. It seemed he had never found himself in a position where his conscience was in direct conflict with his deepest desires. And just at that moment his desire was to carry Decima through into the bedchamber and bury himself in her soft, strong, innocent body.

With an effort that was painful he brought his hands away from the tantalising weight of her breasts, stepped back until her clothing no longer brushed against his body, and back again until he could put a shaking hand on the screen and draw it closed on the image of her standing there, almost naked, quivering for him.

He shut the door into the dressing room and stood looking round at his bedchamber, at the wide bed with its dark green velvet throw. What would she look like stretched on that velvet, her hair loose, her eyes wide with innocent longing? With an oath he flung open the door and strode out onto the landing.

'My lord?' It was Bates. Damn. Adam looked down at himself. The soaked buckskins did nothing to hide the state of agonising arousal he was in. He yanked his shirt out, ran a hand through his hair and walked into the room.

'How are you feeling, Bates?' Hell, Pru was there, too, still curled up in the chair, her eyes wide as she took in his appearance. Her gaze flickered to the groom's and they both looked studiously away.

'Very well, thank you, my lord. The leg aches, but Pru—Miss Staples, that is—fetched me something from the still-room that helped. I was just wondering if you'd help me shift position a bit. I've slid down.'

'Where's Miss Dessy, my lord?' Pru asked.

'Having a bath.' He bent to help Bates, grateful that his back was turned to the maid's scrutiny. 'She is using the tub in my dressing room because it is deeper and she got rather chilled outside.'

He shook out the pillows quite unnecessarily, controlling the urge to talk on, justifying himself.

'Of course, that's why you can't go and get changed,' Pru said in a tone that suggested she accepted his explanation—just. 'I had better go and give her a hand.'

Adam froze. Had Decima had enough time to compose herself? Had he left stubble burns on the soft skin of her throat? 'I think she has everything she needs,' he said finally, straightening up. Either Decima was going to confide in her maid or she was not, but he was not going to say anything to provoke the girl to hurry off in search of her mistress any sooner than necessary.

'I'll go and set her clothes out then, my lord.' Pru got to her feet a little unsteadily. Adam thought of telling her she should still be resting, then decided he would be chancing his luck; Miss Staples would no doubt enquire if he thought *he* should be helping her mistress to find her change of underwear.

Both men watched her make her way out. Adam could feel Bates's eyes boring into him. 'Well?' he demanded irritably. It seemed to be his day for justifying himself to the staff.

Bates shrugged. 'Not my place to say, my lord, but, as you're asking, I'd say that trifling with virgins isn't your usual kick. Bit risky, that.'

'I am not trifling—' Adam broke off. It was exactly what he was doing. It was not his intention, but it was certainly the effect. 'Damn you, Bates.'

'As you say, my lord.' Bates was never so compliant unless he was deeply disapproving—and he was usually acute enough to be right, which was why Adam tolerated the not infrequent censorious comment. This was different.

'Miss Ross is a gentlewoman. One does not trifle with gentlewomen.' Or virgins of any description come to that, but he was not discussing Decima's state of innocence. Bates received this lofty statement in silence, leaving Adam nothing to do with himself other than to stalk out with all the dignity he could muster.

Which was not much, he decided, catching a glimpse of himself in the landing mirror on his way downstairs. His clothing was dishevelled, his groin was in a state of acute discomfort that seemed unlikely ever to subside, his heart beat like a drum, and his conscience was positively screaming at him for his unrepentant desire to drag Decima out of the hot water and make love to her until they both dropped from exhaustion.

Snarling at himself, he threw open the larder door and began to lift out platters and jars, banging food down on the table as though to knock out an opponent. He had made her cold, wet, shocked and embarrassed. And all he could do to make up for it was to try to give her a decent meal.

Decima eased herself into the hot water, letting the physical shock of it on her chilled skin drive away the other shocks her body had experienced for a fleeting moment. The respite did not last. She slid under the water until it lapped her chin and her hair was soaking. Her arms lay by her sides.

She felt too self-conscious even to risk touching herself; everything throbbed or tingled in an overwhelming manner.

She had wanted a kiss, just a kiss. She could admit that to herself. In her innocence she had expected it to be pleasantly intimate, full of the scent and warmth she had experienced when Adam had carried her. She had not expected it to devour every sense, to overturn her mind until she was almost screaming with desire for him to touch her, stroke her, everywhere. To do things she could not begin to understand, let alone find words for.

Of course she knew the basic facts of life. But somehow she had expected all of *that* to be confined to the actual marriage bed. Surely kissing was simply a mildly amorous gesture? It seemed not. How was she ever going to face him again?

The water was beginning to cool. Cautiously Decima lifted the tablet of soap and began to wash. Face, arms, hands. All safe. She swallowed and slicked foam rapidly over the swell of her breasts, gasping as they seemed to turn heavy and full under her palms. Feet, those were safer—except for the memory of Adam's big hands rubbing them back to life. Calves, thighs…her hands trembled and stilled above the soft tangle of curls. He hadn't touched her intimately, so where had that hot, heavy yearning feeling come from? From the feel of his hard weight pressed against her, that was where. *Pull yourself together, Decima, you cannot go through life not washing properly!*

A few hasty, soapy swipes later she scrambled out of the bath, snatching up towels from the pile and swathing herself in them as though Adam was still in the room. No dressing gown. Now what should she do?

There was complete silence in the adjoining room. Decima peeped round the door, then scuttled for her own room, bursting in to find Pru with her hands full of petticoats and a disapproving expression on her pale face.

'Pru, you should be resting.'

'I'm well enough if I sit down now and again. I've put clean clothes out for you, Miss Dessy.'

'Thank you. Now, please, sit down. How did you know I needed them?' Oh Lord, Adam hadn't said anything to Pru, had he?

Pru perched on the edge of a chair and regarded her. 'His lordship said you'd got wet.'

'Well, so I did. There is no need to look so starched up, Pru.'

'I *saw* his lordship. I'd say you got more than wet, Miss Dessy.'

'Pru! What do you mean?' Decima began to pull on her clothes, suddenly shy in front of the other woman as she had never been before.

'His shirt was all pulled out—covers a multitude of sins, that does—his colour was up, breathing like he'd run round the house ten times and not very happy at meeting my eye. And look at you, Miss Dessy. All of a fluster, mouth that looks as though you've been rouging it—and see your neck.'

Decima looked reluctantly into the mirror her handmaid thrust at her. A new Decima stared back. A wanton-looking creature with wide eyes, swollen mouth and, up the column of her neck, reddened patches. She lifted her hand to them, horrified to find her tentative touch produced not so much a feeling of pain as one of acute sensitivity.

'That's a man who needs to shave twice a day if he's going to do that sort of thing,' Pru pronounced. 'Honestly, Miss Dessy, I thought he was a gentleman. Just goes to show you can't trust any of them,' she added darkly.

'Pru, it's not like that.' Decima turned her back while her stay laces were jerked punishingly tight. 'I am just as much to blame, and it was only a kiss.' She saw Pru's disbelieving face. 'Goodness, you don't think he…that we… Certainly not!'

'If you say so, Miss Dessy.' Pru handed her the petticoat.

'I *do* say so, Pru. And it was certainly improper, I admit, but I am glad he did kiss me because at least I know what it is like and I will not be seeing him again once we leave here anyways.' Decima dragged her gown over her head and emerged flushed and breathless. *I will not be seeing him again. Ever.*

'Hmm. Well, I'd better get changed and come downstairs, Miss Dessy. This gown's all crumpled.'

Decima stared at her. The thought of Pru sitting there, a silent, disapproving chaperon all evening, filled her with horror. It was going to be hard enough facing Adam again, but to do it with a witness was impossible.

'No, Pru. I would be too embarrassed. He and I need to…to agree some things between us. You stay here and rest and I will bring you your dinner up.'

She went downstairs half an hour later, immaculate and quivering with nerves, to be greeted by a wave of succulent odours as she pushed open the kitchen door. Adam was uncorking a bottle of red wine; as she watched, he tipped it into a deep pan which was simmering on the range.

At the sound of the door closing he looked up at her, then went slowly to put the empty bottle on the table. The silence crackled between them, filled with unformed words, unspoken thoughts. 'You are cooking dinner,' Decima managed at last, wincing at the banality of the obvious.

'I thought the least I could do, having soaked you through with icy water and frightened you half to death, was to feed you something hot. There was some pigeon left, and a rabbit.' He ran his hand abruptly through his hair and moved away a few steps as though to give her space. 'Where is Pru?'

'Upstairs. I don't need her here. You didn't frighten me, and you don't now. I frightened myself.'

'Decima. I am sorry.' She had not heard him going back

to his room, but Adam had changed his clothing for the dark elegance of evening dress, as though to reassure her with its formality. 'I cannot pretend I didn't want to kiss you, but I never meant for it to go so far.'

'I…I liked it. It would be unfair of me to say I did not. But it was too much, all at once, so I didn't know how to stop.' She made herself keep her eyes on his face. He was being honest, so should she. 'But you did, so that's all right.'

Adam turned away sharply. 'You really are a quite remarkable woman.'

Decima flushed. 'A wanton one, you mean. Perhaps I led you on, I am sorry—'

'Don't apologise!' He swung back to face her, his face full of an anger that she knew was not directed at her. 'I said extraordinary—I mean just that. Why aren't you having the vapours, threatening me with your brother?'

'I told you,' she said patiently, going over to dip a spoon in the fragrant, bubbling stew. 'It was at least as much my fault as yours, it was extremely…interesting and there is nothing to have the vapours about. This is very good stew. Shall I peel some potatoes?'

Suddenly it was all right again. Adam was obviously unconvinced, but she felt quite calm and almost at ease. True, her knees were knocking and her skin felt as though someone was caressing it with thousands of tiny feathers and, if they touched again, she thought she would probably swoon, but other than that she was all right. Of course she was. *I am an independent grown-up woman*, she told herself, *and I can learn to cope with new situations*.

Adam hefted another pan onto the stove and reached for the salt box. 'I've done them. Pru seems better.'

'Yes, she does.' Decima gathered up cutlery. 'I will lay the table in the dining room. How is Bates?'

They were having a perfectly ordinary domestic conversation while underneath her mind was whirling and her body behaving in ways she had never believed possible. Did Adam feel like this? Presumably all sorts of people went through life feeling like this on occasion; it was amazing what went on under the bland face of everyday life.

The evening passed pleasantly enough. Any invisible onlooker would have observed the unusual sight of a lady and gentleman waiting on their own servants, and then on themselves at dinner. But they would have been hard put to detect either the slightest impropriety or even undue familiarity in the rest of the evening, which was passed by the lady and her companion in desultory conversation, the reading of somewhat out-of-date journals and the exchange of opinion from time to time upon clues in the acrostic the lady was attempting to complete.

Or perhaps the unseen watcher would have noticed the way the lady's eyes would rest on the gentleman's bent head, or the manner in which her lashes would sweep down to disguise her interest the moment he moved. And they might also have noticed the way in which he shifted restlessly in his chair and the tight line of his mouth when he caught himself doing so.

As the hall clock struck ten Decima looked up from the *Ladies' Journal* with an arrested expression. 'What is that noise?'

Adam got to his feet and moved to the window, flicking aside the heavy drapes. 'Rain. The thaw has come.' He turned and looked at her and Decima struggled to read the message in eyes suddenly the colour of dark flint. 'The outside world may well reach us tomorrow.'

'The end of our sojourn out of time and away from reality,' she said, trying to make the remark light—and realising almost too late that she wanted to cry.

Decima got to her feet, holding on to the arm of the chair as though she, and not Pru, was weak from a fever. She had the strangest feeling that if she held out her arms now he would come to her and to hell with the consequences. Last time he had had the strength to step away. Now it was her turn to be strong.

'I think I am probably keeping Pru up,' she said with a firm smile. 'And if there is travelling to do tomorrow, we must both get some rest. Goodnight, Adam.'

He took two long strides across the room to her side and did something he had never done before, lifting her hand in his and lightly kissing her fingertips. 'Goodbye, Decima.'

She was halfway up the stairs before she had got her reaction to the fleeting touch of his lips under control and thought about what he had just said. *Goodbye?*

Decima went to bed, expecting a night filled with restless dreams and tormenting longings. Instead she woke to the sound of the landing clock striking seven and the relentless sound of heavy rain against the window. She should be glad, she knew. But was it so very wicked to want this strange holiday from reality to continue for ever?

When she padded into her maid's room in bare feet, wrapped in the gorgeous Oriental dressing gown, she discovered that Pru was already up. Up, dressed and in full flow, arguing with Bates in his bedchamber by the sound of it.

'His lordship's downstairs cooking breakfast, which is where I should be if I didn't have my lady to get dressed, so why you can't have the sense you were born with and let me fetch you your hot water I don't know.'

A low grumble was all Decima could hear of Bates's views on the matter. 'I'm not offering to wash you, you stubborn man.' Decima stepped back as the door swung open and Pru marched out. 'Honestly, Miss Dessy—*men.*' She looked her up and down sharply. 'I'll go and get your water then. The snow's almost gone, you know.'

Decima went back into her room and looked out of the window and the slush that yesterday had been the white yard. She could just see the remnants of their snowman, hat drooping, body already half-eaten away by the rain: nothing lasted, it seemed.

Adam flipped the bacon over, wondering how long it would be before they could get fresh supplies of food. Not much longer, if this rain continued. And then Decima would be gone. After a restless night spent tossing and turning, in between dreams that were either guilt-racked or wildly erotic, he almost welcomed the thought of their separation.

They both needed time, distance and a remedial dose of ordinary life. Perhaps then he could work out what he truly felt for her. He filled the kettle and put it on the hob, caught himself doing it without a second thought, and smiled at how rapidly the basic routines of kitchen life had become second nature.

Decima. He desired her. Oh, how he desired her. But she was a gentlewoman—he could not make her his mistress. What did that leave? A chaste friendship? He grimaced. Marriage?

The bacon was burning. He pulled the pan off the heat and stood there looking at it. He didn't *need* to get married, not with his fifteen-year-old cousin Peregrine all a man could hope for in an heir, and more. He had his freedom now; that would be lost with marriage. The thought of losing that freedom, of finding himself leg-shackled to just one woman for the rest of his life had always seemed intolerable.

On the other hand, he had spent several days cooped up in a snowbound house with just one particular female companion and there had not been a boring moment. Long hours of aching physical frustration, yes, but no boredom.

He was contemplating exactly what that might mean when the back door banged open and his missing domestic staff bundled in, dripping wet and laden with parcels.

'My lord!' Mrs Chitty stopped dead in her tracks and stared at him. 'What in the world are you doing in my kitchen?'

'Cooking breakfast,' Adam admitted, feeling as though he had been caught stealing cake from the pantry.

'Never tell me your guests have arrived!' The housekeeper took in the four plates on the table. 'The only thing that kept my mind at rest these past few days was the thought that none of you would be able to get here.' She cast off her vast bonnet and cloak and shook out her apron with a snap. 'Who has been wearing this, might I ask, my lord?'

'I have, and Miss Ross.' That did it.

'*Miss* Ross?'

'Yes, Mrs Chitty. I need to have a word with you about that.'

'Indeed, my lord? Emily Jane, get outside and fetch the rest of the provisions and look sharp, girl.' The silent kitchen maid scuttled back out into the rain.

'Mrs Chitty, I almost did not manage to get here through the snow. On the way Bates and I helped a lady and her maid who were trapped in their carriage and brought them here. No one else has reached us.'

'Well, at least she had her maid,' the housekeeper observed, burrowing in her basket and producing a loaf. 'And Bates—not that he'd be much use for keeping propriety.'

There was no point in trying to put a fine gloss on the situation. 'Miss Ross's maid has been bedridden with a fever the whole time and Bates broke his leg the night we arrived here.'

'Ah.' Mrs Chitty regarded him with a trace of amusement tweaking at the corner of her mouth. 'I'd say you were in a bit of a pickle, my lord, especially as I've no doubt your houseguests will be here shortly. The roads are mostly passable now, that we could see.'

Oh, hell. Adam realised he had not thought about that. The arrival of four eminently respectable members of London society, two of whom he did not know well enough to confide in, was quite sufficient to ensure Decima was ruined.

Even as he thought it, Emily Jane hurried in, hung about with more shopping. 'There's two carriages coming up the drive, my lord.'

Chapter Ten

'Then it's a good thing I've been here all the time and only Emily Jane and William went into town, isn't it, my lord?' Mrs Chitty finished tying her apron strings round her plump middle and took the frying pan firmly from Adam's hand.

'Emily Jane, take off those wet things and go and open the front door. And no gossiping, mind.' She turned back to Adam. 'You'd better hurry and put your coat and neckcloth on, my lord, and warn the young lady what's happening. And don't you worry about Emily Jane and William, they won't be saying anything out of turn, I'll see to that.'

'Mrs Chitty, you are a paragon. Whatever I pay you, you are going to get a raise.' He bent and planted a kiss on her red cheek. 'And what makes you think it's a *young* lady?'

The housekeeper merely looked at him; a long, slow stare that produced the first blush Adam was conscious of in over ten years. With a rueful grin he strode out of the room and up the stairs, just in time as the knocker thudded on the front door.

Decima sat at the dressing table, guiltily enjoying having her hair properly dressed for the first time since she had left

Charlton's house. She had protested, but Pru refused to sit down and rest, so she gave in and allowed herself to be fussed over.

The knock at the door startled them both. 'Decima? Are you decent?' Adam slipped inside before Decima had a chance to check whether she was or not.

'My lord!' Pru managed to sound like the most outraged chaperon, only to bridle indignantly as she was completely ignored.

'Mrs Chitty, the kitchen maid and the footman are back—and my guests are at the front door now. Pru, are you well enough to come downstairs? Good. Mrs Chitty has, of course, been here the entire time. We have not been cooking, we have not been looking after ourselves and, Pru, you have not left Miss Ross's side.

'Mrs Chitty is cooking breakfast, and whatever the others need—I don't know where they've come from this morning. I will go and warn Bates. Perhaps you and Pru can come down in about twenty minutes.'

He vanished before they had the chance to reply. 'Well, Pru…' Decima took a deep breath and regarded her reflection carefully. Her mouth felt dry and her stomach contracted painfully. Strangers—that was enough under normal circumstances to send her into an agony of self-conscious shyness. But these strangers could ruin her. 'Fetch my jewellery case, please, Pru, I can see that this is an occasion for the utmost respectability. Can you act like a dresser? I want you to pretend to be the sort of upper servant who could chaperon me.'

'What, like Lady Ambridge's dresser?' Pru's eyes widened at the recollection of the stately dame in the employ of one of Decima's cousins. 'All starched up and top lofty?' Her eyes sparkled. 'I can do that, I reckon. Ooh, yes.'

When Decima descended the staircase she was followed by a haughty little person who looked down her nose at the footman and completely ignored the nervous kitchen maid who was carrying plates into the dining room.

Decima hesitated outside the door. Strangers. The familiar panic and shyness swept through her and she could feel her shoulders rounding into the defensive stoop that falsely promised invisibility.

No. She could not skulk out here and she could not appear in the dining room behaving as though she had something to hide. At least, after one look at her, Adam's guests would never suspect for a moment that anything untoward had been going on. If a gentleman was going to indulge in dalliance, he was not going to chose a gawky spinster who was almost thirty years of age. For once her failings would stand her in good stead.

She stood up straight and walked in. By the fireplace two couples dressed in the height of fashion were talking animat-edly to Adam, who turned at her entrance. His jaw dropped, just slightly, and she smiled, realising that with her hair up, her pearls glistening with expensive restraint and her one re-maining respectable morning dress on she looked every inch a lady and not like the hoyden who had been rolling in the snow or grooming horses.

She turned to Pru. 'You may take your breakfast with Mrs Chitty this morning, Staples.'

'Very good, Miss Ross.' Pru dropped a starchy curtsy and followed it with an inclination of her head towards Adam. 'Good morning, your lordship.'

Her exit seemed to bring Adam to his senses. 'Miss Ross, please allow me to introduce you to my friends. My cousin, Lady Wendover, and her husband, Lord Wendover.' A lively-looking lady of about five and twenty with an older husband with a grave expression and amused eyes. 'Mr and Mrs Highton.' A slightly older couple, beautifully dressed and she with languorous blue eyes. 'This is Miss Ross, who has been snowed up here and must be delighted to see some new faces after three days of boredom.'

'Not at all, my lord. I am delighted to meet your friends, of course, but I have been far from bored.' Decima smiled her thanks to Mr Highton, who pulled out a chair for her. 'You and Mrs Chitty have looked after us admirably.' She looked round at the others as they took their places. 'My only refuge until Lord Weston came to my aid was a most disreputable alehouse. You may imagine my relief at finding shelter here. Were you snowed up, too?'

Conversation flowed easily. It seemed Adam's guests had reached Grantham before they wisely decided to go no further than a comfortable inn and had set out early that morning. 'We were looking forward to Mrs Chitty's cooking,' Lord Wendover remarked, helping himself lavishly from the platter of ham, eggs and sliced sausage the footman presented.

'Indeed, yes,' Decima agreed. 'It is excellent, is it not?' This was all right, she could manage. They were too polite to stare at her height, in such a small group they could not whisper about her gawky plainness, and best of all, none of them were trying to marry her off.

After the meal she got to her feet. 'If you will excuse me, I think I should go and oversee my packing. I imagine my carriage should be here shortly.'

Pru was already upstairs, but, although the portmanteaux were out and open and several drawers had already been emptied onto the bed, there was no sign of her, only the sound of all-too-familiar bickering from the room across the landing.

'Pru!'

'Yes, ma'am.' Pru positively flounced out of Bates's room and into her own. 'That man!'

'I see you have started the packing.'

'Yes, Miss Dessy.'

'Then shall we finish before the postilions arrive?' she suggested briskly.

At last, leaving Pru to organise William the footman into carrying down the bags, she went to rejoin the guests. It would seem odd to avoid doing so any longer. Voices led her towards the drawing room and she slipped in unnoticed, taking a chair by the door. The others were all grouped facing towards the fireplace with its cheerful blaze, and seemed to be engaged in ragging Adam.

'So, was Sally as intent on finding you a bride as you feared, Adam?' Lady Wendover asked with teasing laughter in her voice.

'She was indeed, although I was completely lulled at first,' Adam answered ruefully. 'I was in the house for two days and there was not the hint of danger. No ingenuous young house-guest, no visiting bluestocking, no intimate parties threatened. I had let down my guard and then, out of the blue, the casual announcement that we were to expect a visit from some neighbours.'

'Who proved to be accompanied by whom? An unmarried daughter? A plain niece?' Mrs Highton enquired, much amused.

'No, worse.' Adam shuddered. 'An unmarried, middle-aged sister. A lady, I was assured, of fortune and possessed of intelligence and amiability. I took to my heels before they arrived and ended up in a snowdrift for my pains.'

'Oh, Lord!' Mrs Highton produced a trill of knowing laughter. 'A plain Jane, in other words. What *was* Sally thinking of? She must know what a high stickler you are.'

The shocked anger burned through Decima's veins. *How could he?* How could Adam joke with them about it? Oh, no names had been said, of course, he was too much the *gentle-man* for that. Somewhere there was another woman, just like her, breathing a sigh of relief because her unwanted 'suitor' had fled. And no doubt she was having to endure her relatives' endless lamentations that another 'opportunity' had been missed.

She heard the sound of her own voice sounding coolly amused. 'I should imagine she was thinking—like so many matchmakers think when they meddle in their single friends' lives—that she was doing it for the sake of the people concerned, when in fact it is something that neither party would want.'

The five people around the fire turned as one to gaze at her in surprise. As well they might, she realised in horror. As soon as the words were out of her mouth she knew how rude she was being about Adam's sister.

Adam's face went blank, but Lady Wendover recovered herself with a laugh. 'You are too severe, Miss Ross. Surely a sister must be concerned for her brother's welfare?'

'And this can be achieved by trying to fob an unwilling lady off on him? I am sure Lord Weston is more than capable of finding himself an entirely eligible bride, when he wishes to do so.' She had already unforgivably accused his sister of meddling, she might as well face this out and say what she thought for once.

'Well, I agree Adam might be unwilling to be party to such a thing, but surely not the lady? Presumably she is at her last prayers,' Lord Wendover observed.

'Is the married state so desirable that the humiliation of being paraded around by one's relatives is a price worth paying to achieve it? It is nothing but a mortification for the lady concerned and a source of discomfort to any man of sensibility. And, in fact, I am sure many men who remain bachelors for perfectly sound reasons of their own also suffer this sort of interference.' She was in full flow now, her new, strong inner voice carrying her along in the face of their surprise.

'You do not approve of matchmakers, then, Miss Ross?' Mr Highton enquired.

'I *despise* matchmakers,' she said roundly, then caught sight of Adam's frozen expression. She had gone too far. 'I beg your pardon, Lord Weston, if I have spoken disrespectfully of your sister. I am sure her motives are purely those of family affection.' The lady probably could not help herself, any more than Hermione could; it seemed that, once married, any female was immediately seized with the urge to see her entire acquaintance paired off.

Adam grimaced, apparently unoffended. 'Sally is certainly motivated by a strong concern for my interests. Unfortunately she does not take my views of what those are into account one jot. As for the lady in this case, probably Sally can imagine no greater felicity than being married to me and would be incredulous to learn she might not wish for such a meeting.'

'Dear Lady Jardine.' Mrs Highton smiled affectionately. 'I do miss her now she has moved to Nottinghamshire.'

'Lord Weston's sister Lady Jardine lives in Nottinghamshire?' Decima repeated blankly. She could feel the sickening certainty taking hold of her stomach. Suddenly she wished she had not eaten breakfast. It could not be a coincidence. There could not be two Lady Jardines in Nottinghamshire who had both tried to introduce an eligible brother to someone's spinster sister in the week before New Year. *She* was the lady 'at her last prayers' from whom Adam had run.

'Yes, they have recently moved there,' Adam said. 'Have you met them? I have just realised I never asked you where you had come from, the day we met in the snow. Had you come from Nottinghamshire?'

'No.' Her friend Henry always said that if one was going to tell a lie, it might as well be a wholehearted one. 'No,

Leicestershire. I regret I have not had the pleasure of Lady Jardine's acquaintance.'

She was saved by the footman entering. 'Miss Ross's carriage has arrived, my lord. I have brought in your baggage that was left with it. Everything appears to be in order.'

Decima rose to her feet. 'Then I must be on my way. Thank you so much, Lord Weston, for rescuing me from a most uncomfortable predicament. If you will excuse me, I must just go and thank Mrs Chitty.' She exchanged farewells with Adam's guests and escaped into the kitchen where Pru was organising the footman.

'All those bags inside the carriage, I don't want my lady's things getting cold and damp… Miss Dessy, I'll just run up and get our cloaks.'

Her head was still buzzing with shock and emotion, but Decima made herself speak pleasantly to the housekeeper. 'You must be Mrs Chitty. I have to thank you for your discretion, and also for your wonderfully well-stocked stillroom. I do trust we have not wreaked too much havoc with your domestic arrangements.'

'I'm only too glad it was of help, ma'am.' Mrs Chitty's eyes were regarding Decima with sharp intelligence, but her voice was entirely respectful as she added, 'I'm sure his lordship took great care of you.'

'Will you allow me to escort you to the front door, Miss Ross?' It was Adam, entering soundlessly behind her.

Somehow Decima managed to turn round and look at him. This man—the man she had laughed with, worried with, almost lost her virtue to—this man was the one who had fled his sister's house rather than meet her and exchange a few stilted pleasantries. And who, all unknowing, mocked her to his friends.

'I do not stand on ceremony, Lord Weston,' she replied coolly. 'The back door will do very well.' Where had that girl got to? 'Mrs Chitty, would you be so very kind as to find what has delayed my dresser?'

As the housekeeper bustled off, Decima held out her hand. 'My thanks once more, Lord Weston. I shudder to think what several days cooped up in the Red Cock would have been like, or the effect upon Pru's health. I was most fortunate indeed to have been rescued by you. Please give Bates my best wishes for a speedy recovery.'

He ignored her careful formality. 'You are angry with me; I should not have spoken so lightly of my sister's schemes and my reaction to them.'

'Not at all, and I must apologise for my intemperate response. You simply chanced upon one of my prejudices, my lord. I feel for the lady in the case; those of us who do not regard the married state as the be-all and end-all of existence must support each other, do you not agree? Ah, Pru, there you are.' The maid was pink-faced, clutching the cloaks bundled together.

'Goodbye, Decima.' Adam caught her hand in his, the warmth of his grasp penetrating her winter gloves with ease. 'I wish we had been able to talk together longer—there are things I would have wished to say.'

It was difficult to hold his gaze. Decima felt her own eyes waver and then fall before his. 'Nothing of any import, I trust. Now, I really must go. Goodbye.'

For a second she thought he was going to bend and kiss her, but Mrs Chitty came in, and Pru was holding out her cloak, and the moment was gone.

In the yard the snow had turned to muddy slush and to one side all that remained of their snowman was a pile of snow with an incongruous carrot sticking out of it and a battered tricorne perched on the top.

Decima let the postilion assist them into the carriage, only turning to look at Adam when they were settled with the rugs over their knees. He was standing in the snow, his expression unfathomable as it rested on her. Did he feel as wretched as she that their days of intimacy and informality had ended in this chilly, formal farewell?

She raised her hand as the carriage began to move and Adam lifted his in acknowledgement. Did he stand looking after her, or did he turn at once on his heel and go back to the safe familiarity of his friends, putting this whole bizarre episode out of his mind?

Blankly she stared out of the window onto sodden fields and melting drifts as the carriage made its way through the lanes, onto the turnpike road and headed east. Would they reach Swaffham, and home, today? It would be a long journey, and all would depend on how bad the roads were and how good the horses they obtained at the changes. There were excellent inns along the way—that was not a problem—but Decima ached now for this journey to be over and for the safety of her own room, her own bed, her old life. Her old innocence.

Their luck held, with the roads in a reasonable state and horses that held a good pace. Decima was just thinking that at this rate they could count on taking a late luncheon at Wisbech, when something made her glance across at Pru.

The maid looked woebegone, huddled in her corner, her nose pink and one large tear running down her plump cheek.

'Oh, Pru! Are you feeling poorly? I should never have dragged you out today,' she exclaimed remorsefully. 'I will pull the check string and tell the men to stop at the next respectable inn we come to.'

Pru gulped and shook her head. 'It's not that, Miss Dessy, I feel fine, honestly I do. I'm nice and warm and the carriage is ever so comfortable.'

'Then whatever is it?' Decima changed seats so she could sit beside Pru and feel her forehead. Quite normal. 'Tell me,

Pru, we will sort it out, whatever it is.' She took the maid's hand and patted it.

'There's nothing you can do, Miss Dessy.' Pru scrabbled for her handkerchief and blew her nose miserably. 'It's just foolishness.'

'Of course there is something to be done, Pru. I refuse to believe there is not, whatever the problem. Now tell me.'

'It's Jethro,' Pru quavered.

'Jethro?' Who on earth was Jethro?

'Bates, Miss Dessy. His name's Jethro.'

'Has he said something to upset you?' Decima felt quite at sea. The two of them had spent hours together, apparently in a state of constant bickering, but what was there in that to produce tears now?

'Oh, no, Miss Dessy.' Pru's face crumpled. 'I think I'm in love with him.'

'You are in love with Bates?' Decima stared at her. 'But I didn't think you liked him much. You seemed to argue a lot and be exasperated with him...' Her voice trailed off. 'He is rather older than you,' she suggested cautiously after a pause.

'A bit,' Pru admitted. 'Doesn't matter, though.'

'No, of course not,' Decima agreed hastily. 'But does he feel the same way?'

'I don't know.' Pru's lip trembled in a way that made Decima's quiver in sympathy. 'I think so. He's not what you'd call chatty.'

'That is certainly true. Did you agree to correspond?'

Pru shook her head. 'It was all a bit sudden, leaving, and I didn't think.' She sniffed again, her cheeks flushed, and an uneasy thought crept into Decima's mind.

'Pru, you didn't...you haven't done anything...unwise? Have you?' Then she remembered. 'No, of course not, how silly of me, you couldn't have, even if you had been so imprudent, not with his broken leg.' There was a silence, then

Pru slid a sideways look at Decima. 'Pru! Truly? How? No…do not tell me, I do *not* want to know.'

What if Pru becomes pregnant? With that thought came the treacherous memory of Adam's body hard against hers, her own newly sensitised flesh quivering towards surrender. She could so easily have been worrying about exactly the same thing for herself. At least she would never have to face him again, never find herself laid open to either the temptation or the rejection that encounter would bring.

The tears were rolling fatly down the maid's cheeks now. *Oh, Lord! Now what am I to do?* Charlton would say she should instantly dismiss Pru, but then Charlton could be the most unblushing hypocrite. 'Pru, if you still feel the same way about him in a month or two, then I promise we will go and find some way to be close to Lord Weston so you can see Bates again.' And what if Pru was with child and Bates was not prepared to do the right thing? That was a bridge to be crossed if they came to it.

Pru gripped her hands convulsively, too upset to speak her thanks. Decima smiled at her, as comfortingly as she could. But inside she quaked; there was no way she could bring Bates and Pru together again without Adam's help. And that meant seeing him again.

Chapter Eleven

Augusta was, predictably, delighted to see her back, completely incurious about her journey and hardly interested to learn how Hermione and Charlton were. But she did blink vaguely at Decima as they stood in her new glasshouse and observe, 'You are looking different, dear. Have you changed your hair?'

That was typical of Augusta and Decima took no notice. But she *was* shaken by her dear friend Henry. Sir Henry Freshford rode over from his neighbouring estate the next day, alerted by the infallible country grapevine that she was back.

'Henry!' Decima stooped to receive his brotherly kiss on her cheek, so much more welcome than any salutation of Charlton's. 'Did you have a good Christmas?'

'Yes, fine,' he replied, looking at her oddly. 'Dessy, what have you been up to?'

'Me? Why, nothing. Do come and see Augusta's latest extravagance.' She tugged his arm until he followed her through to the glasshouse, built out at an angle from the house so that it formed a conservatory extension to one of the sitting rooms. 'Isn't it wonderful? She is planning to put ferns and palms and even orchids in here.'

She expected Henry to be immediately interested, to look at the heating pipes and ask about the water supply. Instead he stood regarding her, his head on one side and a smile quirking the corner of his mouth.

Henry Freshford, baronet, was the best-looking man Decima had ever met. Although his height was below the average, his features were classically perfect, his colouring blonde, his eyes a periwinkle blue and his figure elegant. His looks in themselves were enough to draw many female admirers, but his breeding and wealth attracted the young ladies' mamas even more.

The short man who had to fight off lures and the tall woman who no one would consider marrying had formed an unlikely, but deep, friendship. For Decima he was the brother she would have chosen; for him, she seemed to be the perfect feminine confidante.

'Why are you staring?' she demanded, sinking down onto one of the new sofas that had been bought for the glasshouse. 'I thought you would be interested in what Augusta has been doing.'

'I'm much more interested in what you've been doing, Dessy.' He sat opposite her and crossed his legs, leaning back to study her face.

'What do you mean? And, please, do not call me Dessy. I've just realised how much I hate it.'

'Of course, Decima.' Normally he would have been distracted enough by this to demand to know all about her sudden decision. Not today. 'Now, stop changing the subject and tell me who he is.'

'Who?' It came out as a startled squeak and she knew she had blushed. 'What *can* you mean, Henry?'

Now Henry seemed embarrassed. 'I'm not sure how to put this delicately. I mean you have a sort of…glow about you. A new sort of awareness of yourself. As you know—' colour touched his cheekbones too '—I regard you with absolutely brotherly feelings, but even I am aware of a certain...*frisson* about you.' He coughed and tugged at his cuffs. 'I assumed there was a man who had, um, stirred up some inner, er, emotions.' He ground to a halt.

'It *shows*?' Decima was horrified. 'I mean, I have not the slightest idea what you are talking about. Anyone would think I had taken a lover.'

'And you have not?' Henry seemed to have recovered from his embarrassment.

'No!' Decima looked at his sceptical, trustworthy face and gave up. 'No, I haven't, but I nearly did. If you promise not to tell anyone, it would be so good to confide.'

When she had poured out the tale of everything that had happened since that last breakfast with Charlton and Hermione—shorn of a considerable amount of completely unmentionable detail—Henry was positively rubbing his hands together with delight.

'You see? I have been telling you that there is absolutely nothing wrong with your appearance as far as anyone but your idiotic relatives and a handful of equally idiotic snobs are concerned. And this man proves it.'

'But nobody else has ever seemed to find me remotely attractive,' Decima wailed, wanting to be convinced and fearing it was only Henry's partisanship speaking.

'I expect this time you had too much else to think about to be working yourself up into being an unattractive spinster,' he retorted brutally. 'He saw you as you really are, not round-shouldered and self-effacing and with all your charm and character hidden.'

'He is very tall. He doesn't realise what a gawky beanpole I am.'

'Society is full of men at least as tall as you, and taller. That won't wash.'

'And he is very odd—he likes my freckles. And he doesn't

seem to think my mouth is too big. In fact, he said I should not pout because he wanted to—' She stopped, blushing furiously.

'What?' Henry enquired, interested. 'Bite it?'

'Yes! Now you cannot tell me that's normal.'

'It's perfectly normal. This is an extremely improper conversation, Dess...Decima, but as we've gone so far, it is a entirely predictable thing for him to want to do. And liking your freckles does not make him odd. *I* like your freckles. He sounds a completely typical man with his due measure of healthy masculine desires, to me.'

'Goodness.' How did that make her feel? Decima tried to sort out her emotions. Adam wasn't some oddity who found her attractive for weird reasons of his own or because he was stranded with her and anything was better than nothing. He had kissed her because, according to Henry—who was the most reassuringly down-to-earth male of her acquaintance— any normal man would want to. Her friend was speaking again. 'I beg your pardon. I missed what you said.'

'I asked you what is going to happen next.'

'Why, nothing. Obviously I do not think it would be a good idea to see him again.' Henry didn't have to say anything, one raised eyebrow was enough. 'I told you, he was perfectly horrible about me when he was talking to his friends. He admits he ran away rather than meet me.'

'But he hadn't met you then, before he ran, so in what way was he being horrible?' Henry enquired. 'You were just as horrible—you ran away rather than meet him and I'll wager that if you had got here without misadventure you would have indignantly told me all about how your family tried to match you up with some ghastly man you would be sure to take an instant dislike to.'

'That is *not* fair!' Decima stopped, thought, regarded Henry's face. 'Oh dear, it is fair, isn't it? I would never have thought of it like that.'

'Are you in love with him?'

'I don't know.' Decima stared at him, a frown wrinkling her brow. Something inside her became hollow. 'How do I tell?'

'Damned if I know either,' Henry retorted cheerfully. 'It hasn't happened to me, more's the pity. I imagine when it does, you just think "I'm in love". Or you go off your food, or dream about the other person all day. Anyways, what are you going to do about him?'

'I wasn't going to do anything,' Decima admitted. 'I can hardly go chasing after him, now can I? Even if I wanted to,' she added doubtfully. 'But the complicating factor is that Pru seems to have fallen for his groom—in fact, quite literally fallen, and I may find myself having to do something about *that* before very long.'

'Hmm.' Henry did not seem to have anything much to contribute to that problem. 'You need something to take your mind off this, Des…sorry, Decima. Mama's going to open up the London house for the Season to fire off Caroline into society. I will be going up as well—why don't you come too and stay with us? Mama would appreciate your company. We are going up at the end of February to get all Caro's gowns and fallals sorted out early. What do you say?'

It was very tempting. She had already thought about going up for the Season, if only to horrify Charlton, who would be scandalised at the thought of her under any chaperonage other than that provided by one of their aunts or cousins. Decima gave herself a little shake. If she was going to do things only in reaction to her half-brother, then she was just as much in his thrall as she had ever been. She must do what she wanted, for herself. And she wanted to go to London, and find out if what Henry said was true. Could it be that if she was not shy and did not think about being odd, then other people wouldn't think it either?

And then there was a very good chance that Adam would be in town for the Season as well. Not that she wanted to see him for herself, of course, but if Pru needed help with her improbable romance, then she had to do her best to assist her.

'Yes, Henry, thank you very much. I would love to come to London and stay with your mama.'

'What the hell do you mean, you can't find them?' Adam Grantham glowered at his agent who stood the other side of the broad desk, a sheaf of papers clutched in his hands. 'How hard can it be to trace one English gentleman and his family? You have been looking for three weeks, damn it.'

The man went red, but kept his composure. Adam reined in his temper. He had never found Franklin negligent in his duties and had no reason to suspect he was not applying himself now. 'Sit down, man, show me what you have done so far.'

The agent took the proffered chair and spread out his papers. 'You told me the gentleman was called Charlton Ross, my lord, but you did not know whether he has a title. His wife's name is Hermione and he has a sister Decima. He has a house somewhere near enough to Whissendine for his sister's carriage to have reached the point where you met in one morning in poor travelling conditions. Miss Ross said it was in Leicestershire.

'So I searched the *Peerage*, the *Landed Gentry* and even *Crockford's Clerical Directory* just in case he was a clergyman. Nothing. Then I tried the various county directories—including Nottinghamshire to be on the safe side. There is not a sign of a Charlton Ross. There are plenty of entries for Ross, and I checked second names where they were given. Nothing that matches. The carriage appears to have been owned by the family as there is no record of it being hired at any livery stable I can find.

'Then I tried the Norfolk end of things, but I couldn't find any single ladies or widows by the name of Ross who might match—and, of course, the lady's cousin might easily be a widow, or a maiden lady of a different surname. The only trace I have is of a party that matched your description taking luncheon at the Rising Sun just outside Wisbech. After that, they vanish. The number of carriages on the post roads that day was considerable, what with people getting themselves back home after being held up by the bad weather. We tried the turnpikes in all directions, but no one recalled them. I am sorry, my lord.'

'Thank you, Franklin. I'm sure you have been extremely thorough.' The man bowed himself out, leaving Adam brooding at the desk he had borrowed in his host's study. He poured himself a large brandy and thought.

Longminster House, the rural seat of the Earl of Minster, Adam's uncle by marriage, was *en fête* for the christening of the first of the Minster grandchildren and Adam had resigned himself to a week of baby-worshipping, dancing attendance on numerous relatives and avoiding lectures on his unwed state.

One of the few avenues of escape he had found was in trying to cheer up a distant relative of his Aunt Minster's, Olivia Channing. He remembered her from her schoolroom days as tiny and shy. Now she was a little beauty—still tiny, but with all the blonde loveliness of a fairy. Add to that the best of good breeding and exquisite manners and one had the perfect eligible, albeit desperately shy, young lady. But Olivia's problem was that her family was extremely hard up. Adam suspected that if her dowry amounted to a few hundred, that was all it was.

And she was being dragged about, pushed into society by her desperate mama, when she believed all she could expect was to be snubbed, despite her looks and her sweetness. A month ago he would have shrugged and taken no notice of her. Now, with Decima's bitter words about matchmakers still ringing in his ears, he regarded her with sympathy and tried to make up to her for the fact that she found herself constantly on the outside of things.

She was a funny little thing, he thought. Even now she was used to him and had begun to chat to him with less constraint, he always had the feeling that she was glancing over his shoulder, checking for something.

He refilled his glass, dismissing Olivia as an insoluble problem. The presence of Peregrine Grantham, the son of his father's late younger brother, was another matter altogether—both the silver lining to the visit and a heartening reminder that lectures on his duty to produce an heir could be met by pointing out young Perry's numerous admirable qualities. Not that Perry, or his mother, were holding their breath at the thought of him stepping into his cousin's shoes.

'I do wish you'd get married, Adam,' Perry had complained the day before as they trudged across a muddy field, retrievers at their heels and a dozen pigeons hanging from their shot belts. 'Here I am, wanting to join up, and all I get from my guardians is lectures on how the heir to a viscounty doesn't go risking his neck in the army.'

Adam had grinned at him and informed him that he had no intention of getting leg-shackled for his sake and he would just have to wait another couple of years until he could do as he chose.

'The war'll be over by then,' Perry had retorted with good humour. 'No, the answer is to get you married off, Adam.'

That evening, stretching long legs in front of a blazing fire and sipping Minster's best liqueur brandy, Adam found himself contemplating matrimony seriously for perhaps the first time.

He was not staying single for Perry's sake; the lad had too much intelligence and ambition to wait around for dead men's shoes. No, Adam was unwed simply because no lady had ever piqued his interest enough to give up his independence and privacy. Except one.

He had set Franklin on Decima's trail as soon as he had realised he could not find any mention of her brother in any of his reference books and that the polite note of thanks he had received three days after her departure gave no address. At the time he had not asked himself why he wanted to find her, only that he needed to make sure she was all right. The fact that her note left him in no doubt of that was beside the point.

Now Adam reluctantly faced the fact that he missed her. It was not just that his body ached for her, although it certainly did. He wanted to get to know her better, to hear that rich, wicked chuckle again, to dance a waltz with her and tease her about her cookery. He wanted to make her blush and cajole her out of her sudden fits of shyness. And he wanted to find out whether this unfamiliar ache around his heart was love.

And now, with the paperwork spread out before him detailing false trail after false trail, it seemed she had vanished. The only thing he could think was that she had not given him her true surname and, if that was the case, even setting the Bow Street Runners on her was not likely to be productive. It seemed that she was not as interested in resuming their strange friendship as he was himself.

He roused himself at the sound of the changing gong and made his way upstairs, only to remember that tonight was the occasion of the dance Aunt Minster was throwing to celebrate not only the arrival of her first grandchild, but also the betrothal of her last and youngest daughter, Sylvia.

There would be a family dinner first, then the arrival of guests and the prospect of a long night of dancing and making conversation in an overheated ballroom.

'What are you about, Greaves?' His valet was stropping a

razor and regarding with some satisfaction his master's newest and most elegant evening clothes laid out on the bed.

'I had made sure your lordship would require to shave before dinner.' He shook out a towel and waited patiently beside the chair, managing to ignore the singular lack of enthusiasm on his employer's face.

With a sigh Adam cast himself down on the chair and did his best to suppress his bad humour. Greaves did not deserve having his employer's disappointment and frustration taken out on him, nor was it his fault that Adam was in the worst possible state of mind to appreciate the elegance of the new satin knee breeches or the gloss the valet had achieved on the dancing pumps.

'I'm not in the mood for a party, Greaves,' he observed mildly as the man whipped up a lather and began to apply it to his face.

'No, my lord. I have observed, if I might be so bold, that dances at which most of the partners are in some way related to a gentleman rarely offer him as much entertainment, however select the company.'

Despite himself Adam grinned. No, this was not likely to be the sort of party at which one could entertain oneself with dashing matrons or semi-respectable widows.

He went down to dinner only to realise that more guests had arrived, necessitating the butler to order all the extra leaves to be put in the dining table.

Perry wandered up to him, looking disgruntled. 'I say, Adam, all the card tables are set out for whist for the old tabbies; we're going to have to *dance* all evening.'

'Well, find yourself some pretty girls to flirt with,' Adam retorted unsympathetically. Perry was still at an age when girls were at best incomprehensible and at worst frightening. 'What about Olivia over there? I'm sure she is your type. We'll go over and you can practise on her.'

Perry, suspecting teasing, shot a hunted look in the direction of Adam's gaze and relaxed. 'Oh, Olivia Channing. I'm sure she'll take no interest in me with you around.'

Adam put this down to adolescent insecurity and ignored it. The chit looked suitable for helping overcome Perry's awkwardness—there was a sweet expression on her face and an air of modest shyness about her that was appealing. She would gaze at Perry as though he were wonderful and not make him feel threatened.

Adam took his cousin firmly by the elbow and began to make his way through the dinner guests, only for them to be hailed imperiously by his Aunt Minster.

'There you are, Peregrine. Stop gossiping to Adam about shooting or horses or whatever you are doing and come and talk to the admiral.' She detached Perry from his grip, hooked her own hand through his arm and carried on in the direction she had been heading.

Deprived of his companion, Adam carried on to Olivia's side. She bobbed a curtsy. 'My lord.' Her voice was soft and slightly breathless and she regarded him with wide eyes.

Too young, too spiritless and far too short, Adam thought, his mind suddenly full of a tall, unconventional lady a good eight or nine years older than this child. And her mama should never have dressed Olivia in that daring style with such low-set sleeves. It was more suited to a married woman. Then his natural kindness took over and he set himself to charm her out of the worst of her nerves.

She certainly opened up a little in the interval before dinner was announced, although Adam once again had the uneasy feeling that she was constantly looking behind him at someone or something. As he took her arm to take her to find her dinner partner, he glanced back and recognised her parents. They seemed to be keeping a very close eye on her, although, with her seeming so nervous, perhaps that was only to be expected.

Dinner was as boring as he expected, trapped between an aunt who twittered and a matron who showed a disconcerting inclination to flirt with him. Adam was aware of drinking steadily and of an overwhelming desire to escape as soon as the covers were drawn. What he wanted was an unconventional lady to talk to, to tease, to—

'Grantham!'

He looked up, startled out of his reverie.

'You are chased,' his uncle said sternly and he found that, indeed, the decanters were at his elbow. With a careless hand he filled his glass and pushed them on down the table.

When the gentlemen made their way through to the ballroom he looked around for escape. Good, the conservatory looked like a shaded haven of palms, comfortable seating and solitude. It was too early in the evening for daring couples to seek it out for a little dalliance or for desperate wallflowers to retreat there to hide.

Snagging a glass of champagne off a tray as the footman passed, Adam slid in through the nearest door and retreated as far into the leafy sanctuary as he could.

Now, at last, he could sit and think in peace about what he was going to do about Decima. A swish of skirts made him stiffen and draw back. He could glimpse a blonde head through the foliage and the sound of a bravely suppressed sob.

Damn it. It was Olivia. Adam eased round until he could see her, head bent, applying a fragile scrap of lace to her eyes. With a sigh he reached into his pocket and found a clean handkerchief.

'Olivia?' She started dramatically and stared at him.

'Oh, thank you, my lord.' As he pressed the linen into her hand her fingers gripped his and he found himself on the seat beside her.

'Olivia? What is wrong?' *Hell, what did one say to weeping girls?* 'There, there.' He patted her shoulder, wishing he hadn't had quite so much to drink and could think about what to do for the best. Fetch her mama? She gave a gasping sob and the next thing he knew he had an armful of quivering young lady.

Instinct took over and Adam gathered her into a comforting embrace, only to find that her gown appeared to have a life of its own and was sliding off her shoulders. Under his palms he could feel soft, bare, heated skin.

'Olivia? You must try and...' Her face tipped up to his, piquant with some trembling emotion he did not understand. Her lashes were spiked with tears, her soft pink lips parted. So he kissed her, a gentle, chaste kiss intended purely to comfort.

'*My lord*!'

'Adam!'

Startled, he twisted round, instinctively sheltering Olivia in his arm. Facing him were both her parents and his Aunt Minster. And even as he stared at them he realised that Olivia was tugging at the neckline of a bodice which had fallen quite scandalously low over her pretty breasts.

'Well, my lord,' Mr Channing uttered in outraged tones, 'just what do you think you are about?' Beside him his wife could not quite keep the look of triumph off her face.

Under the circumstances, what was there to say? Or even to do? He was caught by the oldest trick in the book. 'Mr Channing.' Adam got to his feet, keeping his body between himself and Olivia, who was frantically trying to rearrange her bodice. 'I will do myself the honour of speaking to you tomorrow morning.'

Chapter Twelve

Adam refixed the interested and attentive expression on his face and made himself concentrate on what Lady Brotherton was saying. Four weeks as an engaged man was already trying his patience to the utmost, and finding himself kicking his heels waiting for Olivia to return from a shopping expedition with her cousin Sophie Brotherton was definitely not to his taste.

'They *are* naughty girls,' Lady Brotherton clucked indulgently. 'But I am sure you will forgive Olivia her excitement…it is not every day a girl is shopping for her trousseau.'

In Adam's experience so far it seemed to be occupying Olivia's every waking moment, which suited him very well, except when he was having to wait for her.

'But you know what girls are,' his hostess continued indulgently.

'Well, I do have two sisters,' Adam admitted.

'Only the two?' Lady Brotherton looked pitying. 'Dear Sophie is the youngest of six.'

'And all as lovely as she, I dare say,' Adam responded, knowing what was expected of him.

'To be sure, although it is boastful of me to say so. And all well married, too—I have high hopes for little Sophie.' Lady Brotherton got to her feet. 'Would you care to see their portrait?'

What Adam wanted to be doing was exercising his horses in his new curricle. He smiled with every appearance of delight and followed her to the other end of the room where a group portrait hung. The breath caught in his throat and time stopped.

Six charming versions of Sophie at various ages sat and stood, arms around each other, and at the back was a seventh girl. Head and shoulders taller than the others, a brunette with her hair scraped back into an unflattering plain style, her shoulders hunched and rounded and an expression quite lacking in any emotion. Her lids were hooded, hiding her eyes, but Adam was left with the impression of an animal, cornered and baited, retreating into its own blank misery.

'Who is the seventh girl?' he asked indifferently when he had control of his voice, knowing as he spoke what the answer would be.

'Oh, that is Dessy Ross. Her mother's first husband was some sort of connection of Lord Brotherton's—I really cannot recall now what it was. But her brother Charlton was quite in despair about what to do with her, so we brought her out with our girls—one after the other. One tried one's best to find her a match. Quite hopeless, of course—you might not be able to tell from the portrait, but she is impossibly tall and dreadfully freckled. And, of course, that unfortunate mouth. Sweet girl, although very quiet.'

Lady Brotherton went back to her chair, leaving Adam staring at the portrait. No wonder Decima was so self-conscious about her height, her looks. She had been brought up thinking she was not just plain, but irredeemably ineligible as a result. Her remarks about matchmakers hit Adam like a flick from a whip; her own experience of snubs and humiliations must be deep indeed—scars on her soul.

'Charlton Ross,' Adam said cautiously as he walked back to his seat. It would not do to let slip he knew Decima. 'That sounds familiar. I wonder if I know him.' He raised an interrogative eyebrow and Lady Brotherton shook her head.

'No, my lord, it cannot be the man you know. Charlton is Dessy's half-brother—Lord Carmichael. He lives in Nottinghamshire. Poor dear Dessy,' she added with a pitying expression on her face. 'I believe the Carmichaels have still not given up hope of finding her a husband. So optimistic of them, for what can one do about such handicaps? It is hardly as though it were spots—anyone might grow out of those.' She regarded Adam with concern. 'Are you quite well, my lord? You seem a little pale.'

As well I might, Adam thought bitterly. *Decima Ross was the woman I joked about escaping from—and she knows it.* And then he realised just what he had learned and what it meant.

He knew now why Decima had been so cold to him that last day, he knew how to find her—and that there was no honourable way he *could* seek her out. For he was betrothed to Olivia and he saw, with painful clarity, that what he wanted from Decima Ross was, quite simply, her hand in marriage.

Decima perched on the edge of the bed, sorting silk stockings from cotton ones while Pru carried her unpacked clothes from trunk to clothes presses.

'Well, here we are, Pru. London again after so long. It must be four years since I managed to escape being dragged round by poor Lady Brotherton, doing the Season. Goodness, I had forgotten how noisy it is—and Lady Freshford was so pleased to tell me this was a nice quiet room!'

She scooped up the rolled stockings and went to drop them in a drawer, then turned to watch the maid. Four weeks ago Pru had confided stiffly that there was no unplanned consequence from her unwise dalliance with Bates, but since then had said nothing more about him.

Decima could tell she was not happy though, and sighed inwardly. 'Pru, now we are in London, do you wish me to discover whether Lord Weston is in town, too?'

Pru hesitated, biting her lip, then sat down on the bed. 'Yes, please, Miss Des…Miss Decima. But you won't say anything to Bates, will you?'

'I doubt I would see him,' Decima soothed her. 'If I can talk to Lord Weston, I will tell him that there appears to be some affection between the two of you and ask him to let drop, quite casually, where we are living. Then Bates can make up his own mind and will never know you are concerned.'

Pru nodded. 'Yes, that would do it. I wouldn't want him to think I was chasing him. But how will you find out about his lordship?'

'I'll ask Sir Henry,' Decima said. 'He will be sure to know.' And before she went calling upon anyone she was going to send for a *coiffeur* and do some very serious shopping. She might be a spinster, but Decima was firmly decided that from now on she was going to be a very stylish spinster indeed. *After all*, she had told herself in the long days and nights of January and February as she brooded on her New Year's resolution, *I have no one to please but myself now*. If she was no longer in the marriage mart, then she had nothing to prove, no one to compete with. There was no one whose opinion she had to pander to, and she had all the money she needed to indulge herself. And indulge herself she would.

Wanting to look her absolute best for a certain tall gentleman with grey eyes had nothing whatsoever to do with it.

Adam retreated into his study in his London town house to recover from the latest descent of his future mother-in-law,

Olivia in tow, to discuss wedding plans. The wedding, it appeared, would take place in June; it did not seem she considered it necessary to consult his wishes in the matter. The announcement of the betrothal would go into the papers the next day—a suitable length of time from the compromising incident at the ball to ensure there was no talk.

On any other subject, with any other person, Adam would have no more stood for such Turkish treatment than he would have stood still to have his foot driven over. With Mrs Channing he had no wish to start her on one of her lectures on his libertine and rakish behaviour and how he should indulge Olivia in every way possible to make up for his outrageous attempt at seduction.

Considering that he knew all too well that he had been stalked and entrapped, and that she must know he knew, Adam wondered at her hypocrisy. All that stopped him retaliating was a chivalrous concern for Olivia, whom he knew had been merely a browbeaten pawn in her parents' machinations. She would never dare to stand out against them, just as he knew, with a sinking heart, that, once married, his word would be law and she would never, ever, argue with him.

What he wanted was a bride who would argue, with her elbows on the table, waving her cutlery for emphasis if need be. He wanted a wife who would tease him, would join in foolish whims with a twinkle in her eye and would come into his arms with—

'A lady has called my lord.' It was Dalrymple, his butler.

'What?' Adam stared, aware that he had not even heard him come in.

'A lady, my lord. She declined to give me her name.'

Adam felt both his eyebrows rise. It was not like Dalrymple to make such an elementary error of judgement. 'Are you sure you mean a *lady*?'

'Certainly, my lord. A most well-bred lady, if I might venture an opinion. With her maid in attendance.'

So, not an ex-mistress hoping to presume on past favours, then. 'Show her in, Dalrymple.'

'In here, my lord? Into your study?' The man looked scandalised.

'Certainly in here.' It would be just like Mrs Channing to discover she had forgotten her parasol and return unexpectedly, and he had no intention of being found entertaining strange ladies in his drawing room. The butler bowed stiffly and went out.

'Madam,' he announced frigidly, holding the door for her to enter, then left, shutting it behind him with a decided click. The lady was alone.

Adam stared at his visitor for several seconds, half-convinced he was hallucinating. If it were not for her height, he would have thought he was looking at a complete stranger, an exquisitely dressed, elegantly coiffed young matron.

Then she smiled, curving her wide, generous mouth. Freckles danced across her cheeks as they rounded with the smile and the cool grey eyes sparkled. 'My lord.'

'Decima.' Adam was across the room and had caught her in his arms before he could think. She gave a little gasp, but did not resist him, and her face tipped trustingly up to his. 'Oh, God. I thought I'd never find you again.'

Her mouth was soft under his hard kiss, opening to him with an innocence that his previous embraces had still not taught to be knowing. It was that very innocence, the sweet scent of her, the way her palm fluttered against his cheek, that brought him to himself.

'Decima,' he said again, stepping back. 'Forgive me, I was taken by surprise at seeing you. Please, will you not sit down.' He gestured towards a chair, feeling hideously gauche, as formal now he had just been unforgivably free with her.

'Thank you.' She sank down gracefully and sat poised, watching him. She smiled suddenly, her nose wrinkling endearingly, and the elegant lady vanished to be replaced by the hoyden who groomed her own horses. 'I was pleased to see you, too.'

Adam tugged at the bell pull before sitting opposite her. His heart was beating like a drum. Nothing mattered except that she was there.

'Refreshments,' he said impatiently as the butler appeared. He wanted to be alone with her, talk to her, put her at her ease—put himself at his ease, if it came to that.

'You look…' He struggled for the right word. 'You look incredible. I hardly recognised you.' *Oh, no, that was hardly the most tactful thing to have said!*

Decima produced the gurgle of laughter that never failed to make his heart stutter. 'Better than when I was grooming horses, perhaps? Or perhaps better than my kitchen-maid look?'

'Not better, just different.' What was the matter with him? Normally he had the smooth tongue and the flattering touch of the accomplished rake. Decima reduced him to a gibbering idiot in seconds. 'Have you forgiven me?' Better get it over with. 'I now know your brother's name and who it was I fled from rather than meet before New Year.'

'Oh.' She looked at him, her head slightly tipped to one side like a curious robin. 'How?'

'I saw your portrait at Lady Brotherton's.'

'Oh,' she said again, dropping her gaze to her clasped hands. 'Hideous, is it not?'

'I thought it was sad that no one seemed capable of seeing your true beauty,' he said gently, and was rewarded by a glowing look from her grey eyes.

'Thank you. You seem to see something that other people do not, which is kind of you.'

'I am not kind,' he retorted roughly. 'Why have you come?'

Damn it, Adam, why not show a complete lack of finesse while you're about it?

'Ah. Now that is difficult.' Her gaze dropped again and the colour mounted in her cheeks. 'It was hard to come and speak to you like this, I don't deny it. Especially after all the things I said about marriage and matchmakers.'

Her colour was positively hectic now. With a visible effort she raised her eyes to his face and said, 'You might not be...happy about what I have to say, but I think one should be...honest about...about love.'

Love? She was telling him she loved him? 'Decima.' He reached out and took her hands in his. 'Decima, I think you had better say what you mean.'

'This is very difficult. Has Bates said anything to you?'

'Bates? Go away,' he snapped at Dalrymple, who opened the door, a tray of refreshments neatly balanced on one gloved hand.

'Very good, my lord.' The butler executed a smart turn and removed himself.

'What the hell has Bates got to do with anything?' She was going to tell him she had fallen passionately for Bates, that was it. His life could hardly be in more of a mess.

'It is Pru. I think she is in love with him. But you know what he's like—so taciturn. I thought if you could drop a hint, let him know where she was to be found—then, if he was interested in her, he might make contact.'

'I see,' Adam said flatly, sitting back in his chair. 'So this is all about Bates and Pru. You would not have come to find me if it had not been for that. Just how serious is it?'

He seemed to have flustered her. *Good*, Adam thought viciously, then hated himself.

'Things apparently became quite...that is...I did worry at one point that she might be with child,' Decima admitted, her high colour returning. 'But fortunately not. But I have no idea if his affections are engaged, or simply his, er, physical reactions.'

Well, good for Bates, Adam thought bitterly. To manage a seduction with a broken leg argued a determination and aplomb he had been unaware of. In fact, he doubted he could have accomplished it himself. *And the old devil had the nerve to lecture me about propriety!*

'By all means let us put ourselves about to secure the happiness of others,' he said, hating the sarcastic edge to his voice. Decima looked bemused at his tone. *Of course,* he thought, *she has no idea what I feel for her. How could she? She thinks she has had a salutary experience with a rake, that is all.* 'Are you sure it would not be—let me be sure I have the words right—a piece of meddling?'

'Yes, I am sure,' Decima snapped back, her understandable anger at his tone finally overcoming her good manners. 'Pru wants to find out what he feels for her, that is all. He can choose to ignore the information if he so wishes—she has far too much pride to pursue him.'

She got to her feet in a swirl of skirts, so suddenly that he had to scramble to stand, too. 'If you wish to have nothing to do with it, then I will go down to the mews and see him on the pretext of asking about Fox. You have absolutely no need to trouble yourself about the emotional well-being of your servants or mine, my lord. Good day to you.'

'Decima.' Adam managed to get between her and the door before she could swing it open and stalk out. 'I beg your pardon. I was so taken aback at seeing you.' Her eyebrows rose haughtily. 'Yes, I know, that is no excuse. I feel guilty about how I behaved at my sister's. I feel worse about what I said in your hearing. And I wanted to find you and could not and that hurt.'

'So you were sulking?' she suggested sweetly.

'I do not—' He met her eyes, saw the wicked glint in them and smiled ruefully. 'Probably,' he admitted. Now they were so close, the urge to take her in his arms again was a tangible force, as though someone was pushing him towards her. He knew how her skin would taste, how her mouth would feel under his, how her long, lovely body would fit and slide against his. He wanted to make love to her until she screamed his name and begged him never to stop. He wanted all the things he could not have.

'Shall we go down to the mews, or would you like some refreshments first?'

'Oh, the mews, please. Have you brought Fox up to town with you?' She shot him a slanting, sideways look as he opened the door for her. 'Will you still agree to put him to my mare, now we have made up our quarrel?'

'Have we been quarrelling?'

'Just a little bit, I think. Margery, come along, we are going down to the mews with his lordship.' The maid, a quiet girl who had been sitting on a hard chair in the hall, stood and helped Decima into her pelisse, then curtsied to Adam. 'I thought it better not to bring Pru,' she confided quietly. 'Now, if you wait until we are close to Bates before you ask me my direction, that should do it.'

Decima slipped her hand into the crook of Adam's arm and let him guide her down the steps and along the pavement of Portman Square. Margery, borrowed from Lady Freshford, followed behind at a discreet distance like the well-trained attendant she was.

The luxury of being close to Adam, of touching him, made her pulse race. She tried not think about his kiss, but all the strange new feelings she had been suppressing flooded back to swamp her body. Her breathing was short, heat seemed to run up and down her body and an intimate pulse of arousal beat distractingly.

With him she felt different, strangely confident, able to show her real feelings whether they were shyness or anger. It was an intoxicating sensation, to be herself. And then she realised why he made her feel like this. With a dawning sense of wonder Decima turned her head to look at the strong profile of the man beside her. *I love him.*

Bates had Fox tied up outside and was grooming him as they walked into the mews yard. He straightened up and stared for a long moment, then put down his brushes and limped towards her, tugging off his hat. 'Good day to you, Miss Decima, ma'am.'

'Good day to you, Bates! And how is your leg? Still troubling you, I see.' It made things easier, having to focus on someone else, to think about managing this carefully for Pru's sake. Anything rather than think about the implications of what she had just discovered about herself.

'Getting better, I thank you, ma'am. I expect I'll be a bit of a Hopping Giles all my days, but it could be worse.'

'His lordship and I did not make too bad a job of it, then?'

'No, ma'am, and I'm powerful sorry my language wasn't all it might have been either.' He glanced behind her as he spoke and Decima watched his expression stiffen as he saw who was accompanying her. He had been expecting to see Pru and was disconcerted that she was not there. *Good.*

'It was very educational, Bates,' she said lightly, stepping past him to stroke Fox. 'How's my favourite boy, then?' The stallion rewarded her with a gentle butt with his nose. Decima turned back to Adam. 'We really must make arrangements for putting him to my mare, my lord. I will be staying in town for the Season and I will be in touch before I go back to Norfolk.'

She delved in her reticule and then produced a realistic smile of realisation. 'Of course, I have no card with my London address. I am staying with Lady Freshford in Green Street. Number Eleven. Green Street.'

Adam turned as though to escort her out of the mews. 'And is Miss Prudence with you? I trust she recovered from her illness.'

'Oh, yes. She is with me. She seemed a little cast down—the after-effects of the fever, I expect—so I thought the change of scene would do her good. Goodbye, Bates. I do hope your leg continues to improve.'

Adam took her arm and began to guide her back out of the yard. 'Let me take you back to the house and Dalrymple will call you a hackney.'

Decima said little on their way back other than to whisper, 'That should have done the trick. If he does nothing now, at least Pru knows where she stands.' But what of her? Would Adam make the slightest push to see her again?

As they neared the front steps Decima saw that a barouche had drawn up and the footman was just helping down an exquisite blonde lady. She started slightly when she saw them, and stood waiting, a look of somewhat nervous anticipation on her face.

'What a beautiful young woman,' Decima murmured. 'She is like a little fairy.'

'Exquisite,' Adam rejoined. Curious, Decima glanced at him; he had sounded almost sardonic.

Then she saw the lady more clearly. 'But I know her, surely!' She let go of Adam's arm and hurried forward. 'Olivia? Miss Channing, I should say. I am sure you do not remember me, but I stayed for several Seasons with your cousins, the Brothertons.'

The blue eyes widened with recognition and the apprehensive half smile was replaced by a genuine look of pleasure. 'But of course I remember you—Dessy Ross, isn't it? You were so kind to me, even though I was still in the schoolroom. You used to help me with my French recitation when I found it so hard.'

'You are most certainly out of the schoolroom now,' Decima observed admiringly. 'I almost did not recognise you.' Olivia blushed and demurred and Decima remembered her manners. 'Forgive me, I should perhaps introduce you to Viscount Weston. My lord…'

'That is quite all right.' Adam stepped forward and took Olivia's little kid-gloved hand in his. 'I already know Miss Channing. We are betrothed.'

Chapter Thirteen

For a moment Decima felt as though she had received a blow to the stomach. All the air had left her lungs and words froze on her lips. She stared at Olivia as the realisation sank in.

Of *course* Adam was betrothed to her—one only had to look at her to see why. Fragile, petite, ethereally blonde, with a rosebud mouth and a complexion like a white peach. Even when she blushed, as she was doing now, her skin simply flushed a delicate pink with not a blotch in sight. She was the perfect eligible bride. And, if he had set out to find a woman who looked the opposite of Decima, he could not have found better.

Her voice came back and with it her pride, stiffening her backbone and putting a smile on her lips. 'Congratulations, my lord! And Olivia, I am so happy for you.'

'Thank you,' Adam said gravely. 'Olivia, is something amiss that you are back so soon?'

'Oh, only that Mama left her library book—she must have put it down on the table in the drawing room.' Oddly she looked somewhat nervous at the admission.

'Then I must not keep you standing here talking,' Decima observed briskly. 'Good day, my lord, thank you for your assistance with that little matter. Goodbye, Olivia, it is delightful to have met you again. Come along, Margery.'

The distance from Portman Square to Green Street was far enough for her to regret not taking a hackney carriage—not for the walking involved, but because she was forced to keep a pleasant countenance and not display any of the emotions that were threatening to swamp her.

She dismissed Margery as they reached the hall of the Freshfords' house and turned to run upstairs to her bedchamber.

'Decima.' It was Henry, emerging from the drawing room. 'Did you find Weston at home?'

'Yes,' she said tightly. 'He was at home.'

'What is wrong?' Henry came to the foot of the stairs and looked up at her in concern. 'Decima, what has upset you?'

And suddenly she was angry, seething with a blistering hot anger that she had never felt in her life before. 'Is your mama here?'

'No.' Henry looked surprised. 'She's just gone out. Why?'

'Because I want to lose my temper, and probably throw things and shout.'

'Be my guest.' He gestured towards the drawing room and followed her in. 'I've never seen you lose your temper.'

'I do not think I ever have. I felt so many bad things sometimes that, if I *had* lost it, I would probably have said the most unforgivable, horrible words and made it even worse. I have always been meek and quiet and swallowed it all up. But Henry, Adam *kissed* me.'

'Um, you're losing me here.' Henry frowned. 'I thought he had kissed you before and you liked it, and you were wondering if you were in love with him. Do you mean he violently assaulted you? Because if that's the case, I'm going straight round there—'

'No! I liked it, and I *am* in love with him, I realised it today.

But when we came back from the mews and seeing Bates, there was Olivia Channing, who I used to know when she was still in the schoolroom. And Henry, he's going to marry her.' The rising temper caught up with her and she choked, 'He kissed me today and he is betrothed! He didn't say anything about Olivia—does he think I'm so desperate that he can kiss me and I'll be grateful?' She wrenched off her gloves, splitting a seam, and hurled them at a flower arrangement. They missed it by a foot.

'You are a man—tell me what he's thinking. That he can make me his mistress? I would be a laughable contrast with Olivia, that's for sure. Or probably he just finds it amusing that I let him kiss me.' She took a rapid turn round the room, causing Henry to step back abruptly.

'I might be a man,' he protested, 'but I certainly cannot understand or condone that behaviour. Goodness knows what he thought he was about.'

'Of course he wasn't thinking of making me his mistress,' Decima muttered, tugging at her pelisse buttons and breaking a nail in the process. 'That is a stupid idea.'

'He would know better than to think you would even consider it,' Henry said stoutly.

'No, he wouldn't,' Decima snapped miserably. 'I almost let him seduce me at the hunting lodge. He probably thinks I would be pathetically grateful and flattered for the attention.'

'Whatever his motives, this is completely unacceptable behaviour. I'm going to call him out.' Henry straightened his cuffs, his brows drawn together in thought. 'Now, who can I ask to act as my second? It will have to be someone discreet.'

'No! Henry, you cannot possibly call him out. He never made me any promises, and today I kissed him just as much as he kissed me. I should never have been such a naïve idiot as to think he really found me attractive—it was just the strange circumstances at the time.'

'Oh yes?' Henry enquired sarcastically. 'Being snowed in made you five inches shorter, removed your freckles and gave you a Cupid's bow mouth, did it? Or perhaps he was dazzled by the snow?'

'No, of course not. But we were snowed up alone with no chaperon, and it must have been days since he...er...'

'Unless the man's a ravening satyr, I am sure he could contain his lust for a week at least before setting out to ravish the nearest female.' Decima glared at him. 'And Grantham has no reputation for toying with innocents, either. Pricey mistresses, dashing widows, the odd opera dancer are his style. All perfectly unexceptionable.'

'Most respectable,' Decima said between gritted teeth, then recalled asking Adam about his mistresses and subsided with a complete lack of elegance onto the sofa. 'Henry, you cannot call him out. Leaving aside the risk of scandal and the chance you might get hurt, there is still Pru and Bates to consider. And Spindrift.'

'What about the mare?' Henry sounded baffled.

'I want to breed from her with Adam's stallion.'

'And you have discussed it with him? Give me strength, Decima—ladies do *not* talk about horse breeding with gentlemen.' He came and sat down at the other end of the sofa and regarded her with exasperated affection.

'I discuss it with you.'

'I am the nearest thing you've got to a brother and I have given up being shocked by you. At least, I believed I had,' he added thoughtfully. 'Feel better now?'

'Not really. Losing one's temper is horrid, isn't it?'

Henry appeared to take this as rhetorical. 'Tell me about this Miss Channing, then—you might as well get all the misery over in one go.'

'She's tiny,' Decima said, trying not to sound jealous and resentful. 'Really petite with little hands and feet. And she has blonde hair and blue eyes and a rosebud mouth and skin like cream and she is well behaved and gentle and shy with beautiful deportment—perfect, in fact.'

'Strewth.' Henry looked stunned. 'She sounds amazing. What's the family like?'

'Oh, very well-bred—cousins of the Brothertons. The only thing against her is the fact that I believe they haven't a penny to rub together. A lack of a reasonable dowry is probably Olivia's only handicap.'

'And looking like that, it probably doesn't make much difference,' Henry observed with an unusual lack of tact.

Whereas the size of my dowry doesn't make the slightest difference to my lack *of attraction*, Decima thought bitterly.

'What do you want to do?' Henry asked. 'Go home?'

Two months ago that was exactly what she would have done, Decima realised. Fled and taken her wounds home to lick in privacy. Well, she was a new Decima now and she was not running away from anyone, not even herself.

'Run away? No, I shall stay here and do exactly what I said I would do—enjoy the London Season without any pressure to be a success or do anything I do not want to do. I hope to be useful to your mama, spend far too much on clothes, go with you to galleries and show off Spindrift in the parks. And with any luck, Pru and Bates can meet and resolve things between them without Adam Grantham needing to know anything more about it.'

'Good for you.' Henry held out a hand to help her to her feet. 'Sounds an excellent programme.' She must have looked less confident than she had tried to sound, for he grinned, lifted a hand and chucked her under the chin. 'Chin up, Decima, let's give polite society something to talk about.'

The first thing she needed to do, Decima realised with a grimace as she went up to her room, was to call on Lady Brotherton. She had lived in the household for so many

Seasons it was only polite to visit as soon as possible. No doubt she would hear all about Olivia's wonderful good fortune from her, but then, it was likely to be much talked about in any case. She had better simply get used to it.

'Oh, Adam,' she sighed, sitting down on the window seat and propping her chin on her hand to gaze out at the street. She was a fool, she told herself. What on earth had she hoped for from him? Certainly not marriage, which was the only acceptable way in which she could become more than a casual acquaintance. She'd hoped for nothing, she realised.

Before she had come up to London she had just been thinking about him in a romantic haze as an unobtainable figure of fantasy. He was the man who had awakened all her latent sensuality, had given her the astonishing gift of realising that she was not the freakishly plain girl she had been brought up to believe she was. And as a result she had fallen head over heels.

Or had she? Decima bit her lip in thought. She had been almost instantly attracted to Adam physically, she had liked his sense of humour and his down-to-earth practicality and she had found him so very easy to talk to. Perhaps there was more to her feelings than some sort of pathetic gratitude that a handsome man had paid her attention. She was certainly in love with him. Nothing else, surely, could hurt quite so much? And hurt with a deep longing, not to avoid the source of the pain, but to expose herself to it, over and over again, for ever.

But did it matter whether her feelings were reality or fantasy? Adam could never be hers whatever she thought about it. Presumably other people learned to live with broken hearts—how hard could it be? She caught herself up with a wry smile. She had last thought that about cooking and she hadn't proved any use at that at all. In fact, Adam had proved to be a much more effective cook than she.

After luncheon she would visit Lady Brotherton, combining duty with the desire to swallow the nasty medicine as soon as possible. Then she could just get on with the rest of her life. Her new, wonderful, independent life, she reminded herself firmly.

Lady Brotherton's amazement as she greeted Decima should have given her much quiet satisfaction, if only she had not been feeling in such low spirits.

'My dear Dessy! My goodness, you look so...so...' She blinked, obviously struggling to find a word that was not completely at odds with every preconception she had ever had about her guest. It proved impossible. 'Elegant,' she finally conceded, somewhat breathlessly.

'Thank you, Lady Brotherton,' Decima said demurely. That was worth every minute she had endured with Pru fussing over her smart new hairstyle and the severe tight lacing her afternoon gown required. She caught sight of herself in the long glass over the fireplace and forced her shoulders down, making herself relax. Lady Brotherton was in no position to lecture her on posture or anything else now.

'I do hope you are well, ma'am. And Lord Brotherton, and all the girls, of course. It is Sophie's year to come out, is it not? She must be so excited.'

'Yes, we are all in perfect health, thank you, Dessy. Antonia is in an interesting condition, but apart from that they are all out and about—' Lady Brotherton broke off as the tea tray was brought in. 'And you are staying with Lady Freshford, I believe you wrote?'

'Yes, her only daughter Caroline is making her come-out.'

'Only one daughter. Oh, well, not everyone can have my good fortune. But, Dessy dear, there is the most exciting news—you recall Olivia Channing, my niece?'

Decima suddenly realised she could not claim ignorance of this news. If Olivia said something, then Lady Brotherton would immediately start speculating about what Decima had been doing with Lord Weston. 'Indeed, yes. I met her this morning in the street, quite by chance, with Lord Weston. What a fine match to be sure, you must be delighted, ma'am, for I recall how fond you have always been of her.'

'Indeed I have. Her parents have worked so hard to bring this about.'

'Olivia has known Lord Weston long?'

'No, their acquaintance is fairly recent. They met at a house party.' Why Lady Brotherton was looking uncomfortable about this Decima could not guess, but her speculation was cut short by the arrival of Miss Sophie Brotherton, positively agog with gossip. At the sight of Decima her face fell comically.

'Oh, I wanted to surprise Mama with the news that you had arrived,' she complained. 'But it is lovely to see you. How fine you look, Dessy. Mama, I have seen Olivia and she told me Dessy had arrived—and guess what, Dessy knows Lord Weston! Isn't that wonderful?' She turned an eager face to Decima. 'You see, none of us know him, not really, and we want to know all about him.'

'You *know* Lord Weston?' Lady Brotherton turned a look on her that Decima could only think of as calculating.

'Yes. Not well.' Only as well as having stood half-naked in his dressing room while he caressed her body. But then, they had never been formally introduced, so possibly it did not count. Half afraid she was going to giggle hysterically, Decima added, 'I was visiting Charlton and Hermione for Christmas—you recall I wrote to you from there? I met him during that trip.'

'Olivia thought you had business together.' *Damn.* Now what to say?

'It is probably something your mama would not wish me to mention in front of you, Sophie.' Decima grabbed for the only possible half-truth. 'It is to do with horse breeding. Lord

Weston has a sta—' she caught Lady Brotherton's eye '—a male horse.'

'Oh, dull stuff.' Sophie wrinkled her nose. 'So is there anything you know about him, or is it just horses?'

'Not really. But Olivia will tell you all about him, won't she?'

'She doesn't know him. I mean, they have hardly had time. They are very distant cousins of some sort and he was kind to her at the Minsters' house party, but that's all.'

'It is not a love match, then?'

'No,' said Sophie wistfully.

'Nothing so vulgar,' her mother interjected forcefully.

'But the viscount is so handsome.' Sophie sighed. 'It would be wonderful if they were in love. I think Olivia is frightened of him, though.'

'Nonsense.' Lady Brotherton frowned at her daughter. 'Olivia is merely showing a proper reserve. And as for handsome men and love matches—I hope your papa does not catch you talking such foolishness, young lady.'

Decima made her way home with much to think about. It was not a love match, Olivia knew little about her husband-to-be and Sophie thought she was frightened of him.

But what was there to be frightened of? Adam had never shown an irritable or unreasonable side to his character, and the sort of situation they had found themselves in was almost guaranteed to expose such characteristics. Perhaps Olivia was simply overwhelmed by the sheer physical presence of the man. Decima shivered pleasurably at the recollected sensations of being held in his arms, kissed with that much passion and conviction.

But then, she was tall, almost able to stare him in the eye. What would it be like to be possessed by all that maleness if one were a tiny woman? Perhaps that was all it was. Why she should feel the desire to reassure Olivia when the girl was taking the man she loved was confusing. But that desire was there, none the less.

Decima shook her head, wondering at herself. A few months ago these thoughts, the experience that lay behind them, would have been inconceivable. What she needed was to shake the fidgets out of her bones, get back to what was familiar and safe.

Henry was climbing the steps as she alighted from her hackney carriage. 'Shall we ride tomorrow morning?' she asked impulsively as he held the door for her. 'In Hyde Park? Early, so we can gallop and not be told off by all the old pussies. Surely it will not rain.' Yes, that was it; something she was confident with and could share with Henry.

Adam did up one more coat button against the dank chill of an early February morning and turned Ajax's head through the Stanhope Street entrance to Hyde Park. The discomfort of getting up at such an hour and riding out just as the reluctant light was penetrating the mist was more than rewarded by the prospect of an almost empty park.

The gelding fidgeted and he held him in check, more for the sake of discipline than anything else, as he scanned the expanse of greensward. Bates had reported that Fox had a loose shoe and the farrier had been sent for. He would have to be taken out that afternoon when the crowds made the prospect of exercising a high-blooded stallion something of a challenge.

The way was clear, right to the carriage road, so Adam let the horse have his head and urged him into a gallop. The cold rush of the wind against his face, the surge of muscle between his thighs and the drumming of the gelding's hooves was a physical release he hadn't realised he so badly needed.

He pulled up the reluctant horse as they reached the tan surface of the roadway and made it walk steadily, turning from side to side and changing legs to build suppleness and obedience. The trouble was, that did not occupy his brain or still the restlessness in his blood.

Try as he might, he could not rid his mind of the look of polite contempt on Decima's face as he had told her of his betrothal. If he had not kissed her, had told her at once of his impending marriage… But no, he had taken her in his arms in a rush of relief at finding her and then, somehow, he had forgotten Olivia entirely.

The fact that he spent most of his waking time wishing he could forget about Miss Channing was no excuse. He had been well and truly caught and, whatever his feelings for his future in-laws, he could not take them out on Olivia. It was his duty as a gentleman to marry her. Which meant that he had to forget Decima.

He had paid off his mistress, knowing that Olivia would be distressed if she ever learned of her existence. How much more would she feel it if she came to suspect his feelings for her old friend?

Decima would go back to Norfolk soon—she had left him in no doubt that she disliked London and society. After all, she had only come up to town because of Bates and Pru.

Ajax snickered, pricking his ears to look down the carriage drive, and Adam saw another horse emerging from the swirls of mist that still hung low over the park.

It was a leggy grey, galloping in defiance of all the rules of good conduct in the park, and on its back, riding as though she was part of the horse, was a tall woman in a green habit.

'Decima.'

Chapter Fourteen

With the wind whipping her veil tight to her face, Decima glanced back over her shoulder to where Henry, no doubt cursing comprehensively, was attempting to fix a broken stirrup leather. Seeing that Spindrift was in no mood to stand quietly by, he had waved Decima off to have her gallop, but she had no intention of doing more than making a loop round and coming back to his side. It wasn't fair to abandon him, and, even in a virtually empty park, it was not the thing for ladies to be riding without an escort.

Oh, but this felt so good, to be doing the one thing where she had always felt utterly confident. 'Drat.' She spoke aloud as she saw the other rider through the mist. He was seemingly intent on schooling his mount and out of simple good manners she would have to slow down to a decorous trot to pass him.

Spindrift tossed her head at the pressure on her bit, but slowed obediently, only to risk speeding up again when her mistress's hands suddenly went slack on the reins.

It was Adam and there was absolutely no way to avoid him. 'Steady!' Decima brought the mare to a trot and then to a walk, reining in as she came alongside Ajax. 'Good morning, my lord.' Try as she might, that sounded cool. She was still angry with him, but the thought he might suspect why was hateful.

'Good morning, Miss Ross.' Adam halted Ajax. 'We are very formal this morning,' he observed, with a glint in his eyes that she could not read.

'It seems appropriate,' she rejoined.

'You are angry with me.' Damn him, why could he not have talked of indifferent things? Now what? To pretend not to know what he was referring to would only made her seem insufferably coy.

'Are you surprised, my lord? I do not absolve myself from blame—to have returned your embrace was immodest and unwise, but you should have told me that you were engaged. Even if you did not tell me, it was outrageous of you to kiss me.'

'I had forgotten,' he said with such breathtaking simplicity she could only stare at him.

'*Forgotten?* How could you forget you are engaged to be married? Poor Olivia—it is bad enough that she will have to put up with your mistress, but if she ever suspected that you could forget her so easily, to trifle with another woman...'

'I was not trifling.' Ajax shifted suddenly as though his rider had closed his hands hard on the reins. 'I would never trifle with you. I simply forgot everything because I was so pleased to see you, and then I wanted to know what you were doing in London. If we had not been talking about Pru and Bates, I would have remembered to tell you about Olivia.'

'Indeed?' She wanted to believe him so badly. The thought that the man she loved might act dishonourably was intolerable.

'Indeed,' he echoed her haughty tone. 'And, since you raise the subject, I have parted company with my mistress.'

'Oh, good.' Decima felt her face relax into a smile, only then realising just how tense she had been. 'I knew I could not be mistaken in you, Adam. We will forget all about yesterday in your study.' Not that she ever could forget it: the last time she would be in his arms, the last time his lips would crush down on hers, stealing her heart along with her breath.

The ironic twist of his lips filled her with a sudden doubt that he would forget it either, but she pushed the thought away. Provided Olivia never guessed for a moment that there had ever been anything between them, that was all that mattered.

'I was speaking to Lady Brotherton,' she said, anxious to move the conversation on along conventional lines. 'Olivia's relatives are all so very happy about this match.'

'So I understand.' The words were ordinary enough, his tone quite inoffensive, but Decima saw a flash of anger turning his grey eyes greenish with that betraying colour she had come to know, if not to understand. As she puzzled over it, Adam turned his head and she became aware of approaching hoof beats. It was Henry.

Henry made no concession to his stature in his choice of horses and his mount this morning was a raking hunter as high to the withers as Ajax. Decima smiled fondly at the sight of her friend's approach; he was a fine rider.

'You mended it?' she called out as he drew alongside them.

'Yes, I managed to make another hole with the knife in my saddlebag.' Henry reined in and circled his bay alongside Spindrift. 'Good day, sir.'

'Henry, may I make you known to Viscount Weston? My lord, Sir Henry Freshford. Or perhaps you gentlemen know each other already?' The air was crackling with tension, which was puzzling. Henry might well be poised to defend her against insult, but what was causing Adam to look down his nose with the air of a man about to issue a challenge?

'His lordship is, of course, well known to me by reputation,' Henry said smoothly with a pleasant smile that did not reach his eyes. Knowing him, Decima caught her breath. *Oh, Lord!*

Adam's eyes narrowed. 'I regret we have not met before. You are staying in London for the Season, Freshford?'

'For as long as my mother, my sister and Miss Ross require my presence.'

'You recall I told you I was staying with Lady Freshford, my lord,' Decima intervened.

'So you did, Miss Ross. And has there been any meeting yet between the star-crossed lovers whose cause you are championing?' He met her gaze blandly, but Decima knew he was vividly conscious of Henry, his position by her side, of the way they spoke to each other. And beside her Henry still bristled with protectiveness under his urbane exterior.

'Not that I am aware of, but I do not choose to interrogate my staff about their personal affairs,' she replied coolly. 'Nor do I find the situation as amusing as you apparently do. I would not have Pru made unhappy for the world.'

'And love will make her happy?' Adam's tone was mocking, but Decima sensed a real edge beneath the surface. 'This is something of a reversal of your previous position, is it not?'

'You are accusing me of matchmaking, Lord Weston?' She kept her tone as light as his. 'Then you cannot have been listening to me before—I have been acting at the wish of one party and giving the other information only. Bates is free to act on it as he will.'

'Lucky devil. I must bid you good day, Miss Ross, Sir Henry. I imagine none of us wishes to keep our horses standing in this chill.' He touched his whip to his hat and turned Ajax to canter away across the grass towards the Serpentine.

'My goodness, that was uncomfortable.' Decima let out a long breath and tried to keep her voice light. Inside she felt slightly queasy from the tension that had been crackling between the three of them, and miserable that Adam seemed so distant.

Henry tore his eyes away from the figure vanishing into the mist and remarked, 'He is jealous, of course.' Meeting Decima's puzzled eyes, he added, 'Of us. With me mounted he probably doesn't realise how short I am and thinks I'm courting you.'

'That's nonsense.' Decima was instantly prickly, as she always was on Henry's behalf if someone dismissed him because of his height. 'My feelings for you would not be any different if you were six foot six or five foot nothing. We are friends. Anyways,' she added firmly as they turned their horses' heads and began to walk back down the drive, 'he is in no position to be jealous of anyone except Olivia.'

Was Henry smiling? She looked hard at him and the quirk of his lips vanished. 'Men are strange, possessive animals,' he remarked. 'You two were almost lovers. He feels he has put his mark on you, that's all.'

'*All*? That's scandalous.' Decima found she was truly shocked. 'I am not a mare to be branded or a book where he has written his name on the flyleaf.'

'Actually, the book is a very good analogy. Are you ever going to be able to open the volume of memories of this year without recalling him, seeing his name, as it were?'

Decima knew her cheeks were burning. 'He can write his name in the wedding register, next to Olivia's, nowhere else, and certainly not on anything of mine. Why, what you are suggesting is positively indecent—as if men really want to keep a harem of all the women they have ever…ever…'

'Made love to?' Henry supplied. 'You are probably right. We are very unsatisfactory creatures compared to women.' And he dug his heels into his mount's flanks and cantered off, chuckling, before she could retaliate.

Decima dressed for Lady Cantline's ball that evening in a spirit of half-terrified bravado. It must be—she counted on her fingers, frowning—almost five years since she had been to a large-scale dress ball. Five years in which she had been heartily grateful to be spared the humiliation of always being a wallflower, or, very occasionally, stumbling round the floor as the reluctant partner of some unfortunate man.

She had no intention of dancing tonight, either, but she did have the firm resolve of holding her head up amidst the matrons and the chaperons, knowing she was impeccably gowned and had absolutely nothing to apologise for. She was no longer a shop-worn piece of merchandise on the marriage mart, she was not even on the shelf any longer, because she would not allow anyone to categorise her that way. She was single and happy to be so.

Brave words butter no parsnips, she thought, nervously picking up the powder puff and dusting again at the freckles that were sprinkled across her bosom. And an alarming amount of that bosom seemed to be on show tonight. Decima tugged at the lace trim of the low-scooped neckline and Pru put down the hairbrush and tugged it back into place again.

'Leave it, do, Miss Dessy…Miss Decima.' She still had not got used to Decima's insistence on her full name. 'It's a lovely gown, don't go pulling it out of shape.'

'I will fall out,' Decima moaned faintly. 'It didn't look this indecent in the modiste's.'

'You're a grown-up lady, now; you can show off your boobies,' Pru said stoutly. 'They aren't all that big, but they're a perfectly nice pair and your shoulders are lovely and white.'

'Freckles,' Decima said despairingly as Pru fastened her necklace and handed her the pearl bob earrings. *Your freckles. I wondered if they went all the way down and they do…* Adam's voice as his fingers had traced across her skin. And she had at least had her back to him. What would have happened if he had seen the dusting of freckles across the swell of her bosom and disappearing down into her cleavage?

She closed her eyes tight against the picture her treacherous mind conjured up, then opened them again wide as the image of Adam's face appeared like magic on the inside of her lids.

'There now, you look lovely.' Pru stepped back for Decima to stand and look at herself in the long cheval glass.

Oh, my. This was not her at all. Instinctively Decima rounded her shoulders and saw, to her horror, that the bodice of the gown gaped alarmingly. There was nothing for it but perfect deportment: head up, shoulders back and a startling show of bosom at the front. Pru was talking, wrenching her attention away from her own reflection.

'I was wondering what time you'd be coming in, Miss Decima.' She was fiddling with things on the dressing table, but the casual air did not deceive Decima.

'Not before one, I should think. Why? Would you like to go out?' Pru's neck went pink. 'Oh, Pru—is it Bates? Has he asked you out this evening?'

'Mmm,' Pru mumbled. 'Just round to this tavern he knows, not far from here. He says it is quite respectable and we can have a bite of supper and a chat, sort of thing.'

'That is nice,' Decima said, sounding ridiculously bracing to her own ears, like a mother encouraging her reluctant offspring to try something new. 'You want to go, don't you?'

'Suppose so. I'm just…' Pru stood scrubbing one toe into the carpet '…shy. It's different here, not like it was at the lodge, somehow.'

'I know exactly what you mean,' Decima replied with feeling. 'Never mind, go and have supper and, if that is all it leads to, well, at least you won't be left wondering about might-have-beens.' How easy it was to give advice to other people, even advice one was ignoring oneself.

The drive to Lady Cantline's town mansion seemed unreal. Lady Freshford and Caroline chattered happily about who

Caroline might meet at this, her very first big ball, and Henry sat next to Decima, looking exquisitely elegant, and conversing about any number of unexceptional subjects. All Decima wanted to do was hold his hand and whimper with nerves.

But she was twenty-seven years old, had made a New Year's resolution that she must live up to and Lady Freshford would think her quite mad to be clinging to poor Henry's hand.

Getting out of the carriage while maintaining her modesty in the new gown was a challenge that kept her mind off her terror until they were all climbing the stairs to the receiving line. Then sheer pride came to her aid.

I am not *going to flee down these stairs,* Decima told herself, linking her hand through Caroline's elbow and squeezing encouragingly. Caroline turned wide, nervous eyes on her and Decima found herself smiling reassurance.

'You look wonderful,' she whispered. 'You will be fighting the young men off the moment they see you. Now, don't forget you must not waltz because you have not yet been approved by one of the Patronesses of Almack's, and we do not know if any of them will be here this evening. And do not, whatever you do, dance more than twice with the same man.'

She spoke with the confidence of a woman who had had to deal with these social prohibitions on a regular basis and smiled at herself. Never mind, as long as it gave Caro reassurance, that was all that mattered.

Lady Freshford led the way confidently around the edge of the ballroom until she found a position that suited her and sank onto a satin chaise, waving her unmarried charges to the flanking chairs. Henry, as was expected, took up his position behind them. Decima glanced at him and he lowered one eyelid in the ghost of a wink; she strongly suspected he would slide away to the card room once he was confident his mama was comfortably settled. She wished she could go with him.

And then she looked across the room and saw Adam and the silly little fears and nerves vanished, swept away by an avalanche of conflicting emotions.

Pleasure, just to see him. Desire. Oh, the sheer, shaming heat of it, surging through her blood, leaving her tingling with urgency. Shyness about what he might think of her looks, of her gown. A faint hope that he might think well of her for facing down her fears and appearing at a ball at all. And love, and the knowledge that she must look away at once, now, or her feelings were going to be written on her face for all to see.

But, as her eyes dropped, she saw Adam was there for exactly the same reason as Henry—standing sentry over his little party of ladies—and the shameful jealousy swallowed all those other feelings. Olivia already had looks and youth, why should she have Adam Grantham, too? Other than the undeniable reason that she was exactly the sort of bride a viscount must be looking for.

Decima fought a silent battle with herself and won, just. If Lady Freshford or Caroline noticed the stains of colour on her cheekbones or the way her hands had twisted suddenly in her lap, they gave no sign of it. Decima took a long, steadying breath and blinked until the blurring had gone from her eyes. Then she fixed a smile on her lips and turned to watch the ebb and flow of arrivals with every sign of interest.

Across the room Adam fitted one shoulder more comfortably against a pillar and regarded the turbaned head of Mrs Channing, seated just in front of him, with cold dislike. He was going to keep his temper with her tonight, and on every occasion until he was married to Olivia, and then she would discover that her son-in-law was not going to dance to her tune, however neatly she had entrapped him.

But that could wait. His falling out with Mrs Channing would distress Olivia deeply—he already knew that raised voices, or even mild sarcasm, reduced her to miserable, quaking silence. There was no way he could teach her to show some backbone before the wedding; it would have to wait until afterwards.

And the damnable thing was, if he had never met Decima Ross he might very well have considered Olivia as a bride. She was exactly what everyone would consider suitable. Even her lack of dowry was a negligible factor given his wealth. Yes, BD—Before Decima, as he was beginning to think of it—Olivia fulfilled all his criteria. Well-bred, compliant, pretty, raised to make an excellent housekeeper and wife. If he was to yield to everyone's wishes, including young Perry's, and dutifully marry, Olivia Channing was just perfect.

Adam kept his face smoothly pleasant, nodding to acquaintances, straightening up to be introduced to the numerous ladies Mrs Channing was determined to gloat over, now the engagement notices had gone to the papers. Years of card playing had taught him the trick of an unreadable expression. Even the sanctuary of the card room was out of bounds tonight, he realised. It would be his duty to dance on several occasions with Olivia. In fact, she would probably expect to be able to demonstrate to her less fortunate friends that there was now one man she could dance with as often as she pleased, without causing the slightest scandal.

He bent over Olivia's chair, turning his shoulder to exclude Mrs Channing. 'Which dances will you permit me to have this evening?' he murmured in her ear, deliberately making his voice slightly husky.

She smelt sweetly of roses; her blonde hair was caught up, exposing the soft delicacy of her throat, the fragile skin of her temples. Hidden by the lace of her bodice, the swell of her breasts curved with promise. She was utterly lovely, innocent and fresh. His. And he felt not one iota of desire for her.

'Oh.' She blushed, sent a desperate look in her mother's direction for guidance and found no help, only his very close proximity. 'Which would you like?' Rather desperately she showed him her dance card and Adam pencilled his name against four, including one waltz.

'Four? Is that not rather…I mean, I have not been approved by one of the Patronesses for waltzing…'

'We will create a scandal,' Adam said solemnly. 'There is nothing for it, we will have to get married.' If he had said such a thing to Decima, she would have caught him up in an instant. Laughed at his teasing, punished him in some way for his jest. Olivia simply looked terrified.

Damn. 'I was only teasing you,' he reassured her, smiling ruefully as the panic ebbed out of her face. Could he live with a woman who had no sense of humour? Or perhaps she was just frightened of the whole idea of marriage and would relax and show a different side to her character once they were wed. He could only pray it were true.

Then he straightened up to look round the room and saw her. Decima. Sitting almost opposite with a Roman-nosed matron he did not know, a very young lady and that damned starched-up *friend* of hers, Henry Freshford.

The madness seemed to sweep through him. He would cross the dance floor, catch her up in his arms, stride out of the house, into the night, take her away, make love to her until she sobbed with ecstasy, begged him never to stop—and the world could go hang.

Then he looked down and saw Olivia looking around her with innocent, nervous delight. He had compromised her, however unwittingly. He maintained he was a gentleman, he would fight any man who impugned his honour. And his honour required that he marry Olivia Channing.

He watched Decima shake her head as a gentleman bowed, obviously requesting a dance. It happened again. She was going to refuse to dance and sit out the ball as one of the chaperons, that was clear.

All his desires focused down, quite simply, on the need to have her in his arms one last time. To talk to her, to know she had forgiven him. He wasn't given to prayer, considering that the life he led was not particularly deserving of any higher powers listening to erratic, and doubtless selfish, pleas from time to time. No. If he was going to achieve this, then he was going to have to manage it by himself.

Adam looked around the room for inspiration and his gaze lighted on one copper shock of hair, head and shoulders above the group of scarlet-coated army officers around it. Yes, there was George Mays, an unsuspecting good fairy. He bent over the ladies. 'Would you excuse me for a moment? I have just seen a very old friend.'

Chapter Fifteen

〜∽✦∽〜

Thank goodness. The steady trickle of gentlemen requesting her hand for a dance had finally dried up. Decima sat back and began to fan herself with short, nervous jerks. She had not been prepared for it, expecting all the attention to be lavished on Caro. And certainly *her* card would soon be full.

'How well she looks on the dance floor,' she remarked to Caro's fond mama, who was observing Caroline's progress through the measures of a cotillion with justifiable pride. Henry had slid away ten minutes ago, ostensibly in search of refreshments.

'She does, does she not? I am not without hope that she will take very well indeed.' Lady Freshford shot her a sharp glance. 'And why have you not accepted any gentlemen, Decima? You have received some very flattering attention.'

'They have no idea that I would step on their toes at every turn, and, in any case, I am sitting down. They would swoon when I stood up and they saw how tall I am,' she said lightly. It did not hurt to admit it, she realised. Somehow that ridiculous waltz in the kitchen with Adam had given her the confidence to shrug aside the years of hurt and humiliation. In any case, it was probably this dratted dress with its indecent neckline attracting them. Until they got close enough to spot the freckles...

'Ma'am? I realise it is quite outrageous of me to approach you without an introduction, but might I have the honour of a dance?' It was a tall—a very tall—redheaded man with a pleasantly ugly face who was positively towering over her. 'George Mays. Lady Freshford.' He bowed. 'I think my mama is possibly a connection on your father's side?'

'Of course. You must be Georgiana Stapleford's son.' Lady Freshford beamed. 'How is she?'

'Yes, ma'am, you are correct, and she is very well, I thank you. She and my father are in Scotland at the moment.' He produced a charming smile, transforming his face. 'Might I hope you will introduce me to this lady?'

Lady Freshford smiled indulgently. 'Mr Mays, Miss Ross. Dear Decima is a friend of ours from Norfolk and is kindly supporting me through Caroline's first Season.'

'Miss Ross.' They exchanged bows. 'Is there any chance that you might fit me into your dance card?'

'Thank you, but I am not dancing this evening, Mr Mays.'

'Oh.' He seemed cast down. 'Might I...' He gestured to the chair beside her.

'Yes, of course.'

'Miss Ross, may I confide in you?' When Decima murmured something inarticulate, he bent his head over his clasped hands and blurted out, 'I never usually dance either. But when I saw you, I thought perhaps you would understand.'

'Understand? I am sorry, Mr Mays...'

'It was foolish of me, for I could see how many invitations you were turning down—obviously you would *not* understand. But you see, I am so very tall, most ladies do not wish to dance with me—they feel awkward about it. I saw you were...forgive me, I am making a mull of this.'

He looked wretched. Impetuously Decima said, 'You thought I might not feel the same way?' He nodded. 'Because I am tall, too?' Another nod. How on earth could she refuse him? 'Of course I will dance with you, Mr Mays. I would be delighted.'

'The next dance?' he asked eagerly.

Decima knew she should make some show of consulting her card, or at least make sure it was something she could recall the steps to. 'The next dance,' she agreed with a smile she did not have to force.

The dance proved to be a waltz and Mr Mays to be a most accomplished dancer. Decima took his hand, managed to fight the urge to gaze at her feet, and allowed herself to be swept into the dance with a partner who was a highly energetic waltzer.

After the first sweep around the floor she managed to unfix her gaze from his lapels and glance upwards. He looked down, his eyes lighting with a sudden appreciative warmth and she recalled her low-cut gown—goodness, he must be able to see right down it! Hastily she pushed back her shoulders and smiled brightly. At least the freckles appeared not to repulse him. This was actually very good fun.

'We are well matched, Miss Ross,' he confided. 'I cannot tell you how refreshing it is to be able to talk to the young lady I am dancing with instead of looking at the top of her head.'

'And for me too—oh!' He assayed a daring swoop around a corner and her skirts flew out, brushing against Olivia's modest white muslin as she circled in Adam's embrace. Their eyes met for a second and she found herself smiling at him, a wide beam of pure enjoyment. At least there was no kitchen table or butter churn to avoid here and, with slippers on her feet and skirts of taffeta, she felt as light as a bird.

Mr Mays whirled her to a halt at the opposite end of the room from where they had started. 'How inept of me,' he apologised as they walked off the floor. 'Allow me to take you back to Lady Freshford.' Their way was blocked by a number of military men and one moved as Mr Mays tapped him on the shoulder to make his way through. 'Hello again, Fredericks, Peterson.'

They turned, their scarlet coats taut across well-muscled backs, and Decima caught her breath at finding herself surrounded by quite so much tall masculinity. Her partner grinned at them. 'Allow me to introduce Miss Ross. Miss Ross, Colonel Lord Peterson, Major Fredericks.'

Decima bobbed a curtsy, expecting them to smile politely and resume their conversation. Instead they both, to her astonishment, asked her to dance. 'Anyone who can make Mays look elegant on the dance floor is the partner for me,' the Colonel declared, managing to get in before his more junior colleague.

Half an hour later Decima was delivered back to Lady Freshford and Henry, breathless and more than a little inclined to giggle. It felt as though she had been drinking champagne, which was ridiculous as not a drop had passed her lips.

And then the desire to laugh quite left her. Adam was approaching, Olivia clinging to his arm. 'Miss Channing! Lord Weston, how do you do?' Decima hastily performed the introductions.

'We were just going in to supper,' Olivia murmured shyly. 'Would you join us?'

Decima was expecting a resumption of the morning's tension between the two men. Instead, Adam was looking as though a pleasant idea had just struck him, and Henry was staring at Olivia as though he had seen a ghost. He saw Decima watching him and the look vanished, to be replaced by one of polite interest.

'Yes, do run along, dears.' Lady Freshford was gathering up her fan and reticule. 'I can see Augusta Wimpole over there. We can have supper together and a good gossip. Caro is there already with some young friends.'

Adam led the way to a table in the refreshment room and settled Olivia beside Decima, before departing with Henry to raid the buffet on their behalf.

'What a lovely dress,' Olivia said shyly. 'Mama would never let me wear such a pretty colour.'

'I am sure it would not suit you as well as the gown you are wearing. It looks quite exquisite with your colouring. Besides,' Decima confided, lowering her voice, 'I am regretting this neckline—I have never felt so exposed in my life.'

'It is a little bit daring, but you do have such nice shoulders,' Olivia said.

She is sweet, Decima thought, smiling at the compliment. Would she make Adam a good wife? She would be sure to try and do her duty. How chilly that sounded.

'Is Sir Henry—?' Olivia broke off, blushing. 'Do you and he have an understanding?'

'Goodness, no!' Decima laughed, then saw Adam turn to look at her as the sound cut through the babble of conversation. 'No, indeed not,' she added, lowering her voice. 'We are just very good friends. He is one of the nicest people I know.'

'Oh.' Olivia dropped her gaze to her hands and fell silent, only rousing herself when the men returned with plates full of delicacies.

'Lemonade, Miss Channing?' Henry asked, bending over Olivia solicitously. No one had asked Decima what she would like, but when the men returned Adam placed a champagne flute in front of her. Startled, she looked from one man to the other, but Henry was chatting easily to Olivia and all Adam did was to raise one dark brow.

'Do you prefer lemonade?'

'Not really, if I am to be honest.' Decima picked it up and took a sip, loving the way the bubbles fizzed up her nose. And the way her blood fizzed in her veins. Adam was so close she could feel the heat of him where his arm rested on the table next to hers.

'Oh, let us be honest at all costs,' he agreed softly, his eyes resting on their companions. 'Tell me Decima, is Fresh-ford...entangled with anyone?'

'No. Not that I know of.' She was startled into answering without thinking. 'And it would be no business of mine if he were—I am certainly not going to answer personal questions about my friends!'

'Just curious.' The champagne swirled in his glass. Decima found herself watching it, watching the long, strong fingers holding the fragile stem and remembering them on her body.

Adam seemed to snap out of his abstraction and shifted in his seat, reaching for a fork. 'These patties look good.'

Decima agreed, nibbling at a corner. Where had her appetite gone? She took another sip of champagne.

'Am I forgiven yet?' Adam had speared an asparagus roll, but his gaze was resting on the swell of her breasts in the low-cut gown.

Decima fought the instinct to hunch her shoulders and managed not to enquire coldly what exactly he meant. 'Of course. We discussed that this morning. I have quite put it from my mind.'

'I wish I had. I suspect I was somewhat...prickly this morning.' One dark brow slanted upwards. Decima could not decide whether he was being satirical.

'You were, certainly. Why?'

It really was hopeless trying to disconcert him with direct questions. He did at least have the grace to lower his voice as he answered, 'Because I assumed that you and Freshford were attached.'

Decima glanced at Henry and Olivia, but they were happily engrossed in an animated conversation. Olivia was pleasingly flushed and was waving her hands around in a way that seemed quite out of character while she described something. 'Well, we are not,' she snapped. 'We are very good friends. And anyway, whatever concern is it of yours?'

'I can see you are not, now I see him on foot,' Adam commented, low voiced. 'After all, he only comes up to your...' He waved a hand graphically at her upper-chest level.

'If I loved him, height would not be an issue,' Decima retorted stiffly. 'And I repeat, what business is it of yours?'

'Why, I am jealous, of course.' He said it in exactly the tone he might have used to comment on the weather.

Decima gazed at him blankly, realised her mouth was open and shut it. Henry was quite correct—Adam had added her to his collection and was feeling proprietorial about her, despite his being engaged to another woman.

'Do I have to remind you that you are an engaged man?' she whispered fiercely.

'I know. What a pity that harems have not caught on in England.'

'You are outrageous,' Decima scolded, feeling quite ridiculous, lecturing a man in a whisper over lobster patties. The wretch was no doubt only teasing her, but she could not let him get away with this. 'Poor Olivia—'

'Is flirting,' Adam whispered back, inclining his head towards his fiancée.

'Of course she...is.' Goodness, who would have thought it? Meek little Olivia was gazing into Henry's eyes and positively batting her lashes at him. What would Adam do? Expecting him to intervene at any moment, Decima watched aghast.

'The poor child never managed to get away from her mama long enough to indulge in a little harmless flirtation,' Adam murmured into Decima's ear, making the fine hairs on the back of her neck rise and tingle deliciously. 'I am certainly not going to start lecturing her in the same spirit.'

So, he was so confident about Olivia that he was relaxed about her flirting with a man of Henry's quite exceptional good looks. Why, then, had he been so prickly when he thought she and Henry were in some way involved?

'Why are you frowning?' Adam snapped his fingers at a passing footman and secured two more glasses of champagne.

'Because I don't understand you,' Decima admitted frankly. 'You seem positively inconsistent.'

'Thank you.' Adam bowed slightly. 'But ladies are inconsistent. I strive to be enigmatic.'

'Piffle,' Decima retorted. 'You know perfectly well that you don't put on airs to be interesting, so stop trying to tell me you do.' She had forgotten to keep her voice low and both Olivia and Henry turned to regard her in surprise. 'Lord Weston is bamming me,' she explained, taking a restorative draught from her wine glass.

'Would either of you ladies like an ice?' Henry said, hastily flashing Decima a warning glance. She wrinkled her nose at him. Goodness, the champagne was making her positively light-headed. It was a delightful feeling, so unlike the way she had always felt at balls in the past, huddled in the wallflowers' corner with the spotty, the fat and the poorly dowered.

She took another sip and shook her head. 'No, thank you, Sir Henry.'

'Then perhaps you will dance with me?' Adam asked her, catching her dance card as it hung on her wrist and flipping it open. 'The next dance is a waltz, if I am not mistaken.'

'I am not dancing, my lord.' The words slipped out before she realised she no longer had that defence.

'Obviously not. Just at the moment you are partaking of supper. But as you say, you have finished—'

'You choose to misunderstand me.' Decima felt the blush mounting and fought it. 'I am not intending to dance.'

'But you have been—all evening. Are you rejecting me as a partner, Miss Ross? I am wounded.'

'I...no...I mean...' Decima gazed hopelessly at his bland countenance as he waited patiently for her to dither herself to a stop. She had been dancing. Rather a lot. With a number of different men. And there was absolutely no reason—short of becoming suddenly indisposed—why she should refuse Adam. She gave in. 'Thank you, Lord Weston.'

Beside her she realised that Henry was asking Olivia to partner him and the four of them reached the floor just as the first notes sounded. Decima stood uncertainly, the confidence that had filled her ever since Mr Mays had led her out quite deserting her.

'Decima?' Adam was waiting patiently, and with a sensation of breathlessness she stepped into his arms and took his hand. When she could breathe again the familiar scent of him was such a shock that she almost stumbled—citrus and man and, quite simply, Adam. His arm held her firmly, as he might have collected a horse that had stumbled, and they were dancing.

'That is a particularly fetching gown,' Adam remarked. She could hear the smile in his voice and it brought her eyes up sharply to his face, but mercifully he was not regarding the embarrassing swell of exposed bosom. He grinned at her. 'Those freckles get everywhere, don't they?'

'No, they do not,' she retorted. 'I believe you have now seen every freckle I possess and I would be obliged if you would not refer to them again—it is most unseemly.'

'You make me feel unseemly,' he remarked plaintively, whirling her around a slower pair of dancers. For a second their bodies pressed together. A flash of heat, of hot liquid yearning, ran through her loins and Decima drew back with a gasp.

She said the first thing she could think of to bring them both back to earth and to a sense of their obligations. 'When is the wedding to be?'

'June the eighteenth.'

'Oh.' Now what to say? 'And where will it be?'

'I have no idea. My future mother-in-law has not yet vouchsafed her decision on the matter.'

'Does Olivia not have a say?' Surely a bride would have very decided ideas about every aspect of the ceremony.

'Olivia does exactly what her mother tells her,' Adam said, with a suggestion of gritted teeth.

That did make sense, and could account for some of Adam's apparent coolness on the subject of his marriage. From what Decima knew of Mrs Channing, she imagined she would not make an easy mama-in-law.

'I would lay odds on you winning any future encounters with the lady,' she remarked outrageously.

'I have every intention of doing so. But until Olivia is removed from her orbit, nothing is gained by coming to cuffs with her, other than to make Olivia miserable.'

'You are concerned how Olivia feels?' It was the first time she had heard him say anything that showed any feeling for his fiancée.

'You think me cold? I am very fond of Olivia and I want her to be happy.' Adam looked down at her, his grey eyes dark as he regarded her with an expression at odds with the cheerful music. 'She is shy of me—overt shows of affection would disconcert her.'

'I beg your pardon.' Decima bit her lip and forced herself to finish her apology. 'That was inexcusable of me, I have no right to pry.'

He smiled at her then, making her ill-disciplined heart flip against her ribs. 'As my friend, I expect you to lecture me on a regular basis. I am sure you scold Freshford.'

'Henry rarely needs scolding,' Decima rejoined, catching sight of the other couple as they turned. 'Oh!'

'Indeed,' Adam said drily. 'What a very handsome pair they do make, to be sure.'

It was as though an artist had decided to paint the perfect couple. Olivia, tiny as she was, fitted perfectly against Henry's modest height so they could have been made to measure for each other. Their hair shimmered under the lights: hers palest gilt, his a masculine gold. And both of them had the sort of perfectly moulded looks that seemed to come straight from a classical frieze.

'Olivia has a beauty that would look good, whoever she was partnered with,' Decima said quickly. If he wasn't careful, Henry was going to find himself called out by an enraged fiancé. Adam might turn a blind eye to Olivia enjoying a little light flirtation while she was sitting at his side, but to have her circling the dance floor in another man's arms while the two of them gazed deep into each other's eyes was asking rather too much.

'That is very true,' Adam agreed equably. She shot him a suspicious glance, but he seemed to be quite calm about the situation, only pulling her a little closer into his hold as they danced.

It was a dangerous thing to be doing, dancing with Adam like this. Decima knew it, yet felt no more able to stop herself revelling in the sensation of being in his arms than if she were a small child who had found a bag of sugarplums and was gorging herself to the point of sickness.

She had forgotten quite how well matched their bodies seemed to be as they danced, how his height was quite perfect for her, how the hair on his temples grew and the way the skin at the corner of his eyes crinkled when he smiled, how her breath caught in her throat when he looked at her.

Decima dropped her eyes at the sudden panicky thought that he had seen her feelings in them. She had told herself that it was perfectly possible to love Adam and yet to live with that. She had been prepared to see him around in London and had expected to feel a pang, but that was all. In fact, she had been prepared to find that distance had lent enchantment and that meeting Adam again would be in some way a let-down. She had had no idea that love could be so all consuming, that it would feed on his nearness, would be rekindled by his kiss, that the fact that he was betrothed to another woman would not alter the way she felt one iota.

The music stopped and she swept a curtsy. She felt light-headed and reckless, yet one part of her mind was marvelling at the way she was dancing and having such pleasure doing so—one of her darkest, scariest bogeymen vanquished at a stroke. As if reading her thoughts, Adam whispered, 'I can see two Patronesses staring at us. Were they ones who were beastly to you?'

Decima shot them a hunted look, suddenly a gawky eighteen-year-old again. 'Mrs Drummond Burrell and Lady Castlereagh. I was *terrified* of them. They used to look right through me, but you could see what an effort they found it to ignore something as obvious as me, nevertheless.'

'Right.' Adam tucked her arm through his and headed for the two formidable ladies. Only the fact that over a hundred eyes were watching the dance floor stopped Decima gibbering with nerves and tugging her arm free.

Chapter Sixteen

'Ladies.' Adam stopped in front of them and bowed slightly, receiving gracious inclinations of their heads and smiles of welcome. Obviously Viscount Weston was approved of. 'I am sure you know Miss Ross?' Decima found herself the object of two critical examinations. It appeared the ladies did not know what to make of her, then her height must have touched their memories.

'*Decima* Ross?' enquired Mrs Drummond Burrell. 'Carmichael's half-sister?'

'Yes, ma'am.'

'Good God,' Lady Castlereagh murmured, then more loudly, 'You have certainly…developed, Miss Ross.'

'Miss Ross is a quite wonderful dancer,' Adam confided, ignoring manfully the pinching pressure of Decima's fingers on her arm. 'And she tells me she owes it all to your influence over several Seasons.'

'*Our* influence?' Mrs Drummond Burrell was obviously looking back at her recollection of an unsatisfactory débutante. 'I am sure we never gave Miss Ross any encouragement to dance.'

'Exactly,' Adam said sweetly. 'Is it not remarkable how

character building it is to overcome ignorant prejudice and discouragement?' With another, perfectly correct, bow, he walked on, Decima quivering at his side.

'That's wiped the smug smiles off their old pussy faces.' He looked down at her, his own smile vanishing as he saw her face. 'Oh, Lord. Did that upset you? I thought you might enjoy it.'

Decima fought to keep her countenance and found herself pulled sideways through a curtain and out into the screened portico that overlooked the gardens, sheltered from the February weather by removable panes of glass. At the far end a couple were talking, their backs turned to them, otherwise they were alone in the dim and rather chilly interior. She buried her face in her hands and gave way to her feelings.

Adam swore violently under his breath as he watched Decima's shaking shoulders with the sort of blind panic that only female tears can produce in an otherwise courageous man. 'Decima? Sweetheart? I only meant to put the old cats in their place. Don't cry.' He gathered her against his chest and gave himself the luxury of one long, deep inhalation, filling his lungs with the scent of her skin and the floral rinse she used on her hair.

'I'm not.' It came out as a muffled gasp, he had her squashed against him so hard. Cautiously Adam opened his arms and Decima emerged, flushed and giggling. 'That was wonderful. Thank you so much, Adam. I would never have dared be rude to them, but now I can just ignore them. That is two bogeymen slain in one evening, thanks to you and that nice Mr Mays.'

'Two?' Adam produced a spotless white handkerchief— thank goodness for his valet—and regarded her cautiously. 'And what has Mays got to do with anything?'

'He persuaded me to dance. He is such a kind man, and so tall, I felt perfectly at ease with him. So all in one evening I have got over my fear of dancing and I am not going to worry about the Patronesses, either.'

'I've probably scuppered your chances of vouchers for Almack's.' He hadn't thought of that. Nor had he reckoned on her taking a liking to George Mays. Interfering in this predominantly feminine world was more complex than he had counted upon.

'I have already got them, thanks to Lady Freshford. She is good friends with Lady Sefton, who was the only one of them who didn't snub me all those years ago.' Decima mopped her eyes with his handkerchief, folded it up carefully and put it on the table beside her. Adam put out a hand and slid it silently back into his pocket. How juvenile, being reduced to treasuring a handkerchief because she had dried her tears on it. Love was turning him inside out. He was even jealous of George Mays, for goodness' sake.

'I am tall, too.' The words were out before he realised how ridiculous they sounded, and he was rewarded for his foolishness by Decima's twinkling smile of understanding.

'Yes, but not as tall as Mr Mays. Or some of his military friends.' She obviously relented, 'Or perhaps it is the scarlet regimentals—they do flatter a man so.'

'You, Miss Ross, are rapidly becoming a flirt.'

Decima sent him a slanting look from beneath long, dark lashes. His heart turned, painfully. 'I'm not, truly. I'm simply enjoying myself a little before I go back to my comfortable, quiet life in Norfolk.'

'Is that what you want?' He found her answer to his question was vitally important, as though somehow his whole future hung on it. And that was ridiculous, because if he didn't manage something impossible very soon his future was all too plainly set out before him.

'I don't know any more.' She moved away from him restlessly, her gown swishing across the marble of the floor, her shoulders gleaming white in the subdued light.

What would she say if he just snatched her into his arms,

demanded that she run away with him, now, this minute, and to hell with convention and their duty and whatever society might say? He knew, of course—she would look at him out of those clear grey eyes and remind him of his duty to Olivia. Of his honour. And she would be quite correct.

'I think I want to experience things more.' Decima stopped, turned and began to pace back. 'I think I want to do things because I want to, not because my family thinks I should do them. Obviously, I do not want to be difficult.' She broke off, her full underlip caught by her teeth, and thought some more. 'Actually, whenever Charlton wants me to do something then I *do* want to be difficult. Do you know, he wrote and said that under no circumstances should I come to London. I started packing immediately.'

'Why ever should you not come to London?' Charlton's motives were of profound uninterest to Adam, but he was enjoying the sight of Decima's white teeth on the full swell of her lip and the memory of how it had felt to bite it himself. He hitched one hip onto a marble plant stand and folded his arms, waiting to be entertained.

'Other than the fact that I had not asked his advice first?' Decima laughed, producing an exciting swelling of her bosom. Adam dropped his clasped hands strategically and was thankful for the shadows. 'I hadn't thought. Perhaps he thinks I will fall into the hands of an unscrupulous fortune hunter, now I am in control of my own money. Or I might buy dashing gowns.'

'Like this one?'

'It is nice, isn't it?' Decima asked with an innocent enthusiasm. 'I had no idea how difficult it would be to wear, though—I have to keep my shoulders back all the time.'

'You already know I admire it.' He admired it so much that he was calculating how far she would have to lean forward before he could cup the weight of those lovely breasts in his palms.

'Adam.' He raised his eyes and found her regarding him sternly. 'Stop it. I cannot pretend that I am not flattered by your flirting, but it *has* to cease. Olivia might be a complete innocent, and extraordinarily good-natured, but she is going to notice and I would not have her hurt for the world. What if she thought you were serious?'

But I am serious. And Decima was right; by being alone with her, he was playing with fire—and both her reputation and Olivia's happiness could go up in flames.

'We ought to go back.' Decima looked conscious-stricken. 'People will be wondering what has become of us.'

Adam followed her through the curtains with the strange feeling that his senses were heightened. Something gripped his chest in a vice, but it was not, as he had first thought, frustrated desire. This was the edgy anticipation he had felt before each of the three duels he had fought. It was not fear, more the gut-deep knowledge that he had better get this right or the consequences were going to be very, very serious.

Discreetly, he stood back in the shadow of the curtain as Decima made her way back to Lady Freshford, her dark head easily visible as she moved through the throng of shorter young women. If nothing else, he had gifted her the confidence to enjoy society. Or perhaps he was not even responsible for that. Adam felt his mouth curve as he recalled her decisive voice as she explained her New Year's resolution.

The sensation that he was about to duel had not left him. He made himself breathe deeply and evenly. Part of it, if he was honest, was thorough-going arousal, his body telling him it was ready to fight for Decima. The problem was, the only opponent to vanquish was Olivia Channing, and in all honour the only way he could defeat her was to ensure she came out of it better off than they had begun.

Decima had vanished now. Reluctant to move back into the chattering throng, Adam leaned against the door pillar and thought about her. His body ached with the need to possess her, but this was different from anything he had experienced with women in the past. Ruefully he acknowledged there had been plenty to provide a comparison.

But always what he had desired had been the physical satisfaction that they could give each other. With Decima it was different. He wanted her in that way, of course, his body was telling him so quite plainly, but what he *needed* was to look into her eyes as he made love to her, to read her feelings in those depths, to open his soul to her and to glimpse hers.

This was love, it had to be. He shut his eyes and tried to push back the memory of her wide eyes on his as his weight bore her down into the snow.

'Decima.' He was unaware of whispering her name aloud.

'Are you all right, old chap? I mean, talking to yourself and so forth?' Adam's eyes snapped open and he found George Mays gazing at him with concern on his face. 'A bit mellow, are you? Only I thought you'd want to know your future mama-in-law is on your trail and wondering where you've got to.'

'Marvellous. In fact, wonderful. Thought I'd lost her—such a relief to know she's still here.'

George's eyebrows climbed in incredulity. 'Really, old chap? I have to say: fiancée—what a cracker. But mama-in-law's a bit of a dragon in my opinion. Anyways, wanted to mention—thanks for marking my card with Miss Ross, she's a damn fine girl. Enlisting her sympathy about my height did the trick, just like you said it would. I've half a mind to call. In fact, I think I'll send flowers *and* call. What do you think?'

Adam looked at George narrowly. He, Adam, might not be mellow, but Mays certainly was. 'Why not, George? I am sure Miss Ross would be delighted.' He slapped his friend on the back and strolled off in search of the Channings, his spirits suddenly lifted. The game was on.

He stopped a few yards from where Olivia was sitting

with her mother, chatting animatedly with a young man Adam assumed was her next dance partner. She looked up and the vivacity drained from her face, leaving only the perfectly behaved young miss. No. This was not a game, this was at least as serious as a duel.

Decima was perfectly aware that her attention was distracted over the very late breakfast she was sharing with the Freshfords. They were all heavy-eyed from the events of the night before. Caroline had tried to sleep, but had been too excited by her first proper ball, her mother was showing signs of the strain of the event on a lady who was on the shady side of forty-five and Henry looked…well, *grim*, Decima decided.

She studied his hooded eyes, the hard set of his mouth and his lack of sparkle, and concluded that a pile of Caro's bills must have landed upon his desk that morning. It was all she could think of to explain it, although it was unlike Henry to fret about money. Henry was a wealthy man who believed in making his wealth work. Decima knew all about the investments in canals and coalmines and even in the new-fangled steam-powered machinery.

She gave a mental shrug, dismissing the problem for the moment, and went back to brooding on Adam. Part of her was pleased that he had seen her looking her best, that she had danced with him and had succeeded in managing her unruly emotions when she was alone with him. Decima was confident that he had no idea that she felt any more for him than friendship and gratitude for rescuing her.

But how to resist his flirting? Or the effect his steady gaze had on her heart? Decima cut into her ham and eggs and took herself to task. If someone had asked her, as she had sat at Charlton's breakfast table that day after Christmas, if she would be content to be independent, confident, enjoying all that London had to offer her, she would have answered with an unhesitating *yes*. If that same questioner had asked her if she expected to fall in love, she would have laughed in their face and maintained that the summit of her ambitions for happiness was her independence and the company of her good friends.

Decima sighed and Henry's deep blue gaze shifted from a moody contemplation of the paper to her face. 'Are you all right?'

'Just counting my blessings,' Decima answered with a smile.

'It didn't sound like it.' His mother and sister had their heads together over a fashion journal. 'Shall we walk after breakfast?'

'Yes, that would be pleasant, I would welcome the fresh air. Shall I see if your mama and Caro...?'

'No.' Henry shook his head. 'I want to talk with you alone.'

When Decima came downstairs an hour later, dressed for walking, she found him fidgeting moodily around the hall. 'The park?' she queried, tucking her hand into the crook of his arm as they went down the steps.

'Mmm?'

'Henry! Shall we go into the park?'

'Yes, very well, provided your friend Weston isn't exercising his horses again.' Henry, normally easygoing to a fault, sounded positively hostile. Decima watched him out of the corner of her eye as they negotiated the Park Lane traffic.

'Did you enjoy yourself last night?' she asked casually. 'Caro had a great success, I thought. She is so natural and vivacious, yet with such a touching shyness. I am sure she is going to take.'

'Mmm.'

Now what to say? 'Are you intending to go to the Haydons' soirée this evening? I said I would, but I don't believe I will stay very late, not after—'

'Are you still in love with that fellow Weston?' Henry demanded, cutting across her in mid-sentence. Decima doubted he had even realised she was speaking.

'Yes,' she blurted out before she had time to recollect herself and wonder that she should so expose herself. It had been one thing to confide in Henry when Adam was a distant figure. Now her friend knew only too well that the object of her desires was very publicly attached to another woman.

'Then what is he doing engaged to Olivia…Miss Channing?' Henry took a savage swipe at an innocent weed with his cane.

'Intending to marry her, I imagine,' Decima retorted tartly. 'He has no idea—I sincerely hope—that I have any feelings for him other than friendship.' She shot Henry a swift, frowning glance. 'And I want it to stay like that.'

'Is he in love with her?' Henry persisted.

'Well, of course he is! Why would he marry her if he is not?' Decima demanded. She sounded no more certain, to her own ears, than she felt. Adam showed no signs of deep love for Olivia. He treated her with coolly respectful politeness, was obviously squiring her about attentively and appeared to be able to tolerate her mother, but there was no heat in his eyes when he looked at her, no depths of tenderness in his voice when he spoke of her.

'It cannot be for her money,' she added. 'And although her family is perfectly respectable, I am not aware that she has any connections that might be desirable. A viscount is hardly likely to be in need of such in any case.'

'Do you think she loves him?'

'No.' Decima spoke without needing to think about it. 'No,' she added more thoughtfully. 'I think she is in awe of him and very shy. But he is a marvellous match for her.'

'I would say she is terrified,' Henry observed so dispassionately that Decima would have been quite taken in, if another unfortunate plant was not decapitated as he spoke.

'Surely not? What is there to be frightened of?' Decima looked at her friend incredulously. 'Adam has the most even temper—look how he coped with all the problems when we were snowed in. Why, Charlton would have been in a flaming rage after an hour, and I am sure even you would have been somewhat put out.'

'He has high rank, doubtless major households to maintain...'

'Olivia has been raised to be a gentleman's wife. She might be nervous of the responsibility—but *afraid*?'

'Quite, that was my feeling,' Henry agreed with her. 'I was wondering if perhaps...physically...' He stopped speaking and walked on in silence.

'Granted Adam is very tall, and Olivia very tiny...' Decima began, still thinking about how Olivia might feel, confronting such a large specimen of masculinity, especially when he was not in a particularly conciliatory mood. Then her imagination caught up with her and she found herself wondering, not for the first time, what it would be like to lose her virginity to Adam Grantham.

Alarming, she decided. She found herself blushing from head to toe. Surely Henry wasn't referring to *that* aspect of marriage?

Tentatively she ventured, 'If you mean that she might be afraid of the, er...marriage bed, I am sure Olivia is too innocent to be worried about that.'

'Of course she is,' Henry said vehemently. 'I'm not making much sense, am I?' he added, sounding wretched.

'If I didn't know any better,' Decima ventured, 'I would say you were jealous.'

She expected him to deny it. Instead he swung round to face her. 'I am. I am in love with Olivia.'

'But...but you hardly know her! Henry, you cannot be, surely?'

'She is the other half of me,' he said vehemently. 'I looked into her eyes and there it was. When I held her in my arms, danced with her, then I knew.'

'What does she feel?' Decima found it difficult to form the sentence, she felt so breathless.

'I cannot be certain—trust me, I said nothing, of course—but I am sure she felt an affinity, a liking.'

'Henry, you cannot pay court to her,' Decima protested.

'I know it.' He took a vehement stride away, then spun round to face her. 'Unless she breaks off the engagement to Weston, my hands are tied. To do anything else would be dishonourable.'

'What a coil,' she said miserably. 'I love him, you love her—and whatever it is they feel, I cannot believe it is a love match between them. What are we going to do?'

'Do you want to go back to Norfolk, Decima?'

'We cannot. We must stay and support your mama and Caro.'

'You could go.'

'I am not running away. And in any case…' she tucked her arm affectionately through his again and began to walk on '…I am not leaving you to be miserable. After all, who else is there for you to talk to about this?'

They walked in silence for perhaps twenty minutes, then turned back towards Green Street. 'We must avoid them both,' Henry said resolutely as they approached his front door. 'Heaven knows, there's society and diversions enough in town without us needing to run up against two people.'

'Absolutely,' Decima agreed. A carriage passed them and drew up at the steps. 'I wonder who that is?'

'The frustration of a sensible resolution,' Henry replied grimly as the footman opened the door and set down the step for Olivia Channing to alight.

Chapter Seventeen

'Miss Ross, Sir Henry, good morning.' Olivia regarded them shyly from under the brim of an enchanting blue bonnet. 'I am glad I found you at home, I was a little worried this was a trifle early to call.'

'Allow me.' Henry ushered her up the front steps and was rewarded by a sweet smile and a blush. Decima cast her eyes skywards and followed. 'May I offer you refreshment, Miss Channing? I am not sure where my mother and sister are...'

The butler emerged from the shadows to relieve the ladies of their outer garments. 'Her ladyship and Miss Caroline have gone shopping, Sir Henry. They have taken the barouche.'

'It was Miss Ross I came to see,' Olivia confided, allowing herself to be seated in the salon. 'It is just that Mama and I had tickets for a private view at the Wolverton Gallery—some newly arrived studies from the artist's tour of the continent, you understand—and now Mama has to take Cousin Jane to the dentist. She has an abscess.'

'Very painful,' Decima murmured, wondering just why this concerned them.

'Very. And Cousin Jane—she is Mama's companion, you

see—is frightened of dentists, despite Mama telling her that all it requires is a little resolution on her part. So Mama is going with her, to stiffen her resolution.'

'Indeed?' Decima felt she would rather face a dozen dentists alone than have Mrs Channing as supporter.

'So I wondered if you would like to come to the showing this afternoon,' Olivia finished, finally coming to the point.

'Would you not rather go with Lord Weston?' Decima enquired, carefully turning back the cuffs of her gown, which had become slightly crumpled.

'I did think he might enjoy it, but I have three cards, and I remembered you were interested in art, Miss Ross.'

'That's very thoughtful of you, to recall that after so many years. And, please, will you not call me Decima? I would enjoy seeing the show, but I am certain Lord Weston would wish to accompany you.'

'He says he cannot come today. Then, when I said I was going to ask you, he suggested that I also ask Sir Henry, as he said he would feel happier if I had a gentleman with me, rather than just a footman. He said you were rather a high stickler, Miss…Decima, I mean, and would no doubt feel more comfortable as well.

'And as soon as he suggested it, I recalled what you had said last night, Sir Henry, about having enjoyed the Grand Tour, so…' She came to a halt, rather out of breath with shyness. Decima thought she had never heard Olivia say so many words together before.

But what on earth was Adam thinking about? Obviously he had not the slightest suspicion that Henry might entertain warm feelings for his fiancée. Perhaps he was worried about Olivia being alone with her in case she let something slip about their snowbound adventure, or perhaps his motives were exactly as Olivia had described them. And what the wretch was doing describing her as a high stickler she could not imagine, unless he thought that would reach Mrs Channing's ears and stop her fussing.

But, of course, after what Henry had just said, he would refuse. It was the only prudent thing to do.

'How thoughtful of you, Miss Channing. I would be delighted. What time would you like to set out?' Decima was too far away to kick him on the ankle, so instead she opened wide eyes at him. He smiled back ruefully as if to say, *What can I do?*

Invent an appointment, you idiot, she thought, wondering if she should remind him that he had promised to escort his mother that afternoon or invent some other fib, but it was too late, Henry and Olivia were happily making arrangements for them to collect her at two thirty that afternoon.

All Olivia's qualms about an early visit appeared to have vanished as she chatted with Henry. Decima sat, willing her to go so that she could tell him exactly what she thought of his uncharacteristic lack of resolution, but all she could do was to sit there and provide the chaperonage she was certain Mrs Channing would be expecting.

Finally Olivia left. 'Henry Freshford! What do you think you are—'

'A letter for you, Miss Ross.' It was Starling, the butler, proffering her a silver salver.

'Thank you. No, Henry.' He was leaving in the butler's wake. 'Don't you dare sneak away until I have rung a peel over your head for this!'

'Who is the letter from?' Henry appeared uneasy. *As well he might*, she fumed.

'Charlton. Oh dear, I do hope nothing is wrong with Hermione.'

'You had better open it. I won't run away.'

Decima slit the letter, unfolded it and began to read until she threw it down, fuming.

'Bad news?'

'The worst! No, no one is ill or dead, I do not mean that. But, Henry, he writes to say he is appalled that I have come *jauntering* up to London without informing him. It is misguided, extravagant and exactly what he might expect—I wonder he should sound so surprised, then!—and he and Hermione feel it their duty, at great inconvenience, to come up too and open the town house. Now, what can I do?'

'You don't have to do anything, do you?' Henry asked. 'He is no longer your trustee.'

'But he will expect me to go everywhere with Hermione, and he will want to know exactly what I am doing and who I meet. And what about Adam?'

'Well, as you are hardly carrying on a torrid affair with Weston, what is there for Charlton to concern himself with? If he meets him, he won't be any the wiser about your little adventure—and Weston's safely betrothed to Olivia.'

'Which he won't be if you carry on flirting with her,' Decima retorted.

'I am not flirting.'

'You are certainly not doing anything about avoiding her, either. You are in love with her, she certainly enjoys your company—how much more contact will it take for her to feel something more?'

They stared at each other in shocked silence, then Henry said slowly, 'That would solve both our problems.' The words seemed to hang in the space between them, then Henry shook his head. 'I should not even think it, let alone say it. It is dishonourable of me, almost as bad as if she was already his wife.'

'Yes.' Decima moved and took his hand, squeezing it, all her anger ebbing away. 'It would be, and I know you would never countenance such a thing. And, in any case, Adam does not love me—or why would he have proposed to Olivia in the first place? He may not love her either, but that is beside the point. But, Henry, do be careful, for Olivia's sake if nothing else.'

* * *

If her companions were subdued when they collected her that afternoon, Olivia showed no sign of noticing. She chattered happily to Henry, innocently tucking her hand under his elbow as they walked around the exhibition and urging him to tell her which scenes he had viewed in real life and how well the artist had represented them.

Decima went round dutifully behind them, gradually relaxing as she saw the effort Henry was making to treat Olivia with scrupulous detachment—even the most ferocious of chaperons could not have faulted his manner. Her heart bled for her friend and, in worrying about him, she found she could forget her own bruised heart.

It seemed pointless trailing around in their wake; Henry seemed happy describing scenes in detail for Olivia, she hung wide-eyed on his every word and Decima was growing thoroughly bored with set-piece landscapes executed with little originality and less verve.

With her feet hurting her more than her conscience, she sank down gratefully on one of the chaises provided by the gallery and let her unfocused eyes rest on an academic rendition of the Forum.

'My dear Miss Ross, I do declare you are asleep.' The softly chiding voice jerked her upright with a gasp. Adam was lounging elegantly on the chaise next to her.

'Ah! You made me jump! No, of course I was not asleep, I was only—'

'Resting your eyes?' he enquired mockingly.

'Certainly not. That is the sort of thing my grandmama says. I was resting my feet, if you must know. I find dawdling round an exhibition is more tiring than a good brisk walk, although why that should be I cannot imagine.'

Oh, give me strength... Adam was looking particularly handsome. *Positively edible*, a wanton part of her mind commented, making her blush at the thought. And it was painfully stimulating to be bickering with him.

'Such mediocre work would inspire an ache in every part of my body,' he remarked, leaning back and giving her the opportunity to admire long legs in elegant pantaloons, a superb pair of Hessians and—not that any lady should notice—exceptionally well-muscled thighs. 'You may well sigh,' he added, happily unaware of her thoughts. 'And doubtless you are going to reprove me for being the cause of you being here.'

Decima struggled to get a grip on her reactions, if not her emotions. 'I did wonder why, if you are here now, you did not escort Olivia in the first place,' she responded tartly. 'Not that I'm not delighted to have her company.'

Adam sent a quizzical glance down the length of the gallery to where Olivia and Henry were in ardent debate over a vast canvas, but said nothing. Decima wrestled with a defensive remark and wisely decided to stay silent. But there was a subject upon which she could talk, quite unexceptionally, with Adam, and now was an ideal opportunity.

'I wanted to ask you something,' she began, swivelling on the chaise to look at him properly.

'Yes?' he murmured, catching the hand she was beginning to gesture with in his and holding it. His hand was warm and hard and somehow she could not find the resolution to free hers.

'Has Bates said anything about Pru?'

He grimaced. 'What has *she* said?'

'Oh, I declare this is as bad as trying to discuss it with Pru herself! Every time I venture a question about how things are developing she blushes and prevaricates and will not commit herself.'

'Can you blame her?' Adam regarded her with questioning grey eyes.

'No, of course not. I don't want to pry. Only I don't believe she is happy, although they have been out of an evening together several times. I wonder if I should speak to Lady Freshford about allowing Pru to invite Bates into the servants' hall. Perhaps it would help. What is your policy about followers?'

'Good God, I don't have such a thing! I leave that to my butler.'

'But perhaps Bates would not care to apply to him for permission to bring in a friend—after all, he is outside staff and not under the butler's authority.'

'I don't imagine Bates's love life is being in any way inhibited by a lack of permission to take tea in the servants' hall,' Adam said impatiently. 'He has his own rooms here, over the stable. He is a grown man who knows his own mind—he could be entertaining a troop of dancing girls there for all I know or care.'

'You *don't* care, do you?' Decima burst out passionately.

'Yes, I do.' Adam's grip on her hand tightened and she started, suddenly conscious of the impropriety. Somehow the gentle grasp had seemed so safe and unthreatening that she had simply relaxed into the comfort of it. Had anyone passed by and noticed? She tugged and Adam held on. 'I care very much that he is happy, but I don't agree that interfering is going to make things any smoother for them. Would you want Pru meddling in your love life?'

What love life? Decima bit back the words before they could spill from her lips and glared at Adam. 'Let go of my hand this instant, my lord. And I do not want to interfere— do you take me for some meddling matchmaker? I simply want to remove every obstacle from their path that I can. Don't you feel that way about your friends?'

'My friends all seem quite capable of ordering their own affairs, Decima,' Adam said softly, his silver grey eyes resting on her mouth in a lingering look that made her heart thud painfully. 'I would not welcome their interference in mine.'

'No doubt you have your *affairs* all perfectly in order, my lord.' Decima made sure the emphasis was pointed. 'And I imagine that you have very little in your life to restrict you from doing precisely what you want, when you want—unlike your servants.' She got to her feet and jerked her hand out of his clasp. 'And I am equally sure your fiancée will be delighted to know that you have managed to get here after all.'

'I wish you would stop calling me *my lord*,' Adam complained, rising as she did and strolling languidly after her retreating figure. 'And, Decima,' he added, *sotto voce*, 'if you do not slow down I am going to have to raise my voice to carry to you and I am sure you don't want that.' She stopped abruptly and glared at him. 'Are you grinding your teeth?'

'Yes, I am. I'm in a very bad mood, if you must know. Thoroughly blue devilled, although I doubtless should not use the expression. And you, *my lord*, are not helping in the slightest.'

'An attack of the mulligrubs?' He managed to look so innocently serious that Decima laughed aloud, suddenly back in the kitchen in Rutland being teased out of her sudden fit of depression.

'I am afraid not, otherwise I could take myself off to the confectioners and indulge in a healing purchase of sweetmeats, just as your old nurse recommended.' She linked her arm through his and allowed herself to be walked down the long room. 'Unlike the mulligrubs, my bad mood has a number of very real causes.'

'Tell me.' She felt his arm close against his side, pressing her hand against warm cloth. Under her knuckles she fancied she could feel his heart beat, and her own tripped in response. Decima knew that to feel angry with Henry for failing to resist the chance to be with Olivia was being thoroughly hypocritical—she was being just as bad herself.

'I am worried about Pru and Bates. Hen— A friend of mine

is unhappy and there is nothing I can do to help, and, to crown it all, Charlton is coming to town.'

'Wonderful! No, I don't mean the troubles of Pru and your friend, but I will be intrigued to meet the legendary Charlton. I'm sure you have been slandering the man and he will prove to be a fire-eater whose wrath I must dread in case he ever finds out about our previous acquaintance.'

'It would serve you right if I cast myself upon his bosom and told him all about it,' Decima said warmly.

'*All* about it?'

'I thought we were going to forget about that,' Decima said, struggling to keep her voice under control. It was desperately unfair that this was a man with whom she felt she could talk about anything, and yet she was barred by honour and decency from exchanging all but the most superficial banter with him.

'We may have agreed not to refer to it, and I apologise for doing so, but I most certainly did not promise to forget it, Decima.' His voice was warm honey, seductively sweet in her ears.

'I suggest that you do so,' she riposted sharply in an undertone as they came up to the others. 'Olivia, see who has managed to get here after all. Henry, come and show me your favourites.'

She drew him away down the gallery, keeping up a flow of small talk until she judged they were safely out of earshot.

'Why are you trembling?' Henry demanded when they finally stopped in front of a large canvas of the Grand Canal in Venice. 'Has Weston said something to upset you?'

'Yes…no…I don't know! Him just being here upsets me. I am worried that he might guess there is something between you and Olivia, and I am afraid he will guess how I feel about him. I want to be with him so much, but when I am all I can do is bicker and sound fractious.'

* * *

Adam watched Decima while listening to Olivia's animated explanation of how much she was enjoying the exhibition. 'Sir Henry has been telling me all about Vienna, and Paris and the sites of Rome. He is so well-travelled, and describes things so vividly, I can almost imagine myself there.' Adam could not recall her speaking to him with such freedom since their betrothal. 'The heat and the smells and the romance of it all.' She sighed, making the blonde ringlets on either side of her pansy-face bob charmingly. 'I would so love to see it all for myself.'

It pained him to snub her, but it was no part of his plan to have her think him sympathetic; he had too much ground to make up from the time he had spent listening to her recount her woes at the Longminster house party.

'Indeed? I am sorry to disappoint you, Olivia, but I have a fixed disgust of foreign travel.'

'Oh.' Her lower lip quivered pathetically. Any man of the slightest sensibility would want to comfort her, but Adam had been down that road already. 'But I imagine you enjoy travel in the British Isles?' she ventured. 'Scotland, perhaps? I dote upon Sir Walter's romances.'

'Scott? Certainly not. I do hope you are not given to novel reading, Olivia. And as for Scotland, I would as soon sit under a pump for a week—one can then become wet, cold and miserable without the inconveniences of travel.'

'Oh,' she said again, thoroughly crushed. Adam just hoped he was providing a suitable contrast to Freshford, although it felt like kicking a kitten to be doing it.

It had seemed such an ideal solution, to throw Olivia and Freshford together. He was obviously besotted with her despite his efforts to hide it and Adam could not imagine that she could find a more compatible husband. But the combination of Olivia's perfect obedience, her terror of her parents and

Freshford's apparently rigorous sense of honour was going to make this trickier than he thought. It didn't help that Decima seemed so fixed on ensuring he treated Olivia as he should.

What if he did manage to disentangle himself from this coil with honour and she would not have him? Adam closed his eyes briefly, seeing Decima's face against the blackness of his lids. At least he could explain what had happened, how he felt. If he couldn't have her, that would be poor comfort indeed.

He came back to himself to find Olivia was regarding him anxiously 'Do you have a headache, my lord?' He could not persuade her to use his given name. All his attempts met only with a blush and a stammered, 'Mama says it is not proper or respectful.' Not for the first time Adam quailed inwardly at the thought of a wedding night with a bride who could not even bring herself to relax to that extent.

'No, not a headache. Have you seen enough, or would you like to stay a little longer?'

'No, thank you, I am quite ready to go, but I must wait for Decima and Sir Henry.'

'No need. My business meeting this afternoon has had to be cancelled as my agent is unwell; I can escort you home.'

'Oh, Sir Henry promised to lend me some of his foreign sketchbooks—but perhaps you would not care for me to borrow them?' She looked up at him anxiously.

'By all means, if that would give you pleasure.' *Well done, Freshford.* Adam grinned at the approaching baronet, Decima still on his arm. The man's tactics for maintaining perfectly respectable contact with Olivia were excellent, and very encouraging. But he still could not see how, unless Freshford could be persuaded to abduct Olivia and carry her off to the border, he was going to manage the thing. And Freshford did not strike him as the sort of gentleman who would even contemplate such irregularity.

'It seems you have been kind enough to promise Olivia a

sight of your sketch-books, Freshford. Would it be convenient if we return with you now?' Sir Henry agreed immediately, but Decima narrowed her eyes and her brows drew together in a fleeting frown. If he was not careful, she would overset his entire scheme. This called for more dramatic action than he had at first contemplated.

Chapter Eighteen

Decima fretted all the way back to the Freshfords' house, but Olivia's presence in the barouche prevented her giving tongue to anything but careful comment on the exhibition. Olivia had quite naturally climbed into their carriage, only realising as she sat down that perhaps she should have gone with Lord Weston. But he seemed indifferent about the matter, causing Decima even greater anxiety.

Was he so blind? Should she say something? But to do so would be to suggest that Henry might act in a dishonourable manner—and that, of course, was unthinkable. With a sinking heart Decima decided that she would have to have an intimate talk with Olivia.

She was still brooding on exactly what form this embarrassing conversation should take when they arrived back to find Lady Freshford and Caroline entertaining in the green salon.

'Decima, my dear, see who is here!' Lady Freshford welcomed her with a smile that only Decima and her children would have recognised as desperate. 'Your brother and dear Lady Carmichael.' She smiled at her son, who hastened to introduce Olivia and Lord Weston.

Blushing, Olivia protested that she had no wish to disturb Lady Freshford whilst she had company, but Adam accepted the offer of a chair and a cup of tea with alacrity, urging Olivia to sit down beside him. Decima saw the light of unholy glee in his eyes and shut hers in horror. Adam was settling down to become fully acquainted with Charlton.

But Charlton, with his usual single-minded concerns for his own priorities, rapidly returned to what he had obviously been discussing before they had arrived.

'I was just saying to Lady Freshford, it is most kind of her to look after you, Dessy, but now we are in town there is absolutely no need for her to be troubled. In fact, if you pack now, you may return with us immediately.'

'But—'

'But, Lord Carmichael, I would be most distressed if dear Decima were to leave us,' Lady Freshford cut neatly across Decima's protest. 'In fact, I would find myself quite at a stand, for in making my plans to bring Caroline out, I had no idea that Decima would not be able to stay with me for the entire Season.'

'Dessy? She is assisting with Miss Freshford's come-out?' Hermione regarded her hostess blankly.

'Why, yes. I am not strong,' Lady Freshford said, with a brazen disregard for the robust health she enjoyed. 'And dear Decima is able to take much of the burden of chaperonage from me, besides being such a help in showing Caroline how to go on.'

'*Dessy?*' Charlton interjected.

'Why, certainly.' That was Adam, leaning back in his chair and smiling benignly on the astonished Carmichaels. 'Miss Ross's style on the dance floor is much admired—I am sure it is not just Miss Freshford whose mama is pointing her out as an example of grace and deportment.'

'My mama is always very happy when she knows Miss Ross is with me,' Olivia chimed in with her sweet smile.

'But Dessy is single and—'

Adam cut in before Charlton had the opportunity to display his crashing lack of tact. 'But of mature years.' Decima forgot to be grateful for his interjection and glared at him. 'And she has such poise and judgement.'

Charlton spluttered, 'That's as may be…' The glance he shot Decima plainly said he did not believe a word of it and had wandered into a house full of lunatics. '…But I am afraid I must insist. Hermione will depend upon Dessy for her companionship and support, and, as family, that is where she belongs.'

'No,' Decima said baldly, knowing she should have waited to discuss the matter until they were alone. But if she did, she had the terrible fear that Charlton would simply sweep her away with his bullying and she would feebly agree. 'No, I am afraid that would not be convenient. I am fixed here, I promised Lady Freshford; in any case, I have so many engagements I really would be of little use to Hermione.' She smiled at her sister-in-law. 'Would Cousin Gertrude not be free?'

'Engagements? What, pray?'

'Four balls during the next sennight, a luncheon engagement—'

'Lady Hale's At Home,' Caroline chimed in. 'And you promised you would take me for my court-dress fittings because Mama finds that too fatiguing,' she announced inventively.

'And Miss Ross will be chaperoning Miss Channing on an expedition to Richmond,' Adam added. It was the first Decima had heard of it, but she nodded in agreement.

'Then there are my own fittings, and so forth,' she improvised. 'I am sorry, Hermione, not to be able to oblige you at such short notice, but I am sure Cousin Gertrude would be only too happy to join you.'

Charlton surged to his feet, his face red. Decima feared an

outburst, but at the last moment he seemed to recall that he was in company and refrained. With a stiff bow to Lady Freshford and a curt nod to the rest of the company he took his leave, Hermione anxious on his heels.

There was silence, then an almost collective drawing of breath. Adam put down his cup and tactfully took his leave, Olivia pressing Decima's hands and assuring her she was looking forward to seeing her again at the Laxtons' ball tomorrow.

When the door shut behind them Lady Freshford regarded Decima anxiously. 'Did I do right, my dear? Somehow I did not think that you wished to leave us, but if I am wrong, please do not hesitate to say so.'

'I am delighted to stay, if you wish me to, ma'am,' Decima assured her, clasping her hands tightly in her lap to quell their shaking. She would not have heard the last of this from Charlton, and, thankful though she was for the support of her friends, she could have wished for that unpleasant little encounter to have been in private.

She had her opportunity for a private conversation with her half-brother rather sooner than she would have wished for. No sooner had the Freshford party entered Lady Laxton's ballroom for her masquerade ball the following evening, than she saw Charlton and Hermione, deep in conversation with their friends the Fosters.

Decima's hands went instinctively to put on her mask, then she realised that not only would it give rise to ill-bred gossip if she avoided her own family all evening, but her height made her easily distinguishable in any event.

Henry, dressed as Robin Hood, found them a comfortable alcove with sofas from where they could admire the multicoloured throng in front of them. Lady Freshford had been so taken with Henry's costume that she had decreed a greenwood

theme for the party. Caroline was Maid Marion, Lady Freshford was a sweetbriar with rose petals covering her mask and
Decima had decided upon going as a willow tree in a gown
of shimmering fresh green and a mask created out of silk
leaves.

Charlton, so far as they could make out, had unwisely
decided upon dressing as a Roman emperor. The effect was
more pleasing on his wife, who carried off the lines of a classical tunic with somewhat angular elegance.

'Charlton is certainly visible in that outfit,' Decima
observed in a whisper to Henry, who turned, saw him and succumbed to a regrettable fit of stifled laughter.

'I thought it was the Regent for a moment,' he gasped,
snorting despite his mother's reproving look. 'What he needs
are a set of corsets and a much more concealing mask.'

He had to pull himself together rapidly, for the first of a
steady stream of gentlemen began to arrive to beg the hands
of Miss Ross and Miss Freshford in almost equal numbers.

'It is most unfair,' Caro observed teasingly as she viewed
her dance card with complacence. 'You are attracting all the
tall gentlemen, Decima, and I only get the short ones.'

There was one tall gentleman whose name did not appear
on Decima's card, however. Of Adam Grantham there was no
sign. Decima had just concluded that Mrs Channing had
decreed the more free and easy atmosphere of a masquerade
ball unsuitable for Olivia when a familiar dark head appeared
amidst the throng. Decima blinked. Adam seemed taller than
she recalled, then she saw that he was in the dress of the
middle of the last century—severe black, laced with silver,
his coat skirts stiffened with whalebone, his feet in buckled
shoes with red heels. He looked magnificent. By his side
Olivia was in the dress of a Meissen figurine, all bouffant blue
skirts and tight-laced waist, her hair arranged into a cascade
of ringlets. Her mother, nodding graciously from side to side,

was gowned in a rather more restrained version of the same period. Like many of the chaperons, she had dispensed with a mask.

Henry took a step forward, hesitated and remained where he was. 'Are you not going to ask Miss Channing to dance, dear?' his mother asked. 'She is a nice child, is she not?'

Henry hesitated, avoiding Decima's gaze, then took himself off across the room. 'I like Miss Channing, too,' Caro remarked. 'What a pity she is betrothed to Lord Weston—she is just the girl for Henry.'

This innocent observation seemed to hang in the air and Decima saw Lady Freshford's gaze sharpen and focus on her son. She turned slightly, her eyes meeting Decima's with startled realisation.

Decima stayed silent until Caro's partner came to claim her, then said quietly, 'I am sure Henry would do nothing…imprudent.'

'No, of course not,' his mother said stoutly, her anxious gaze fixed on the small group across the floor. 'I expect we are refining too much upon it.' She collected herself and observed, 'Here comes Lord Carmichael.'

Charlton was, indeed, making his way towards them, laurel wreath slipping dangerously on his balding pate, toga draped like a vast bath towel.

'Ma'am.' He bowed to Lady Freshford and glared at his sister. 'Dessy.'

'I hope you have not come to ask me to dance, Charlton,' Decima remarked, sounding regrettably pert to her own ears. 'I believe I have virtually nothing left but country dances and you certainly cannot perform those in that costume.'

'Of course I am not intending to dance,' Charlton fumed. He took Decima's arm and steered her away from Lady Freshford's seat. 'I attended only to accompany Hermione and to remonstrate with you about where your duty should lie.'

'If Hermione had invited me to join her in London when I was with you at Christmas, I would most certainly have been glad to oblige her.' Decima had qualms about whether that was the truth, but she was not going to refine upon the matter now. 'But to expect me to change my plans and to inconvenience Lady Freshford, who has been most kind to me, at no notice whatsoever—why, Charlton, that is the outside of enough.'

Her brother began to splutter, then his face went rigid. Decima was conscious of a presence close behind her and somehow knew who it was before he spoke. 'Miss Ross, Carmichael, good evening.'

'Lord Weston.' She turned and dropped a slight curtsy. 'May I say what a very fine costume group your party makes.'

'Why, thank you, Miss Weston. You present the most elegant of willow trees, if I may be so bold. And, Lord Carmichael, what an admirable guise! But where is your barrel?'

'Barrel?' Charlton boggled at Adam 'What do you mean, sir?'

'Why, you are representing Archimedes, are you not? At the point where you have leapt out of the barrel, wrapped a bath towel around yourself and cried "Eureka"?'

Charlton was becoming puce. Hastily Decima intervened before he had the threatened stroke. 'My brother is representing a Roman emperor, my lord. Surely you observe the wreath upon his brow?'

It was very hard to control her laughter. She fixed Adam with an imploring look and he took her arm.

'But enough of costumes. My dance, I think, Miss Ross; we must make haste or miss the opening notes.'

The formal sets of a cotillion were not the best place to remonstrate with one's partner, but Decima did her best as they came together and parted.

'How could you? Bath towel indeed!'

'A genuine mistake,' Adam observed as the measure brought him back to her side.

'That, my lord, is a complete untruth,' she scolded.

'True,' he agreed maddeningly.

'And this is not your dance, either,' she added.

'Was it anyone else's?'

'No,' she conceded, 'but that is not the point. You are extremely autocratic, my lord.'

They were swept apart by the dance. When he took her hand again Adam was serious. 'Will you give in to your brother on his demands to stay with him?'

'No.' Decima shook her head decisively. 'It makes me feel guilty to defy him—he is the head of the family, after all—but I resolved to be independent, and I will be.'

'Good.' The smile came back to Adam's face and with it a warm glow filled her. His approval meant so much—and it should not, she knew it. She should be guided only by her own conscience and her own sense of duty.

As the dance came to an end he retained her hand as they walked off the floor. Decima turned to thank him and was shocked into silence as he lifted her hand and, turning it in his, dropped a light kiss on the skin of her wrist where the buttons of her long gloves parted.

'Good,' he repeated. 'I would hate to think I had misjudged you, Decima.' And then he was gone, leaving her blushing on the edge of the dance floor. She was only a few steps from Lady Freshford, but Decima felt as though she had been abandoned in the midst of a throng of critical strangers. She glanced round wildly, expecting to see the chaperons all pointing at her and hissing about her wanton behaviour, allowing her bare wrist to be caressed in public.

But no one was looking at her, not even Lady Freshford, who was chatting animatedly to a friend. Still hot-cheeked, Decima escaped to the retiring room and retreated behind a screen to peer anxiously into a mirror and try to restore her countenance. A word of thanks sent the hovering maid away, leaving her alone.

This would not do, it really would not. She was relying too much upon Adam's approval, his very presence, for her happiness and that was madness. He obviously felt so little for her that it never occurred to him that paying her attention might rouse unsuitable feelings in her breast.

Presumably now he was engaged to be married he was able to put aside their lovemaking in the hunting lodge and assumed she could do so as easily. And yet he had seemed jealous of Henry's attachment to her. Men were *very* strange; she must have another talk with Henry.

Decima sighed and began to twirl strands of hair, that had lost a little curl in the warmth of the ballroom, between finger and thumb. They really needed the application of a hot iron again, but the fruitless exercise at least offered her some excuse for not going back out again for a few minutes.

The outer door opened. 'Good evening. May I assist you, ladies?' The maid had obviously stepped forward and this time was requested to find needle and thread for a torn hem. It was Mrs Channing, and as she chatted to her companion, loftily ignoring the maid's presence, it was obvious that the possessor of the damaged dress was Olivia.

'You must try for a little more poise and grace, Olivia. Your hurly-burly manner of going about things was bound to result in some damage to your gown. It is fortunate that it was only a sight tear at the hem.'

'I am sorry, Mama, but there was such a crush of people…'

'You should have stood your ground. You are a lady, it is up to them to make way for you, not for you, engaged to a viscount, to step back in that clumsy self-effacing way. You will have to learn to be more assertive when you are married, my girl.'

'Yes, Mama, but…'

'Do not argue, Olivia!' Decima rolled her eyes at her own reflection. How did the woman expect the girl to behave if she browbeat her every time she tried to speak?

'You should try for a little more *presence*. You could do worse than to copy Miss Ross.'

'But she is older than me, Mama. She knows her way about in the world…'

'She is an unmarried woman—I certainly hope she does *not* know her way about, as you so inelegantly put it, Olivia. I mean that she has poise and a certain something.' *Praise indeed!* Decima suppressed a gasp of sheer amazement. Mrs Channing's approbation was an unexpected honour.

'Mind you,' the matron continued forcibly, 'she has so many faults to overcome that she must have had to learn to make the most of all her good points. And, of course, nothing could possibly win her a husband. Not with her height and those freckles. I wonder if I should recommend Delcroix's *Crème des Sultanes* to her? I hear it worked wonders for Mrs Pettigrew's youngest.'

'Oh…perhaps she might take it amiss?' Olivia ventured, earning an unseen, but vigorous nod of agreement from Decima. She should have known better than to expect unalloyed praise from that source!

There was a further flurry of activity from the other side of the screen and then the sound of the door opening and closing. Decima gave her hair a last tweak and stepped out from her concealment to find Olivia, alone except for the maid who was on her knees finishing off the thread. 'There you are, miss, that should hold.'

'Oh, no!' Olivia was scarlet with embarrassment. 'Oh, Miss Ross…Decima…I had no idea you were there! Oh, dear…'

'It is entirely my fault,' Decima said, trampling down her embarrassment in an effort to quell Olivia's distress. 'I should have made my presence known as soon as your mama began to speak. And, in any case, she spoke most kindly of me.'

'Yes, but…'

'My freckles? Perhaps I should try her thoughtful recommendation.' *But Adam likes my freckles*, the rebellious voice murmured in her ear. All the more reason for getting rid of them then, she thought firmly.

'Decima?' Olivia asked hesitantly.

'Yes?'

'Might I…might I come and speak to you, in confidence?' Olivia was flushed, her head bent, her fingers twisting together.

'Of course.' This would be the ideal opportunity to talk frankly to Olivia about focusing all her attention upon Adam and not allowing her 'friendship' with Henry to develop, but it was hardly a duty Decima felt ready for. 'Why not call tomorrow, about three? I am sure everyone else will be out, so we can have a comfortable talk.' Her heart sank. It would be nice if doing the right thing was easy.

Chapter Nineteen

❦

'**Y**ou do not love Lord Weston *at all*?' Decima regarded Olivia's miserable face with horror. The younger woman must have misread her expression for one of condemnation, for she began to sob quietly, wringing her hands into the fine muslin of her pretty morning gown in her distress.

'I want to be dutiful, and I do not *have* to love him, do I?' she faltered. 'Mama says no gentleman would expect such a thing in any case and I am foolish and wicked to think about it.' She stifled a hiccup in her handkerchief. 'I think he is very kind…at least, he used to be, but I am so silly, Mama says, no wonder he seems strict with me now.'

Oh, lord. Decima cast a hasty glance at the drawing-room door to make sure it was firmly closed and did her best. 'I know that love is not considered a prerequisite for a happy and ful-filling marriage,' she began carefully. 'Between gentlefolk, and especially the aristocracy, I believe it is the exception rather than the rule. But there must be mutual affection and respect, I am sure—do you not feel those things for Lord Weston?'

'He was very kind to me before we became betrothed.' For some reason Olivia blushed scarlet. 'And, of course, I respect him because he is so intelligent and has such a great position.'

'Well, then, I expect this is all nerves and you will be very happy when you are married.' Decima thought she sounded like Hermione. But what else could she say? Should she encourage Olivia in her doubts in the hope that she would jilt Adam? That would be despicable, besides risking ruining the girl's reputation.

'And do not forget he proposed to you despite the fact that you are not titled and—forgive me—perhaps not as richly dowered as some young ladies.'

For some reason that produced an even deeper blush and a look of total misery. 'I am sure he had no intention of proposing to me before the Longminster house party.'

'Then that shows how taken he was with you,' Decima said, attempting to inject a rallying tone into her voice. 'You must know how beautiful you are, and I am sure you have all the skills needed to manage a great house.'

'Th…thank you.' Olivia dabbed at her eyes. 'You do not seem at all afraid of him.'

'Why, no. Why ever should I be? Has he said anything to give you a fear of him?'

'No…' Olivia did not seem too sure. 'He seems very stern sometimes, but then so is Papa.'

Not very romantic. 'Has he *done* anything to alarm you, then?' Decima persisted.

'He…kissed me.'

'Oh. Well, that is to be expected, is it not? I mean, you are engaged to be married.'

'I did not think it would be so…so…' Olivia stammered. 'I thought he might kiss me on the cheek, or my hand, but not on the mouth like…like that.'

'Ah. Er…has your mama explained about…um… marriage?'

'Not really. She says I am a goose.'

'Well, *I* cannot talk to you about it, Olivia. After all, I am

unmarried myself and really do not know about these things.'
Decima could feel the blush rising up her throat and only
hoped the girl would attribute it to the embarrassment of discussing intimate matters. She tried again.

'But don't you think, if you were to attempt to return any
affectionate, or even passionate, gesture by at least not shrink-
ing from him, that might help? He would feel you trust him
and you might sooner become accustomed to his…caresses.'
Olivia nodded thoughtfully, dabbing her eyes. 'And if you
were to confide in him a little, explain that you feel nervous—
not about kissing, but about some subject that is easy to
discuss, say, how you will get on with a large household to
manage—then you will get to know him better and he will
make allowances for your inexperience.'

'I will try,' Olivia said bravely. 'Thank you so very
much, Decima. I would never have dared discuss such
things with Mama.'

'But you were having real doubts about the betrothal? Is
there anyone else?' Decima pursued.

'Oh, no! Mama would be so angry if I were to fall in—I
mean, if I were to do such a thing.' The colour was ebbing
and flowing under Olivia's fine skin as she looked both guilty
and utterly wretched. She was obviously a very poor liar. 'I
could never go against what Mama felt to be right.'

Decima waved goodbye to Olivia as she stepped up into
her carriage with mixed feelings and a crashing headache.
Loving Adam meant she should want what was best for him,
and if that meant Olivia, then so be it. On the other hand, she
still had nagging doubts about whether Miss Channing truly
was the bride for him. Had he simply fallen for a ravishingly
pretty face? But that seemed to suffice for many men. Which
was a lowering thought—one would have hoped that the
object of one's affection had better judgement.

* * *

The Freshfords returned home to find their guest reclining on the sofa, languidly flicking through a book of poetry and fighting what Decima frankly described as a thundering headache. She took herself off to her room rather than dampen everyone's spirits over luncheon and was somewhat cheered by Pru's smiling face.

'I'll make a cold compress for your forehead, shall I?' Pru tiptoed about, finding the hartshorn and the lavender water and humming softly under her breath.

Decima levered herself up against the pillows and regarded her with interest. Pru had been very quiet, and extremely close-lipped, the past few days, and Decima had decided not to pry, but it was such a relief to talk to someone who appeared to be happy that she ventured a question.

'Have you seen Bates lately, Pru?'

'Yes, Miss Decima. Almost every free evening I've had, and my half-days. I don't think we've stopped talking, hardly.'

'Really? Bates talkative? Don't you argue any more?'

'He was just shy, that's all. Bashful, like.' That seemed unlikely, but then, Decima decided, she was not regarding Bates with the eye of love and perhaps Pru was more perceptive about his character. 'We don't argue at all now, not about anything.'

'That is wonderful, Pru.' Headache forgotten, Decima sat up properly. 'Has he said anything about the future?'

'Not yet, but he sort of hinted. He said his lordship might see his way to letting him have a cottage if he ever felt like settling down.' That was promising. It would mean losing Pru, of course, but Decima couldn't begrudge that. 'I think he might say something this evening.' Pru's round face was creased by a beaming smile and Decima thought she had never seen her look so pretty.

'What will you be wearing? Would you like to borrow my Norwich shawl?' Pru's eyes widened in delight—the fine

Paisley-patterned cashmere was a luxury no lady's maid could hope to aspire to buying.

'Oh, Miss Decima! I'll be ever so careful of it.'

Decima felt revived enough to take some soup and fruit in her bedroom, but she refused Lady Freshford's invitation to accompany them on a shopping expedition. She was still trying to forget Adam, Henry and Olivia by thinking about Pru when there was a tap at the door.

Decima opened it and found the Freshfords' butler outside, an expression of rigidly repressed irritation on his face.

'I am sorry to disturb you in your chamber, Miss Ross, but Lord Weston is at the door. I informed him you were not at home, but I regret that Staples, who was passing through the hall at the time, very pertly interrupted me to say that you were in your room with a headache.'

'I am sorry she spoke in such a manner.' It was outrageous of Pru, and a direct attack on the butler's authority and dignity. 'I will speak to her directly.' But the man did not appear mollified.

'His lordship then said that he was sorry you were indisposed, Miss Ross, but that if you were so unwell that you could not come down, he would come up here himself and speak to you.'

'*What?* Has his lordship been drinking?'

'No, Miss Ross. I would venture the opinion that his lordship is exercised, to a high degree, with some irritation of the spirit. I tried to insist, but he refuses to leave, and I am reluctant to employ the footmen in ejecting a peer of the realm without Sir Henry's express orders.'

'No, of course not, Starling, that would never do. You have acted quite correctly. Please show his lordship into the little drawing room and tell him I will be down directly.'

'Certainly, Miss Ross. I will find Staples and have her sent to you.'

Decima hesitated. Whatever had brought Adam here in such a mood, it was unlikely to be trivial, nor something she would want to share with anyone, not even Pru. 'No, Starling. I imagine this is a confidential, family matter. I will see Lord Weston alone.'

She turned back into her room, but not before she had caught a glimpse of the disapproval on the butler's face. He would no doubt complain to his mistress, but, with her headache rapidly returning, Decima was past caring.

She smoothed her hair and her gown and made her way downstairs, past the rigid figure of the butler and into the small drawing room. Why she should be feeling quite so ridiculously apprehensive she could not say, but her stomach appeared to be trying to tie itself into a knot and she felt positively queasy.

'Adam…'

'Do you really have a headache?' He was standing by the cold fireplace, one booted foot on the fender, his brows drawn together as he regarded her.

'A little, it is better than it was.' Decima returned his unsmiling look with a level one of her own. 'What exactly is so important that you must outrage Lady Freshford's butler so?'

'You have had a very busy morning, Decima, have you not?' Adam drew the leather gloves he had been holding in one hand through the other, making a snapping noise that jolted her stretched nerves painfully.

'I have had a visit from Olivia, that's all.' She was becoming angry now, but the apprehension was still there, coiling inside her.

'All? I gather I have you to thank for the transformation of my fiancée from a modest and innocent young lady into one of a highly coming disposition.'

'But…but all I said was…' Decima lost her voice. What on earth had Olivia been saying—and doing?

'Yes, Decima, do enlighten me. At what stage in your discussion of my lovemaking did you suggest that Olivia throw all precepts of well-bred decorum to the winds and hurl herself into my arms?'

'I did no such thing! And I have not been discussing your *lovemaking*, as you put it.' She took a few agitated steps away from him and swung round again, appalled at just how wrong her well-meaning advice had gone. 'Olivia asked to speak to me. She wanted to confide in me. What was I to do? Spurn her? She has no female friend to talk to.'

'She has her mother.' Adam's face was set and hard with anger.

'She is terrified of her mother. Olivia would not say boo to a goose and she certainly could not confide her worries to Mrs Channing, not without receiving such a scolding that the poor child would be prostrated.'

'So, what did she want to talk about?'

'I have no intention of telling you, she spoke to me in confidence.' Decima was uneasily aware that Adam was getting closer, and began to edge away behind the illusory safety of a pie-crust side table.

'Decima, do you want me to get it out of her—or will you tell me?' His voice was dangerously quiet.

'Very well, if you are going to bully her otherwise. She told me that she was sometimes somewhat nervous of you. I put it down to her youth and inexperience and her very sheltered upbringing. Now I do not wonder at it, if you treat her to many of these exhibitions of domineering ill-temper!'

Adam ignored her sweeping insults. 'So, what did you tell her to do?'

'Talk to you, that is all. Explain that she was nervous, using some matter she felt less shy about mentioning than—than intimate topics. I was sure that once she got into the way of confiding in you, her trust would soon grow.'

'Very sound advice, I am sure.' Decima was not lulled into relaxing by his sarcastic tone. Adam sounded far from grateful for her assistance. 'And exactly how might she interpret that as throwing herself into my arms and kissing me passionately? If she had not been so unskilled, I would have taken her for a loose woman.'

'She was also alarmed by your kisses,' Decima blurted out. 'I simply suggested that if she made some effort to return any gestures of affection you made, she might find herself growing accustomed.'

'And you are so very experienced that you can offer advice?' Adam was closer now, almost within arm's reach. Decima edged further back and came up sharply against the lowered flap of Lady Freshford's writing desk.

'You know exactly how experienced I am,' she snapped. 'I don't understand why you are so angry. I would have thought you could have trusted me to try and do what is best for you, as a friend. Olivia is very shy and very sheltered— it would be dreadful if her fears led her to do something…' she hesitated, seeking the right word '…something unwise.'

'You think she would be wise to marry me, or that I would be wise to marry her?' Adam's eyes were very green, very hard, as he watched her face.

Decima shook her head, baffled at the question. 'You asked her to marry you, she accepted. For either of you to cry off would create a scandal. It could ruin Olivia. Why are you speaking like this? You sound almost as though you don't want to marry her!'

Adam watched Decima's face, seeing the confusion chase across her features. She wanted to do the best thing for him, and for Olivia, and he loved her for it. Whether that was coming from her sense of duty, or whether she really did want to see him married to another woman, he could not fathom. He had begun to think he understood Decima Ross—now he was far from sure.

'You think I might have made a mistake?' he asked slowly, trying to read her thoughts in the expressive, wide eyes. The frustrated anger that had driven him to demand to see her was ebbing in the face of that candid gaze, despite the fact that she had put his progress with Olivia back by days, if not a week.

'If you have, there is nothing you can do about it!' She was staring at him, horrified. 'You cannot mean to jilt the poor girl?'

'No, no, of course not,' Adam said slowly. If his plans did not work, then he would have to accept, and make the best of, a marriage to Olivia Channing. But he had no intention of it coming to that, however Decima might unwittingly try to scupper his scheme. He toyed with the idea of telling her the truth, but baulked. She was surprisingly good at hiding her true feelings for him—unless, of course, she had none, only feelings of friendship.

'I am interested in your opinion, that's all.' He turned aside, trying to make his voice light. 'You're right, Olivia is very sheltered—I should take account of that.' And possibly push her further? He might have to, now she was trying to apply Decima's well-meaning advice. He had certainly been seriously taken aback when what had been intended as a kiss designed to send Olivia into nervous, blushing confusion had resulted in her bravely throwing her arms around his neck and pulling his head down so she could return it with clumsy determination.

He was jolted out of his thoughts by Decima. 'You are in a very strange mood today, Adam.' She sounded less angry than exasperated with him; he supposed he deserved that. Goodness knew what she made of all this. 'Promise me you will not jilt poor Olivia.'

'Do you really think I would do such a thing?' It hurt, he

found, to have her believe he might. What would she say when she discovered what he was planning to do? God, he wanted to take her in his arms and hold her—just hold her, so he could smell that elusive jasmine scent, feel her soft warmth against him. He reached out a hand and caught hers. For a moment she resisted him, then allowed him to lead her to the sofa.

'No...no I don't, except that when you act so strangely, I don't understand you at all.' She hesitated, looking down at their clasped hands, then gently pulled her own free. 'Do you love her?'

'No.' He could not lie to her about that. 'No. It is time I married; you heard the views of my family on the subject. Love is not expected when persons of our class wed. You must continue to encourage Bates and Pru if you want to witness a love match.' He had hoped to distract her by talking of the two servants, but she made a little gesture as though to brush that aside and raised troubled eyes to his.

'You will be kind to her though, won't you? Olivia has not had much affection in her life, I think.' She caught his hand in hers again, apparently unconscious of anything but the need to impress upon him the importance of what she was saying. Adam tightened his fingers around hers, feeling the beat of her pulse. It seemed to enter his body, take possession of his own heartbeat.

She turned her face up to his, searching his expression as though to read the truth in it. Adam fought the urge to simply catch her in his arms and kiss her until she understood how he felt for her. But he had fallen into that trap already, consoling Olivia—there was too much at risk now to dare revealing the slightest hint of his feelings for Decima. She was so close his senses were full of her, of the warm scent of her skin, of the touch of her breath on his skin.

'Decima, I promise I will do everything in my power to make things better for Olivia than they are now.'

'Thank you,' she said simply and he placed his other hand over hers, trapping it between both of his. 'Adam—'

The door behind them opened abruptly, swinging back on its hinges. Decima started, instinctively reaching for Adam's lapel with her free hand and he, equally instinctively, turned to shelter her body with his.

Lord Carmichael stood on the threshold, his face red with outrage. Behind him there was a glimpse of the butler and a flurry of skirts, but no one was going to pass Charlton.

'How dare you, my lord! Decima, come here this instant! I can hardly believe my eyes, to find you here, unchaperoned, alone with a man, behaving like the veriest trollop—'

He did not finish the sentence. Adam had heard the expression 'to see red' and had believed it to be merely that, an expression. Now he found, viewing Charlton Carmichael through a blood haze, that it was simple description. He got to his feet, clenched a serviceable right fist and hit the furious baron squarely on the jaw.

Charlton fell back, collided with Starling and the two of them crashed to the floor of the hall, narrowly missing Pru, who jumped back with a squeal of alarm.

Chapter Twenty

'Charlton!' Decima tried to push past Adam to where her brother lay sprawled on the floor, blood coming from his mouth, which was opening and closing like that of a landed carp. Beyond him Pru was helping Starling to his feet, only to be pushed away by the outraged butler.

'Stay there, Miss Ross,' Adam said curtly. He strode forward, took Charlton by the arm and dragged him to his feet and into the drawing room, shutting the door firmly behind him.

Charlton began to gobble with fury as Adam swung round to face him. 'I am sure Miss Ross can do without being further exposed to the impertinent stares of the servants.'

'How dare you!' Charlton dug in his pocket and produced a vast white handkerchief, which he clapped to his face. Decima realised his nose had begun to bleed. 'I find you ravishing my sister and you have the gall to assault me, sir! I will have the law upon you—'

'For defending the good name of a lady who had just been grievously slandered? I will not repeat the phrase that you used to blacken Miss Ross's character, Lord Carmichael, but no gentleman could stand by and hear a lady so insulted.'

'I am her brother, damn you!'

'Then you should be even more sensitive to the lady's honour, and I would further remind you that she is still present and ask you to moderate your language.'

Adam was managing to sound quite ridiculously pompous, Decima realised, marvelling that he could turn the compromising situation around so that it seemed Charlton was in the wrong. But this was a nightmare—at any moment the Freshfords could return, doubtless half the household was already gathered in the hall, and, idiot though he was, Charlton was her brother.

'Naturally, it is regrettable that Miss Ross's attendant should have stepped outside the room for a moment—'

'Moment? Moment?' Charlton's voice was thickening with his nosebleed. 'My sister was unchaperoned, left alone with a rake! I will see that feckless slut of a so-called maidservant dismissed without a character—'

'You will do no such thing!' Decima interjected hotly. Neither man paid her the slightest attention.

'Are you calling me a rake, Lord Carmichael?' Adam enquired dangerously. 'I can hardly call you out over remarks made to your own sister, tempting though it is, but I will have no hesitation in doing so if you blacken my character. Name your friends, my lord.'

'No!' Decima pushed past Adam and stood between the two men, unsure which of them was making her the more angry, or why, under the anger, she was feeling quite so excited and disturbed. 'Stop it, both of you! Charlton, there was not the slightest impropriety in what you just witnessed. Lord Weston, I am in no need of your protection from my own brother, I thank you. I think you should leave. Now.'

From outside the door she could hear the sound of new arrivals on the scene. Starling's voice was quivering with outrage, she was aware of Pru's indignant tones and over it all Henry's firm voice demanding to know what the devil was going on in his front hall.

Decima took a deep breath, stepped around Charlton and threw the door open. Embarrassing though this was, it was better than the risk that it would all end in a fight, either here or on the duelling ground. Under other circumstances Henry's stunned expression would have been amusing.

'Sir Henry,' she said, cutting across all three men, 'there has been a regrettable misunderstanding. My brother requires some medical attention. Lord Weston is just leaving.'

Adam was regarding her with dangerously slitted eyes. 'I have no intention—'

'Of staying, yes, I know, excellent.' She stared back, willing herself to meet his eyes and not to show any of the emotions that were churning inside her. 'Please give my regards to Miss Channing. I believe Starling has your hat, my lord.'

There was a long, dangerous silence, then Adam turned to Sir Henry and said, 'I apologise for being the cause of a certain degree of disturbance amongst your household. Miss Ross, I give you good day.'

As the front door closed behind him Decima pressed a furious Charlton down into an armchair. 'Henry, I can only apologise. Might I presume to call your housekeeper to see what can be done about my brother's nosebleed?'

The sound of a throat being tactfully cleared made them turn. It was Henry's valet. 'Staples apprised me that the gentleman might require some assistance, sir,' he said smoothly, as though bleeding and seething barons were a commonplace occurrence in his master's household. 'If you would care to accompany me, my lord, I am sure I can make you more comfortable.' Charlton appeared mollified by the attention and allowed himself to be helped solicitously to his feet. 'Should I send to your own valet for fresh linen, sir?'

'Yes, yes, do that.' On the threshold Charlton emerged from the shelter of his handkerchief to glower at Decima.

'Dessy, I expect you to be packed ready to accompany me home.' He stomped out.

'Good God, Decima!' Henry took her by the arm and almost dragged her down to sit on the sofa beside him. 'What is going on? I leave you laid upon your bed with the headache and come back to find Starling threatening to hand in his notice, your maid demanding that I go in and rescue you and your brother bleeding all over Mama's favourite carpet.'

'I gave Olivia some advice, which I meant for the best, and she acted upon it rather overenthusiastically,' Decima admitted. Now all the excitement was over, she was feeling more than a little queasy, and guiltily aware that under it all there was the thrill of seeing Adam stand up to defend her. 'Adam was angry with me, we were discussing it and Charlton arrived. Pru wasn't in the room and I think Starling was somewhat put out, so he let Charlton in and we were sitting on the sofa and he put two and two together and said things he should not and Adam hit him.'

'Oh, lord.' Henry regarded her blankly. 'It has all the ingredients of a farce, has it not? Luckily Mama and Caro are not back yet. I'll try and soothe Starling before they do return. Were they on the point of calling each other out?'

'Adam called Charlton out for calling him a rake. I think he realised he could hardly call out my own brother for insulting me.'

'He probably *is* a rake,' Henry pointed out, reasonably.

'Well, I expect he doesn't want to be, now he is betrothed.' She sighed. Adam had looked magnificent as he squared up to Charlton, and the fact that any well-brought-up lady should have had the vapours at the sight of fisticuffs did nothing to diminish the thrill that the memory evoked.

'Are you going to go back with Charlton?'

'No.' Decima shook her head. 'No, I will call tomorrow and apologise when we are all calmer. But I'm not going to allow my life to be dictated by my family, however much I have to admit Charlton has justification this time.'

Charlton's final departure was fraught enough to send Decima back to her room shaking with emotion. Pru regarded her anxiously. 'I'm sorry if I caused that, Miss Decima, but I thought you'd want to see his lordship.'

'You meant well, Pru, but I am afraid you must go and apologise to Mr Starling. He was very put out, and I cannot stay here if we are going to upset Lady Freshford's upper servants.'

'Yes, Miss Decima.' Pru hesitated. 'About his lordship... are you...I mean, is he...? Will it be all right, Miss Decima? He isn't really going to marry Miss Channing, is he?'

'Of course he is, Pru!' Decima swung round from her seat at the dressing table where she had been attempting to redress her hair. 'Whatever makes you think he might not?'

'Jethro says he doesn't love her.' Pru was scuffing her toe in the carpet.

'That is not a consideration when the aristocracy marry,' Decima said repressively, trying to believe it. 'Making a suitable match is what matters.'

'Oh. When will you be seeing him again?' Pru seemed to pull herself together, took the hairbrush from Decima and started to tease out her curls.

'When?' Decima was conscious of a strange, sinking feeling. Dreadful as the last few hours had been, underlying them had been the guilty delight of being with Adam, the revelation that he would defend her honour, physically if need be—even the reprehensible pleasure of knowing that she could stir strong emotions in him. 'I think that it would not be wise to see him again, unless I cannot help but encounter him socially.' As she thought it through, the illicit excitement ebbed away, leaving her feeling more than a little uneasy.

Charlton was head of the household, her brother, and, however infuriating he was, she had to believe that he had her best interests at heart. He had castigated her for behaviour that, looking back at it, was indeed fast. She had swung from being a shy mouse to behaving with unbecoming freedom which ill-befitted a single lady. Probably she had given Adam a disgust of her. Dismally, Decima blinked back a tear.

Adam strode into the mews yard to find Bates perched on a mounting block, mending a length of driving trace. 'Saddle Fox.'

'He's at exercise, my lord.' Bates sawed off the end of the waxed thread he was using, folded his clasp knife and shoved it back into his pocket. 'I told the lad to ride out with Ajax and take Fox on the leading rein, seeing as you said you wouldn't be riding today.' He shook out the leather and eyed it critically, apparently paying not the slightest attention to the thunderous expression on his master's face.

'How long since?' Adam ground out. He'd wanted to ride Fox—fight him—as the only way he could think of to expend the aggression that was burning through him. You did not shout at servants, you did not aim a kick at the cat, and you certainly did not go anywhere near your meek fiancée, not when what you wanted was to land another blow on the nose of a pompous, bacon-faced addle plot, and as for his sister—

'The lad left not ten minutes ago, my lord,' Bates said placidly. 'I told him to give them a good workout, so he'll be at least another hour, I'd say.' He put aside the trace and picked up another strip of leather and a punch. 'Is Miss Ross well, my lord?'

'Miss Ross is perfectly well, thank you, Bates.' Adam managed not to grind it out through clenched teeth. He tugged off his gloves, filled with an uncharacteristic indecision about what to do next—other than to go back to Decima and tell her he loved her. She would probably box his ears, and he wasn't sure he would blame her if she did. It was beginning to sink in that if he couldn't make his peace with her, then his entire strategy for ending his sham of an engagement was in pieces.

'What?' Bates had been asking something. He swung round to face the groom.

'Been in a bit of a mill, have you, my lord?' Bates nodded towards Adam's right hand. He looked at it, surprised to find that the knuckles were raw and grazed. 'You'll need to put a bit of something on that afore long, stop it scarring. How's the other fellow?'

'The other fellow happens to be Miss Ross's brother.' Adam felt the anger drain out of him, leaving him tired and depressed. Of course she didn't love him. Why should she? He had flirted with her, damn near seduced her, gone off and become entangled with another woman and now he was brawling with her brother.

'Tsk.' Bates clicked his tongue in disapproval. 'Not a very good move, my lord.' He shifted along the mounting block to give Adam room to sit down. 'Ladies like being rescued from villains, goes without saying, but decking their own family, now that's quite another kettle of fish.' He drove a bradawl through the leather, squinted at the resulting hole and threaded his needle. 'What did she say?'

'She threw me out.'

'Ah.' Bates knotted the twine. 'What are you going to do now, my lord? I'd be all a mort if I was you.'

'That just about sums it up.' Adam took off his hat and sat turning it round in his hands.

'Don't reckon she'll have you now, not unless you can mend a few bridges.'

'Quite.' Adam blinked and focused on what Bates was saying. He should have known that the groom could read him like a book, but he could hardly admit the truth of what he was implying. Not yet. 'I am engaged to marry Miss Channing. Not Miss Ross.'

'Well, you are now,' Bates observed cynically. 'Best see what you can do about getting back on terms, my lord.'

Adam gathered the shreds of his dignity and stood up. 'And how is your courtship faring, Bates?'

'She's a proper handful is Pru, and a right unaccountable piece,' Bates observed. 'But I'm not complaining—*I'm* only trying to court one woman at a time.'

Clear early spring sunshine cheered Decima as she returned, chastened and emotionally bruised, from a morning visit to her brother and sister-in-law the next day. But at least that unpleasant duty had been performed, and, due apparently to Hermione's pleading, she was not going to be cast off and disowned. Provided, that is, she avoided Lord Weston's contaminating presence like the plague.

She confided something of this to Pru as the carriage rattled back to the Freshfords' house. 'So I believe I must take great care, which is going to be difficult as I have no wish to have Miss Channing think I am cutting her,' she concluded.

'Oh.' Pru stared at her, wide-eyed. 'Then you couldn't talk to his lordship about something?'

'Only the merest commonplaces in passing. Why?' Pru was looking positively dismayed. Now she looked back on the morning, the girl had seemed somewhat subdued ever since she had helped Decima dress.

'It's just that Jethro doesn't think he'll be able to have that cottage after all. In fact, he thinks he might lose his place if he marries me.' Pru sniffed bravely 'It's a good position, he's been there for years. I can't ask him to give it up.'

'When did this change of heart occur?' Decima demanded. 'You were quite happy yesterday.'

'Jethro told me last night. He's proper upset, but he said it wouldn't do to carry on courting, not if he was about to lose his place. He said his lordship was on the high ropes when he came back yesterday. It's all my fault,' she concluded dismally. 'If I hadn't told his lordship you were at home yesterday, none of this would have happened.'

'I don't believe he could be so petty,' Decima exclaimed. 'Does he hope to wound me by spoiling things for you, or is he simply so top lofty that he cannot bear to be thwarted?' She reached up and jerked on the check string. 'We'll see about that!' The coachman's face appeared at the window. 'James, drive at once to Lord Weston's house. He must learn he cannot have everything he wants. Pru, if he remains adamant I will offer Bates a place. I have been intending to increase my stables, perhaps take breeding more seriously. I shall need an experienced groom.'

The detour was short. As Decima stepped down, she saw movement against the study window. So, Adam was at home. 'I shall be a few minutes. Please go down to the mews if you wish, Pru.'

Adam's butler greeted her with a respectful bow, which was cut short when he saw she was without a companion. 'Good morning, madam. I regret that Lord Weston is not at home.'

'I believe he will be to me,' Decima retorted with a smile. 'Do not trouble to announce me.' She slipped past the astonished butler before he could move and was twisting the study door handle by the time he had turned.

'Madam!'

Then she was inside the room, facing Adam, who dropped the newspaper he was holding onto the desk and stared at her. 'Decima!' He took a long stride towards her before she overcame the shock of sensual pleasure that always struck her whenever she saw him.

She threw up her hands. 'Don't you Decima me! How *could* you, Adam? I would not have believed it of you.'

He stopped abruptly and ran his hand through his hair. It needed trimming, she saw, wishing she could follow his hand with her own, tangle their fingers together in the thick, dark hair. Feeling like that did nothing to soothe her temper.

'Look, I can see why you are angry, but you have to admit, the provocation was strong.'

'There is some inconvenience to you, my lord, and you regard it as *provocation*? That it is enough justification to excuse your action?'

'I should hardly call it inconvenience.' He gestured towards a chair. 'Decima, please sit down and let us discuss this. I must confess I was thinking about you, puzzling about how I could mend fences again.'

'A simple word to Bates would have done it, I would have thought.' Decima moved away, trying to focus on a small group of Meissen figures on the mantleshelf to avoid looking at him.

'You feel I use our servants as go-betweens?' He seemed puzzled.

'An apology would have put things to rights, I should imagine?' Decima reached out a finger and lightly touched the sweeping skirts of one little figure. It was exquisite. If she concentrated on that she could keep herself detached from this quarrel, put it onto an impersonal level where the pain would not reach her. 'Pru is very upset.'

'Pru?' He seemed genuinely confused. Could he be so in-different or uncaring about his servants that he did not realise the hurt he had inflicted on Pru and Bates? 'Oh, you mean that her interference yesterday led to that scene. You are fortunate that you have a maid who is so attached to your interests and so conscientious.'

'It is Pru's interests I am concerned with, not mine.' Decima turned sharply to face him. 'And Bates's, of course.'

'Bates?' Adam laid a hand on her arm and frowned. 'Decima, are we completely at cross-purposes? Why are you here?'

If she stood on tiptoe she could brush her lips against his, curl her arms around his neck and be held close to him. She was aware of his cologne, of the faint smell of woollen broadcloth that had been recently pressed with a hot iron, of the scent of clean, warm man. Her eyelids felt heavy and it was as much as she could do not to sway towards him.

'I am here because you have broken Pru's heart and I am very, very angry with you.' Decima's voice shook slightly and she struggled for control. 'And disappointed.'

'I have done nothing to Pru! What the devil is this about? Decima, I'm trying to apologise for hitting your infuriating brother yesterday. I wish I'd done it harder, but I upset you, so now I have to wish I'd never done it at all.'

'But you told Bates he couldn't have the cottage! He and Pru think he would lose his place if they marry—and to do that just because I asked you to go yesterday—that is so unfair.' Decima freed her arm and moved back a little so she could watch Adam's face without the distracting closeness. 'Of course you should not have hit Charlton, and he was quite within his rights to be angry, finding us like that. He is pompous and overbearing, but he is my brother. What else could I do but tell you to leave? What if Olivia had come to hear of it? She still might.' She drew a deep breath. 'But to take it out on poor Pru—I could not believe you would do such a thing.'

Adam's expression had run from puzzlement, through enlightenment to rueful amusement. 'It's not funny,' Decima snapped.

'I agree. I was mocking myself. Do you know, I had been existing under the illusion that I was in control of my life, my household, my destiny, and now I find that I am merely the plaything of my staff. Did Pru tell you in so many words that I had withdrawn the offer of the cottage, or that I had forbidden Bates to marry her?'

'No…' Decima wrinkled her brow in an effort to recall the exact words. 'No, not *exactly*. She said that Jethro—Bates—did not think he would be able to have the cottage after all, and he might lose his place and you were—what was it?—oh, yes, on the high ropes.'

'Decima, my love, has it occurred to you that we are both being manipulated by our servants? Pru and Bates obviously decided that we had quarrelled and that we were unlikely to get back on speaking terms again without a powerful incentive.'

'You mean they are *matchmaking*? But…but… You are engaged! *What* did you call me?'

There was a tap at the door and the butler was inside before Adam could speak. Decima blinked at the man. Knocking at all, let alone sliding into rooms looking decidedly shifty, was not the sort of behaviour one expected of a top-flight butler.

'My lord, Mrs Channing's barouche has just driven up.'

'Hell. Thank you, Dalrymple, I am sure you can make quite a business of taking the ladies' things and showing them into the salon.'

The butler allowed himself a grimace. 'I have never yet succeeded in ushering Mrs Channing anywhere she does not wish to go. She is aware that you normally spend some time in the study in the morning. If the lady would care to come with me, it would be safer—' He broke off at the sound of the knocker, then they all froze. Someone was opening it and there was the sound of voices.

'Peters—I believed him to be in the kitchens.' Dalrymple lowered his voice. 'I can hardly open this door and go out now…'

'Stall.' Adam seized Decima's wrist and pulled her towards a cupboard door in the alcove beside the fireplace. 'There should be room.'

Decima found herself squeezed into a space that seemed

to be half filled with books and boxes. With the pressure of Adam's body against hers she wriggled onto a shelf, managing to perch on the narrow ledge, her face squashed against his shirt front, her knees pressed into his thighs.

The door shut behind them, apparently with Dalrymple's full weight against it, for Adam was pushed even harder against her. Then a familiar voice penetrated the panels.

'There you are, Dalrymple. Where is Lord Weston?'

Chapter Twenty-One

'I regret that his lordship is not at home, ma'am.'

'I saw movement in this room as the carriage arrived.' Decima wondered from whence Mrs Channing got her overwhelming self-confidence.

'You must have glimpsed me, ma'am. I was just ascertaining that his lordship's inkwells had been filled. One cannot rely on new footmen, I regret to say. Would you and Miss Channing care to take some refreshments in the salon, ma'am?'

'When will Lord Weston return?' Mrs Channing was obviously not best pleased to find her quarry not available.

'I really could not say, ma'am. I am quite unable to speculate on what his lordship might be doing at this moment.' The butler's voice faded as the study door was shut.

'The old devil,' Adam muttered against Decima's cheek. '*I am unable to speculate* indeed! Are you giggling?'

'Yes,' Decima admitted, struggling to suppress her chuckles. 'I have to say, you do have the most unconventional servants.'

'I know. That's what comes of inheriting most of them. They have known me since I was a grubby brat in nankeens; although they normally do their utmost to preserve my dignity, I suspect it is for their own self-esteem, not mine. If you could try and giggle without wriggling I would be grateful.'

'S...sorry,' Decima managed to gasp. 'Why? Do you think we might be heard?'

'No, because I very badly want to kiss you.' He said it in a matter-of-fact whisper that effectively stifled the slightest desire to laugh.

'Adam! Olivia is in the next room!' Decima pulled herself together. 'In any case, you should not be thinking such a thing, it is highly improper.'

'I'd have to be a hundred and ten not to be thinking such things in this position,' he said darkly. 'I don't think we could be any closer together unless we removed all our clothes.' Decima gave a small squeak of alarm and felt, more than heard, his gasp of amusement against her neck. 'Relax, I'm not a contortionist.'

There was not much to be said in response to that—nothing that was not repulsively missish or unbecomingly forward. Decima decided that silence was the best tactic and tried to keep still. It was not easy. She was pressed against Adam in a way that was both intimate and uncomfortable; the edge of the shelf on which she was perched was cutting into her behind and what felt like a large volume was digging into the nape of her neck. But, recalling Henry's various pieces of advice on the way that men's minds worked, she supposed that finding himself in such close proximity to any young woman would result in Adam wanting to kiss her. She certainly should not attribute it to any particular desire for herself.

'Do you think it is safe to come out now?' she whispered.

'Probably. Are you uncomfortable?'

'Very.'

'So am I. Delightfully so,' he added, so quietly she thought she must have misheard. There was a crowded minute while Adam attempted to get his hands behind him to open the door. 'Unfortunately there is no handle on the inside and Dalrymple appears to have locked the door.'

Decima succumbed to the cramp in her neck and let her forehead rest on Adam's chest. It felt so good.

'Am I forgiven?' he asked.

'For hitting poor Charlton? Yes, I forgive you, if you will forgive me for believing you would treat Pru and Bates so badly.'

'I think I can do that.' He was smiling, she could hear it in his voice. 'Has your brother forbidden you from having anything to do with me again?'

'Mmm. He is quite right, of course.' Decima wondered if the crick in her back was enough excuse for trying to insinuate her arms around Adam and snuggling closer. She rather thought that a lady of refinement and true modesty would die before doing such a thing. Regrettably this seemed to prove she was neither refined, nor modest, any longer. Fortunately, as her arms were trapped by a stack of files, she was prevented from giving way to temptation.

'Do you intend to obey him?' Decima jerked herself back to attention. She had begun to drift off into an uncomfortable, yet sensual, doze. 'Only I really do need your help.'

'I thought I should,' she replied, trying to sound as businesslike as possible while whispering. 'What do you want?'

There was a pause while Decima decided she could have phrased that better, but Adam made no disconcerting response. 'I wondered if you and Sir Henry might join Olivia and me on a trip out of town one day soon. I've inherited a small estate near Bushey and I cannot decide whether to keep it or not. I want to show it to Olivia, see if she takes a fancy to it, otherwise I will place it on the market.'

There were major objections to this; Decima had to give it no thought at all to see that. It would place her in exactly the position of intimacy with Adam that she knew she should avoid—Charlton would be livid if he found out—and it would throw Henry and Olivia together again. Henry's feelings for Miss Channing had not faded, Decima could tell, however much he tried to cover it up. She wondered if hers for Adam were as obvious to someone who knew her well.

'Please?' Adam injected a wheedling tone into his voice, which made her smile. She doubted that he ever had much need to wheedle and was not convinced it was genuine now. They were playing a game, they both knew it—and she had no idea how they had got there. 'If you don't come, I will have to take Mrs Channing and I really feel another man is necessary, just in case of any problems on the road. Olivia is shy, she would feel more comfortable with you and Freshford.'

'If Henry agrees, yes, I will.' She had opened her mouth, intending to refuse the invitation, but somewhere between drawing in breath and speaking something else had taken over. The rebellious other self was stirring again, dangerously.

As if her capitulation was a signal, there was the grate of a key in the lock and the door swung open. Adam stepped back to save himself from falling and Decima tumbled out into his arms. Dalrymple managed to keep his face straight, despite the unseemly spectacle she knew they must present.

'Mrs and Miss Channing have departed, my lord. They intend returning this afternoon. Mrs Channing was good enough to confide in me that she wished to discuss arrangements for the honeymoon, my lord.'

'Does she, by God?' Adam snarled, steadying Decima, who was staggering slightly as her stiff limbs regained their balance.

'So she gives me to understand,' Dalrymple responded tranquilly. 'Might I fetch you refreshments, Miss Ross? No? I regret the necessity of locking you into the cupboard, but I feared the door might swing open again if I did not.'

'Have you been speaking to Bates?' Adam enquired, regarding the butler with suspicion.

'No, my lord, not for a day, at any rate. Miss Ross's woman is in the kitchen, my lord.' He paused on his way out. 'Mrs Channing was also gracious enough to confide that she is going out of town for a few days, leaving Miss Channing to the chaperonage of her cousin.'

'How very convenient.' Adam stood looking out of the window, all the fun and the teasing gone from his face. 'I will speak to Olivia about the house in Bushey this afternoon. If I were to send you a note, perhaps you would be good enough to let me know when you and Sir Henry could accompany us.'

'Will Mrs Channing not want you to wait so she can go with you?'

'Probably.' He grinned suddenly and Decima forgot all her good resolutions in a swamping tide of love and longing. 'I will tell her I have a good offer and must make up my mind soon—which is true enough. She won't want me selling it, not after I have described it. The more properties Olivia becomes mistress of the better, in her eyes.' He stopped looking out of the window and turned the smile on Decima. 'And she approves of you, so she will not think twice about you chaperoning Olivia. Please, Decima—save me from an entire day of my future mama-in-law.'

The reminder of the role Mrs Channing was destined to play in Adam's life was sobering. Decima hesitated, torn between what she knew was her duty and the temptation of one last day with Adam. 'I will ask Henry,' she temporised. And Henry might either feel the same about being with Olivia, or might think that the pain of being in her company outweighed the pleasure—or the strain on his acting skills in not revealing his feelings. 'It sounds delightful. Will we need a picnic?'

'I will ensure we have the very best,' Adam promised.

'Now, I think we had better see you out through the kitchen door for discretion.' He seemed quite normal, chatting of inconsequential things as he escorted her down the back stairs and into the kitchen, earning a scold from Cook for bringing a lady below stairs.

But Decima, even distracted as she was by Pru's guilty air, noticed something new about him. It was as though he was watching, planning, waiting with a kind of tension that held nothing of apprehension and everything of excitement and determination. She was as conscious of him as a man, of his strength and his will, as when she had been rescued by him in the snow or when he had caught her in his arms and made love to her.

It was an effort to collect herself to greet Cook, nod pleasantly to the kitchen maids and take an indifferent, formal leave of Adam. What his staff thought of her choice of exit she had no idea, but no doubt they were too well-paid and well-managed to presume to either comment or speculate.

Once she and Pru were safely in the carriage and the vehicle in motion, the maid began to fidget. Decima refrained from speaking for a long minute, increasing Pru's discomfort until at last she burst out, 'Is it all right, Miss Decima? You and his lordship are speaking again?'

'No, it is not all right, Pru! You lied to me, did you not? No, don't try and tell me what you said—you may have been very careful, but you deliberately left me with the impression that Lord Weston had warned Bates off marrying you simply because we had had a falling out. Did you not?'

'Yes'm.' Pru had her head down and the reply emerged as a painful mutter. Then she looked up and burst out, 'He ought to be marrying you, Miss Decima, not that washed-out little Miss Channing. You love him.'

Denying it seemed futile. Decima ignored the statement. 'He is engaged to be married. Even if he has made a mistake—which I am not saying he has, so do not quote that back to me, if you please!—he cannot honourably withdraw.'

'*She* ought to,' Pru said mutinously. 'She could if she wasn't so hen-hearted.'

'Would *you* have the courage to disobey Mrs Channing?' Decima enquired tartly. 'Poor Olivia is terrified of her mother and she deserves her chance to make her own life and be happy.'

'Well, and so do you,' Pru retorted. 'Men haven't the wit they were born with, most of them. You have to write a sign and wave it under their noses afore they'll see what a woman's feeling.'

'So you are thinking better of marriage to Bates, are you?' Decima enquired wickedly.

'No. He needs looking after,' Pru declared. 'I'll make something of him.'

Henry was at home when Decima returned and she caught him alone to tell him about her morning. He nodded gravely as she recounted her uncomfortable visit to the Carmichaels.

'I'm glad you've made peace again. Does Charlton insist upon you going to stay with him and Lady Carmichael?'

'He tried to.' Decima pulled off her gloves and went to curl up on the sofa next to Henry's writing desk. He seemed to be working his way through an alarming stack of correspondence, much of which looked like modistes' bills to Decima's newly experienced eye, and did not seem unhappy at being distracted. Doubtless launching a sister into society was not a cheap exercise.

'I refused, but, of course, if you or Lady Freshford would rather I didn't stay after yesterday, I will leave, naturally. I know I am refining too much upon going there—I'm sure it will be all right once he realises that I'm independent.'

'No, please stay.' Henry grinned at her. 'We would hate to lose you—even Starling has consented to withdraw his resignation. Now, tell me about your encounter with Lord Weston.'

Decima did so, not even omitting the episode in the study cupboard, which made Henry roar with laughter. 'Oh, lord! Can you imagine Starling bundling me into a cupboard to save me from a compromising situation?'

Decima had to confess she could not. The image was so ludicrous that she felt she had better stay away from the butler until she could command her face. Then the thought of the rest of her news sobered her.

'That is not all. Adam wishes us to accompany him and Olivia on an expedition to visit an estate at Bushey.' She explained what Adam had told her, watching Henry's reaction. 'I had a stiff wrestle with my conscience,' she admitted, 'and I finally gave in, although I have not told him so yet. It will be a treat to reward myself for exercising the utmost discretion ever afterwards. But I was not sure how you would feel—' She broke off, catching her lower lip between her teeth anxiously. 'I thought perhaps you might feel the same about Olivia. Or it might be too painful…' Henry was silent, tapping the edge of a milliner's bill with one fingernail. 'Or perhaps you no longer feel…'

'Oh, I feel—I feel just the same about her,' he admitted eventually. 'And I expect I will yield to temptation, one last time, just as you intend to. Do you remember we discussed how one knew if one was in love? Ironic, is it not? I wish I had stayed ignorant.'

The bitterness that was suddenly in his voice stung and Decima winced. How could people find sport and entertainment in match-making? For every happy union they brought about, how many broken hearts were there? Still, Pru and Bates would be all right, of that she was certain.

Adam's promised note arrived later that afternoon, suggesting an expedition in two days' time, providing the good weather held. There was a separate note for Henry, who read it with raised brows.

'What is it?' Decima asked, watching his thoughtful face.

'Weston urges me to accompany you as he has some concerns after recent reports of footpads in the area. He says he has no real fears, but would feel happier about going if there was another gentleman to take care of the ladies, as opposed to grooms.'

'Do you think it dangerous?' Decima queried.

'No.' Henry shook his head. 'There have been reports, but only occasional ones, and not of any attempts upon parties. Single riders, or people alone in a gig might perhaps be at risk, but two gentlemen will be quite sufficient, even if Weston does not intend to take a groom as well. I will put my carriage pistols in the curricle.'

'You intend to come with us, then?'

Henry smiled wryly. 'I do not believe there is any danger, but I could not let either you or Olivia go without my escort. Irrational, is it not?'

The morning of the expedition dawned fair with a clear sky and the promise of sunshine. Decima resisted, with a pang, Pru's efforts to persuade her to wear her newest, and very dashing, walking dress, and settled instead for a more modest outfit in moss green with a braided hem and a darker green pelisse and veiled bonnet. She was not going to try and compete with Olivia, as if that were possible. Today she was an onlooker, there to give Olivia feminine company—and to bid farewell to her heart.

Henry seemed in much the same, subdued mood. As Dalrymple showed them into the salon where Olivia and Adam were waiting, Decima saw how his eyes locked with Olivia's and held for a few betraying moments. Then Olivia was her usual sweet, shy self, eyes downcast except for rapid, flickering glances at Adam.

Had he noticed anything? He was discussing the route

with Henry perfectly amicably. Decima puzzled how, when he seemed so observant over everything else, he seemed unconscious of the attraction between his fiancée and Henry. Perhaps it was simply that because his affections were not deeply engaged it made him less sensitive to her. Poor Olivia. For perhaps the first time in her life Decima wondered if remaining single was not an enviable thing.

'Daydreaming, Miss Ross?' Adam enquired. Decima realised the others were all on their feet and making ready to go. She forced a smile and shook her head, 'No, just thinking about tomorrow.' And all the days after that. 'Do you think this fine weather will last?'

Bates and another groom were holding the heads of the horses at the front door. He exchanged nods with Adam, then, when he saw she was looking at him, he knuckled his forehead. 'Morning, Miss Ross, ma'am.'

'Good morning, Bates.' She wondered whether she should show her disapproval for the scheming he and Pru had been up to, then smiled. 'Are you coming with us?'

'No, ma'am. My leg's still playing up too much for a long ride.'

They set off, Adam's carriage in the lead. Both men had chosen to bring ordinary curricles and Decima could only be grateful. Being tooled around Hyde Park by Henry in his high-perch version was all very well on well-rolled tan surfaces and for short distances, but she did not relish the thought of it swaying over country roads, with the passengers sitting several feet off the ground.

She found she was watching Adam's back as he negotiated the traffic, handling the team lightly through the confusion of carriages and carts. But even he seemed taken by surprise as a rapidly moving shape slid soundlessly out of Upper Brook Street. His team sidled and shied, then he had them under control again and the strange vehicle had passed.

'What on earth was that?' Decima craned to see it, but it had vanished.

'A pedestrian hobbyhorse, I believe.' Henry settled his own horses as they took exception to a coal heaver's cart. 'They're supposed to be the next big thing—I think they should be banned. It'll be steam engines on the roads next, frightening the horses.'

'It looked fun,' Decima said wistfully. 'Not as good as a horse, naturally, but think how convenient for town use—no waiting for it to be saddled up and fetched from the mews.'

'They do say there is a ladies' version with three wheels.' Henry checked his team, then followed Adam's lead into Edgware Road. 'But how one could ride one of those things side saddle and still propel it defeats me.'

They bickered amicably over the merits of new inventions, Decima teased Henry about investing in steam engines and then condemning them if they might inconvenience him, and they looked with interest at the route of the new Regent's Canal as they crossed it just before Maida Vale.

Henry gave his team their head as they came to Shoot Up Hill and drew alongside the other curricle as the hamlet of Cricklewood hove into view. Adam looked over and grinned. 'Do you want to race? First past the Dog and Duck in the High Street?'

Decima's eyes sparkled and she took a firm grip on the side rails, but a squeak of alarm from Olivia was greeted by a firm refusal by Henry. 'I think not, Weston—it would alarm the ladies.'

'No, it would not,' Decima said crossly as they dropped back to follow once more. 'Not that you would win, Henry,' she added to take her revenge. 'That is a particularly fine team Adam's driving.'

'Not bad,' Henry admitted grudgingly. 'But mine has the better bone.'

That minor squabble lasted all the way until they crossed

the River Brent, by which time Henry was maintaining that he was blowed if he was going to advise Decima on the purchase of horses in the future if she had so little faith in his judgement.

Decima finally gave in with a laugh. 'Henry, we sound like brother and sister, arguing like this! I yield absolutely— Adam's team will break down with splints and spavins at any moment and I bow unreservedly to you in the selection of a pair for my phaeton.'

'What phaeton?' he enquired suspiciously.

'The one you are going to assist me in purchasing next week,' she responded. 'I intend to cut a dash in the parks.'

'Your brother will have kittens,' Henry observed. 'And I will figure large in his conversation as the man who led you astray. Not a high-perch, I devoutly hope?'

'Not until I have mastered the ordinary type,' Decima promised. 'Then I will take Charlton for a drive. Now what?' Adam had come to a halt and she could not help noticing Henry feeling under his seat as he reined in, as though to reassure himself something was there. His pistols, no doubt.

But it was only a large wain being backed across the road by two heavy horses with an alert-looking lad at their heads. Adam drew abreast as the heavy wagon straightened up and Decima saw the lad pointing up ahead, then tugging his lank forelock as Adam sent a coin spinning in his direction. He caught it neatly and grinned as the two carriages bowled past.

'Where are we?' Decima queried, looking round at the gently rolling countryside. 'I do not think I have ever been so far north on this road.'

'Hendon's over there…' Henry gestured with his whip to their right '…but I don't know what this hamlet is. Looks as though Weston's found us an inn, though.'

Decima, who had been beginning to think that she had drunk too many cups of tea at breakfast for comfort on a long drive, greeted that news with some enthusiasm. It proved to be a substantial, ancient place, rambling with lean-to extensions under a thatched roof.

Decima's discreet questioning of the landlady produced directions to an airy privy at the bottom of the garden, neatly placed between the chicken run and the woodpile. Olivia came with her, blushing frantically at the thought that anyone might guess where they were going.

'Thank you for asking,' she whispered. 'I would never have liked to do so. I feel so conspicuous. Mama says a lady should simply not drink before setting out, but I became so thirsty.'

Decima chuckled. 'It is why so many privies are next to the woodpile. Then the maids can pretend that is all they've come out for and it means they always come back in with an armful of wood. That or they feed the chickens.'

Olivia smiled. 'What a good idea! I do wish I was as brave and as practical as you are, Decima. I know I must disappoint Lord Weston—he admires your spirit so much.'

'He does?' But Olivia had slipped into the privy, pulling the wooden door with its cut-out half-moons shut behind her, and Decima was left addressing a small flock of brown bantams who eyed her hopefully for kitchen scraps.

Chapter Twenty-Two

Back in the parlour that the men had bespoken, Adam was slouched at one end of an ancient settle and Henry was leaning against it. They were drinking ale with the air of men who could companionably sup their drinks for hours on end without any need to do more than grunt at each other occasionally.

Decima felt her lips twitch as they straightened up and stood, then Adam slid back into his corner, long legs stretched out, and Henry passed cups of tea to her and Olivia.

'What are you smiling at?' Adam asked with a lazy lift of one brow.

Decima eyed the dark brown tea with some misgivings as she took the seat next to him. 'You and Henry. Men seem capable of sitting together for hours on end, communicating in grunts. Women talk.'

'I've noticed. Chatter.'

'Communication,' Decima said firmly. 'It makes society go round.' She checked that Olivia was on the other side of the room talking to Henry and lowered her voice. 'Please do not suggest we race again, not with Olivia here. She is very nervous.'

'But you would like to race?' Adam appeared to ignore her reproof, his eyes fixed on the foam on top of his tankard.

'Well, yes. But then I like speed, she does not.'

'You do, I have noticed.' He looked up, his eyes green with sparking amusement. 'Ice skating, riding, sledging…'

'Yes, all of those things.' Decima found she had to look away and began to study a blackened print on the wall with apparent interest.

'And you don't run away from danger, either.' His voice was soft velvet with a reminiscent tone that sent the colour hot into her cheeks. It was not the dangers of speed to which he was referring.

'Charlton would tell you that is because I am a hoyden and have no conduct.'

'But that is new, is it not?' Adam asked, drawing swirling patterns in the spilt ale on the tabletop with one elegant finger. 'You used to be a dutiful young lady who would never step out of line and who always deferred to her relatives. You told me so.' He lifted his hand away from the table, leaving a wet pattern of interlocking hearts. As Decima stared at it, it began to shrink and dry.

'And then I came into control of my affairs and with independence comes freedom, I have found. Within bounds, naturally,' she added in a commendable imitation of Hermione's tone when lecturing on proper conduct.

'Indeed?' Adam was teasing again and the tense moment was past.

'Indeed,' she agreed. 'I am about to purchase a phaeton and a team and Henry has agreed to assist me with that. He will not approve my trying a pedestrian hobbyhorse, though,' she added wistfully. 'He considers that *would* pass all bounds. There are ladies' versions, apparently,' she added when she saw both Adam's eyebrows shoot up. 'With three wheels.'

'Then I am with Freshford on that subject—they would be a truly terrifying addition to London traffic. He is a man of sense.'

Adam glanced across to where Henry was talking to

Olivia. Her charming smile was lighting up her face, transforming her from a pretty but passive statuette into a lovely, vivid young woman. 'Quite beautiful,' Adam observed dispassionately, as though he was admiring a work of art, and a cold chill ran down Decima's spine. Was that really all he wanted? A beautiful trophy wife?

She was still brooding when they resumed their places in the carriages. Adam drew alongside to discuss the route with Henry. 'We turn off to the left at the crest of Brockley Hill, then follow the lane across Stanmore Common. The house is shortly before Bushey Heath.'

With an effort Decima pulled herself together and tried to take an intelligent interest in the purpose of the expedition. 'It is very pleasant around here,' she observed, looking around them as Henry followed Adam's curricle off the main turnpike. She was immediately grateful the men had not chosen to drive high-perch vehicles, as they lurched from one pothole to another. 'But somewhat isolated. If it were me,' she decided, 'I would not think it ideal. It is too far from London to make it easy to drive in and back in the day—not if one wishes to shop or attend a function, that is. But the house may be lovely and make up for that.'

They were crossing an expanse of common land now, with furze bushes and spindly trees in clumps amidst the brown of last year's bracken. Adam turned in his seat and gestured towards some chimney pots that could just be seen rising above a copse fringing the edge of the open land. 'That is the house.'

As he spoke, two riders swung out of the nearest clump of furze and spurred towards them. Their purpose was unmistakable, even without the masks pulled up over their lower faces and the heavy horse pistols in their hands.

Decima heard Olivia's scream, then Adam was turning the curricle, only to be headed off by one of the riders. With the frantic girl clinging to his arm, Decima could see he was having difficulty controlling his team.

'Damn it.' Henry was juggling whip and reins. He thrust them into Decima's hands and reached under his seat, coming up with a pistol in his hand, but the curricle in front cut off a clear shot at the riders and Decima could see he was unable to fire without risking hitting either Adam or Olivia.

Then Adam dropped his whip, thrust Olivia ruthlessly to the floor of the curricle and reached down. Like Henry, he too was carrying pistols under the seat. Despite the plunging team, he stood and took aim. The gun cracked and one of the riders clapped a hand to his shoulder, then his companion fired, wheeling his horse in at close range before Adam could use his other pistol.

'Oh, God!' Decima fought with the reins as the team tried to back away from the noise and confusion and Henry managed to drag the other gun from its fixings. For a moment she could not see what had happened. The scene before her seemed as before the shot was fired, then Adam bent, clutched at his thigh and toppled out of the curricle to the ground.

The unwounded rider swung round, threatening them with his weapon. Henry threw himself across Decima, shielding her body as he tried to find a steady bead on the man.

'Adam!' Decima tried to push Henry away and steady the horses before they bolted, but the riders closed in on the driverless curricle, one on each side. One man bent and seized the rein and then they were away, cantering across the uneven ground, bearing Olivia away from where Adam's still body sprawled on the turf.

Decima regained control and drove the few yards to reach his side. She thrust the reins into Henry's hands and jumped down, stumbling in her long skirts. He was dead, he had to be dead, he lay so still on his back, his right thigh a mass of blood from where the bullet had torn through his buckskins.

As she reached his side Adam groaned and raised himself on one elbow. 'Olivia?'

'They've taken the curricle.' Decima fell to her knees beside him. Thank goodness, the bullet did not appear to have hit an artery, the blood was not spurting. She rummaged under her skirts, seized the edge of her petticoat and tore ruthlessly.

'Go after it,' Adam gasped, looking up at Henry. 'Have you a loaded pistol left?'

'Yes, both.'

'Take her to the house—you can hold two of them off from there.' Adam's breath was coming in painful gasps. 'Hurry.'

Henry brought the whip down with a crack and the team responded, already almost out of control with fear. Decima barely watched him go, her whole attention fixed on the man sprawled in front of her.

'Adam? Can you hear me?' His eyes were closed. 'I must bandage your leg, stop the bleeding.' How was she going to move him? Could she leave him here and go for help or would the men come back…? First things first, she steadied herself. Stop the bleeding.

'Is he out of sight?' Adam spoke clearly. Thank heavens, it would be much more difficult if he were unconscious.

'Yes, try not to worry, Henry will save her, I know he will.' There was the distant sound of a shot.

She looked up from where she was trying to make a pad out of wadded strips of petticoat to meet a pair of calm, lucid grey eyes fixed on her. 'Of course he will,' Adam said, lifting himself onto both elbows with a grunt. 'God, this track's hard. I must be lying on a flint.'

How could he be so calm, so brave? 'Lie still, you'll make it bleed worse. Can you just raise your leg a little, I know it must hurt…'

Adam sat up fully. 'Leave it.' He got to his feet, pulling her up with him. Too amazed to resist, Decima stared at him.

'Your leg—Adam, you must let me bandage it.' But the blood had stopped completely now and the man facing her was standing squarely on both feet, not favouring either leg. The grey eyes watching her were unclouded by pain, or any sign of fear for Olivia's fate.

'You aren't wounded at all!' She stared at the jagged tear in his buckskins, the blood-soaked leather. 'How did you do that?' Her heart was still pounding with the aftermath of fear and frantic action, her arms ached from the effort of holding the plunging team and she felt sick with reaction.

Adam shook his right arm and a knife slid out from the sleeve into the palm of his hand. 'Sausage casing filled with pig's blood in my breeches pocket.'

Decima reacted without any thought. Her right hand went back of its own accord and she hit him, flat on the cheek. 'You idiot! Henry's armed, someone will get killed!'

Adam rocked back on his heels, but made no other move to avoid her blow. 'Bates swapped Henry's ammunition for blanks before we started. The only person with a loaded gun is me, and that's here.' He patted a coat pocket. 'My two assistants have blanks in their pistols as well and by now I imagine they will have proved singularly inept kidnappers and will have abandoned the curricle and Olivia in it. Come on, I am sorry you were frightened, but it's all in a good cause.'

'Frightened? I was terrified. And Olivia—can you imagine how she is feeling?' Decima gathered up her skirts and ran to catch up with him. 'Adam, what do you think you are *doing*?'

He glanced down at her, a smile twisting his mouth. 'Match-making. I am sure Olivia would consider ten minutes of terror a fair exchange for not having to marry me.'

'But…' Decima found she was having to run again. He strode on, leaving her staring after him, her mouth half open. 'But unless you propose to die of your wound and stay dead, how is this charade going to help?'

'I am relying on human nature and on your friend Henry's abilities as a chivalrous hero to carry the day. Now, stop hectoring me for a moment, Decima, you may lecture all you like in a minute.' The two highwaymen were riding out of the copse, masks gone to reveal the grinning faces of young men on a spree. Neither of them looked capable of anything more vicious than an inn brawl over a girl.

'All went according to plan, my lord,' one of them reported, touching his battered tricorne hat to Decima. 'We let go of the curricle just where you said, and made sure the reins got tangled in a bush—it wasn't going anywhere. The young lady's all right, I'd say—shrieking fit to bust, though. Would Henry be the short blonde gentleman?'

'Yes,' Adam agreed.

'He's well in, then,' the groom observed with a grin, remembered Decima's presence, and broke off in confusion.

'Good work. Off you go, and for goodness' sake tidy yourselves up before you hit the turnpike or I'll be bailing you out of the local clink on suspicion of being on the High Toby.'

They rode off in high spirits and Decima took full advantage of his permission to lecture. 'How can you be sure they will hold their tongues? Is this going to be spread all over town? We will be a laughing stock and the scandal will ruin Olivia,' she stormed as they entered the copse.

'They are grooms of mine, they are completely trustworthy and they think they are helping me win a wager with Sir Henry.'

'Of all the improbable stories! They will never fall for that.'

'Decima, they are eighteen years old, ripe for a spree and certain that the nobility can be relied upon to carry on in a completely incalculable manner. This just proves it. Now hush, we are almost at the house and I don't want Henry's attention distracted from calming Olivia down.'

They were emerging where the edge of the thicket met the overgrown pleasure grounds of the house. Adam turned and began to lead Decima towards the back. There was a small rustic summerhouse and he pushed open the door. 'Come in here and let me explain.' Reluctantly Decima let herself be seated on one of the benches that ran around the inside of the little shelter.

Adam shut the door and leaned against it, his face serious in the shadowed room. 'This is not a joke and not something I am doing lightly, whatever you may think. I should never have offered for Olivia. The circumstances made it impossible not to, and I cannot explain more than that—if she feels she can tell you about it, she will. Once we found ourselves in that position I could not withdraw. At first I thought she could, and might if she realised that I was quite the wrong husband for her. But I had no idea at first just what a degree of subjugation she is held in by her parents' influence. Her mother in particular. Olivia could no more defy her mother than fly. And then I saw what was happening between her and Henry Freshford. At last I could see a way out.'

'You saw? I couldn't understand why you were so tolerant!' Decima shook her head, still puzzling. 'Henry loves her, but he is trying to do the honourable thing. Nothing has been said between them, I am sure of it.'

'So am I,' Adam retorted grimly. 'And while I did everything to remind Olivia just how miserable she would be married to me, I did my best to throw her together with Freshford. Your helpful efforts to reconcile her to the match were most unwelcome, I have to say.'

'But I—'

'You acted out of friendship and the most honourable of motives, I know.' He smiled at her and something inside Decima quivered into life. Hope. 'It is one of the things I love about you.'

Love? Did Adam say love? Decima found her hands were twisting tightly in her skirts and she forced herself to relax them. He loved her as a friend, that was all. They had been talking about friendship.

'I could see that nothing was going to undermine Freshford's sense of honour or Olivia's rigid obedience, other than a major crisis, so I engineered one. I could have gone to him, told him I knew of his feelings, and assured him of my support. But we would never have got Olivia to admit the truth and face up to her mama. And what she would see as certain disgrace.' Adam grimaced. 'It took me days to think of something sufficiently convincing, yet that would put none of you at risk.'

'But has it worked?'

'Let's find out.' Adam held out a hand and Decima took it, her fingers enveloped in his. She was still shaken, but her anger had given way to a feeling of deep apprehension. What if this elaborate ruse had not worked?

They crept up to the back door. Adam reached up and retrieved a key from the ledge above and gently opened it, leading Decima into a kitchen, clean, equipped, but cold and unused. Walking with catlike tread despite his boots, Adam began to move out of the kitchen, along a passage and through the heavy baize-lined door that separated the servants' world from that of their masters.

They were in the front hall. All the doors were closed except one, standing ajar on the right-hand side of the front entrance. Adam led the way until they were standing outside. He kept her hand in his and Decima found herself clinging to him, as though bracing herself to hear bad news.

'They have gone.' It was Henry's voice, strong and reassuring. 'They will have no way of knowing who else is here, and one of them is wounded. They will be off, thinking we can summon the constables. It's all right now, Olivia. I am here.'

There was the sound of a muffled sob, then feet moving on the boards and Henry's voice again, less clear. 'There, there, Olivia, you are quite safe with me.'

'I know. You were wonderful.' The adoration in Olivia's voice was touching. Decima shifted, uncomfortable at eavesdropping. 'So wonderful. Oh, Sir...oh, *Henry*!'

Adam, who had been standing with one eye to the narrow hinge opening, grimaced and moved away slightly. As he met Decima's questioning gaze, he smiled and whispered in her ear, 'I think this is going to be all right, but I'm damned if I'm playing the Peeping Tom. Give them a moment.'

He appeared to be counting, then gave Decima's hand a squeeze, released it and pushed the door wide. Henry had Olivia in his arms, her face was tipped up to his and they were kissing with total absorption. Decima found a smile of pure indulgence was spreading across her face and she hastily straightened her expression and coughed. How was Adam intending to play this?

The lovers jumped apart as though a shot had been fired. Olivia went white and burst into tears. Henry, as pale as she, drew himself up to his full height and bowed. 'I am at your disposal, my lord. Please name your friends.'

'I find you ravishing my affianced bride and you expect the honour of a duel?' Adam's voice was icy. 'I should fetch a horsewhip.'

Chapter Twenty-Three

No!' It was Olivia, transformed from a tearful mouse into a spitting cat. 'Henry was not ravishing me, he would do nothing so dishonourable. We love each other!' She turned and took Henry's arm, twining herself close to him. 'I defy you to accuse him. I know I am ruined, but I do not care!'

'Let me be the first to congratulate you,' Adam said warmly.

'What?' It was Henry, one arm tight around Olivia's quivering form. 'Are you making sport with us, my lord? Because I have to warn you that I have no intention of standing by and seeing you insult this lady. All blame for what has just occurred is mine and I insist—'

'Stubble it, do,' Adam interrupted, lapsing into exasperated cant. 'You love her, she loves you. Miss Channing and I find that we were mutually mistaken in our affections and have agreed, on the friendliest of terms, to sever our contract.'

'We were? I mean, we are?' Olivia was staring at him, her pretty face flushed, the snail tracks of tears drying on her cheeks. 'But the scandal…'

'What scandal?' Decima decided it was time to take a hand. 'Lord Weston, and you and Henry, will all appear in public on the friendliest of terms. Lady Freshford will be delighted, and will say so. Your parents will express their approval—'

'They will?' Henry was staring at her, apparently dumbfounded.

'They will when they realise how wealthy you are,' Decima retorted. 'And how generous you will be with the settlements. And, of course, the fact that you will be persuading your cousin the duke to host the wedding at Farleigh. Adam might be a viscount, but he is not closely related to any living dukes, are you?'

'No, although I am a distant connection of Freshford's duke.'

'He's only a second cousin,' Henry protested faintly. 'Once removed.'

'How are we going to tell Mama?' Olivia enquired, going a little pale again and clutching Henry's arm.

'Are both she and your father out of town?' Adam asked.

'Yes, until Wednesday—three days' time.'

'Then we will both talk to them then, together. We will explain how we are mistaken in our feelings and how, although you tried to hide it from me, you loved another. I saw through your honourable deceit, leaving you free to marry the man you love, and so forth. I will exit, looking noble, to be followed by Freshford, hard on my heels before they have time to think of objections.'

'I will be so frightened.' Olivia's eyes were wide. 'I cannot do it, I know I cannot.'

'Do you want to break Henry's heart?' Decima enquired bracingly, satisfied when she saw Olivia's jaw set with determination.

Henry appeared to be a man coming out of a dream. The stunned expression was vanishing rapidly, to be replaced by a look of deep suspicion. 'A word with you, my lord,' he said grimly.

'Not here.' Adam held the door wide and ushered Henry out. 'We do not want to confuse or alarm the ladies, do we?'

Adam closed the door and leant back on the panels. 'Before you ask, yes, that was all a ruse.' It was just beginning to sink in that it had worked, that he was no longer tied to Olivia and that he could at last tell Decima how he felt about her.

'Your leg?' Freshford was still eying him with a degree of suspicious hostility, unwilling to trust him entirely yet.

'A trick.'

'Someone could have been killed, shots were fired, Olivia was alone in that curricle.'

'Every pistol, including yours, was loaded with blanks. The "highwayman" leading the curricle is a highly competent groom and the horses were less than fresh after a long drive. I did what I could.' Suddenly bone weary, he let his eyes close for a moment, then reopened them to find Freshford regarding him quizzically.

'Why did you become engaged to Olivia in the first place?'

Adam shook his head. 'Ask her. If she will not tell you, I cannot. I suggest you drive her home in your curricle now. Take the picnic hamper from mine and have a pleasant journey back.'

'And leave you with Decima?' To Adam's eye, Freshford was looking less like a man in love and more like a suspicious relative. 'Just what are your intentions, my lord? I should tell you, I regard her as my sister. If you hurt her, you will have me to answer to. I am more grateful than I can say for what you have done for Olivia and me, but I won't let that stand in my way.'

'My intentions? To marry her, if she'll have me. Do you think she will?'

Freshford grinned suddenly. 'You'll have to ask her and see.'

Adam reached into his pocket and withdrew the pistol.

'You had better have this, just in case. The ammunition is live. If Decima were to be…delayed this afternoon—'

'I will tell my mother she's staying with a friend.' Henry took the pistol, pocketed it, then held out his hand. 'Good luck.'

Adam stepped aside as he opened the door and called. Olivia came out, too wrapped up in Henry to even notice Adam standing back in the shadows. He shook his head ruefully, wondering what transformation in the pretty little mouse the experience of loving Henry Freshford would bring about. It would be intriguing to watch, but now he had his own fate to put to the touch.

Decima was standing by a cold fireplace, staring down at the empty hearth. She glanced up as he came in, her face serious. 'Olivia has just told me about the house party and why you had to propose to her. She feels so guilty about that.'

'Water under the bridge now.' Adam shrugged. 'At the time I almost welcomed it. I had lost something very precious and I didn't think I had a hope of finding it again, so nothing else really mattered.' Did she understand him?

It seemed she did—the colour was high on her cheekbones and her eyes dropped before his. He pressed on. 'I was running away from love and commitment and marriage. I thought that what I felt for you was desire, just that.' He was doggedly determined to lay it all out, leave nothing unsaid. 'Then when I realised what I really wanted, that I didn't want to run any more, I couldn't find you. When I did discover who you were, it was too late.'

Decima was silent. Had he misjudged it? Should he have taken her back home, waited, tried wooing her with soft words and flowers?

'Decima.' It was four strides to reach her across the room—it seemed like a mile. 'Decima, I love you. Will you marry me?'

'Oh, yes.' She turned to him, her eyes sparkling, her warm, generous mouth curved into a smile that was pure happiness, just for him. 'Yes, I will, and I love you, I've loved you for so long and I never thought you could possibly love me.'

There didn't appear to be any words, or, if there were, his tongue was incapable of articulating them. Adam took Decima by the shoulders, turned her gently into his embrace and kissed her.

This was real, and it was different, quite different from their kisses before, different from the way she had dreamed it would be. As Adam's mouth angled over hers, gently insistent as he caressed her lips with his, she realised what it was. There was no doubt, no guilt, no anxiety about why he was kissing her. She knew he was showing her his love and he knew that was what she wanted, too.

Her lips parted and she shuddered deliciously at the heat, at the shocking, velvet slide of his tongue over hers. She moaned a little, deep in her throat and he shifted his hands to bring her closer, one hand in the small of her back, the other at the back of her head, impelling her into his kiss.

It was not enough. Her hands splayed across the breadth of his shoulders, her fingers spreading as they traced the hard muscle under the broadcloth and linen. He was so big, so strong, so hard, that he frightened her and delighted her all at the same time. But she was strong too, she would match him, keep pace with him, incite him to love her without restraint.

Adam's hands shifted again and she was in his arms, lifted tightly against his chest. Decima muttered a protest as he carried her through into the hall. 'I don't want to go yet.' Her lips found the skin at the edge of his jaw, rough with the start of new stubble, and she nuzzled at it, making him gasp.

'We aren't going.' She felt him begin to climb. 'Decima, stop it or I'll make love to you here and now on the stairs!'

'Mmm,' she murmured encouragingly. Under her lips she could feel the pulse in his neck, hammering.

'Witch.' It was a chuckle, albeit a breathless one. He shouldered open a door, took a few more strides and she found herself laid down on a bed. Reluctantly Decima opened her eyes. She was in a bedroom, but unlike the rooms downstairs that were occupied by only a few items of dust-sheeted furniture, this room was fully furnished with damask drapes at the windows and new candles in the sconces. Adam struck a spark from his tinderbox and set a taper to the fire, which stood ready-made in the grate.

'You see my arrogance exposed,' he said, coming towards her, shrugging out of his coat in a way that dried her mouth with desire. 'I had this room prepared, right down to the fire.'

'Not arrogance,' she managed to say. 'Hope.'

Adam sat on the side of the bed beside her, watching her with eyes that were tender, patient. 'If you want to go back to London now, wait until we are married, then you only have to say.' He clasped his hands together as though to show he was not going to touch her without her consent. 'But if you wish to stay, no one will expect you back.'

'It seems a very long time since that snowy New Year's day,' Decima said slowly. 'You started something I think we should finish.' She smiled at herself. 'I find I am no longer very good at being patient.'

'You will have to be.' Adam began to tug off his neckcloth. 'I have all those freckles to count.' He tossed the crumpled muslin onto the floor and began on his shirt buttons. 'Of course, I could always make love to you *while* I count…'

'That would save time,' Decima agreed solemnly, reaching for his shirt placket to help with the buttons. At last, skin. She slid her hands through the opening in the fine linen, sighing with satisfaction as her palms slid over smooth muscle.

'Hmm.' Adam pulled her close. 'Now then, how does this gown unfasten?' It seemed to be a rhetorical question, for he was managing very well with the tiny buttons and the row of hooks. And then it was sliding from her shoulders and somehow her chemise was going with it.

Decima found herself on her back on the bed, everything but her stockings and garters gone. She gave a little gasp of alarm and tried to cover herself with her hands, only to find them captured and kissed. 'Let me look at you, sweetheart.'

Adam ran his hands gently over her body, down the length of her, his touch a caress, his expression tender. 'You are so beautiful. No, don't shake your head at me. Look at you, so long, so smooth, so rounded.' His palm stroked lightly over the curve of her belly, cupped her hip lightly, dipped into her waist and up to her breasts. 'Oh, yes, now these freckles. I cannot just count, I must kiss.'

He bent his head and began to touch her skin with his lips, down, along her collar bone, down to the swell of her breasts. Decima shifted restlessly under the relentlessly soft caress, then his lips captured one nipple and she arched up in shock. 'Adam!'

'Not so impatient.' His breath teased across to the other breast, the other nipple, rousing an ache that filled her body. He nipped suddenly, gently, with his teeth, then, as she was writhing against his mouth, he released her and she sensed him moving away.

It was momentary. Adam's weight came down on the bed beside her and she felt the whole length of him, naked against her side. His arm went across her body, holding her as she shivered in reaction. Tentatively Decima opened her eyes and found him watching her.

'I love you,' he murmured and his hand moved, slid downwards, cupped for a moment against the tangle of hair and then, as she moaned, unable to take her eyes from his, one finger slid into the secret place that was aching so insistently.

The flood of sensation was overwhelming, shameful, pleasurable, beyond her dreams. Decima closed her eyes and turned into Adam's body, instinctively trying to hide her nakedness against his. He turned and she found herself beneath him, his knee gently urging her thighs to part.

'Trust me, sweetheart.' She nodded, gasped his name, hardly able to think rationally as her body took over, reacted to his hands and his body. She shifted, cradling him between her thighs, restless until his weight came down and she could arch beneath him, secure, held, throbbing with need for him.

'Decima, open your eyes, look at me.' She tried to obey, dragged her lids apart, gazed into the hot, grey-green depths of his and saw desire and need and love and a kind of worship. 'Trust me.' And he thrust, filling her as her body bowed up under his, then withdrawing, returning, while the sudden sharp pain vanished to be replaced by a building, driving need. She cried out, her arms tight around him, letting him sweep her along. It seemed she must die—no one could withstand this. Hazily she remembered thinking she was strong, that she could follow him where he led her.

'Adam!' She cried his name, words of love, gasps that were not words, and something happened, something crested and burst and the black behind her eyes vanished in a blaze of light and she was sinking down, back into a velvet, throbbing darkness.

She came to herself to find she was held against a bare chest. Tentatively she moved her legs and found that Adam was stretched full length beside her. Her body was heavy with the memory of pleasure, relaxed beyond anything she could ever recall. Opening her eyes was hard, but she wanted to see him, wanted to see what expression his eyes would hold.

He was watching her, waiting for her. Their eyes met and words did not seem necessary. His hands began to drift, then his lips found hers again and Decima discovered that it was possible for perfection to become better.

* * *

How much later it was when she woke she had no idea. This time Adam was out of bed, padding round the room in bare feet, his long frame clad in one of his gorgeous Oriental dressing gowns as he touched a taper to the candles.

He turned as he heard her stir and came across, bent and took her mouth with an intensity that had her reaching up for him. 'I love you,' she murmured.

'I love you, too, and, if we don't soon have something to eat, neither of us is going to have the strength to prove it all over again,' he teased.

'We have to cook?' Decima stretched. Her muscles felt oiled and sleek.

'No. Look.' Adam opened a door. Decima got out of bed, blushed all over when she remembered she was naked, and caught a sheet around her. The next chamber was a dressing room and in the middle of it stood a tub, full of steaming water. The dressing table was set out with her brushes and little silver pots and hanging from the doors of the press were dresses and petticoats.

'Pru?'

'And Bates.' Adam pulled aside a curtain. Through the trees Decima could see lights twinkling. 'There's a snug gardener's cottage. We won't see them, but the horses are stabled, there will be food on the table shortly and for two days we can run away from the world.'

'But Pru and Bates aren't... I mean, I shouldn't countenance...' Decima followed Adam's gaze to where the big bed stood, the sheets a rumpled testimony to an afternoon of lovemaking. 'Oh.' She could feel the blush mounting her cheeks and hid her confusion by burying her face in the thick silk of Adam's dressing gown.

'I do love you, Decima Ross,' Adam murmured into her tousled hair. 'And if you could think clearly after I've made love to you I would not take that as much of a compliment. Now, come and let me soap you all over while we congratulate ourselves on our excellent matchmaking skills.'

Decima let him peel away the sheet and slid into the warm, scented water with a soft sigh of pleasure. 'But everyone must get married soon,' she said firmly, trying to resist a whimper of delight as Adam squeezed a soapy sponge over her.

'Absolutely,' he agreed seriously. 'I cannot speak for Bates, or Freshford for that matter, but I have every intention of applying for a licence at the earliest possible opportunity. Meanwhile...' he bent to nibble her earlobe '...meanwhile, I intend practising making love to you as often as I can.'

'Yes, Adam,' Decima agreed meekly. 'It is regrettable that it appears to make us late for meals, but I cannot help but feel it is my duty to practise as much as possible to please you.' She rather spoilt this pious wifely hope by turning to curl wet arms around his shoulders. 'I do love you, Adam.'

'And I love you.' He got to his feet and pulled off the dressing gown. 'Do you think this bathtub will hold both of us? Because I fully intend being very late for dinner.'

Downstairs in the kitchen Pru shut the oven door firmly on a beef casserole, set the bread and butter on the table and smiled at Jethro Bates. 'There, that won't spoil, never mind how late they are. Now, what shall we have for dinner?'

* * * * *

*Rancher Ramsey Westmoreland's temporary cook
is way too attractive for his liking.
Little does he know Chloe Burton came to his ranch
with another agenda entirely....*

That man across the street had to be, without a doubt, the most handsome man she'd ever seen.

Chloe Burton's pulse beat rhythmically as he stopped to talk to another man in front of a feed store. He was tall, dark and every inch of sexy—from his Stetson to the well-worn leather boots on his feet. And from the way his jeans and Western shirt fit his broad muscular shoulders, it was quite obvious he had everything it took to separate the men from the boys. The combination was enough to corrupt any woman's mind and had her weakening even from a distance. Her body felt flushed. It was hot. Unsettled.

Over the past year the only male who had gotten her time and attention had been the e-mail. That was simply pathetic, especially since now she was practically drooling simply at the sight of a man. Even his stance—both hands in his jeans pockets, legs braced apart, was a pose she would carry to her dreams.

And he was smiling, evidently enjoying the conversation being exchanged. He had dimples, incredibly sexy dimples in not one but both cheeks.

"What are you staring at, Clo?"

Chloe nearly jumped. She'd forgotten she had a lunch date. She glanced over the table at her best friend from college, Lucia Conyers.

"Take a look at that man across the street in the blue shirt, Lucia. Will he not be perfect for Denver's first issue of *Simply Irresistible* or what?" Chloe asked with so much excitement she almost couldn't stand it.

She was the owner of *Simply Irresistible*, a magazine for

today's up-and-coming woman. Their once-a-year Irresistible Man cover, which highlighted a man the magazine felt deserved the honor, had increased sales enough for Chloe to open a Denver office.

When Lucia didn't say anything but kept staring, Chloe's smile widened. "Well?"

Lucia glanced across the booth at her. "Since you asked, I'll tell you what I see. One of the Westmorelands—Ramsey Westmoreland. And yes, he'd be perfect for the cover, but he won't do it."

Chloe raised a brow. "He'd get paid for his services, of course."

Lucia laughed and shook her head. "Getting paid won't be the issue, Clo—Ramsey is one of the wealthiest sheep ranchers in this part of Colorado. But everyone knows what a private person he is. Trust me—he won't do it."

Chloe couldn't help but smile. The man was the epitome of what she was looking for in a magazine cover and she was determined that whatever it took, he would be it.

"Umm, I don't like that look on your face, Chloe. I've seen it before and know exactly what it means."

She watched as Ramsey Westmoreland entered the store with a swagger that made her almost breathless. She *would* be seeing him again.

Look for Silhouette Desire's
HOT WESTMORELAND NIGHTS by Brenda Jackson,
available March 9 wherever books are sold.

HARLEQUIN® HISTORICAL:
Where love is timeless

The Horseman's Bride
ELIZABETH LANE

After taking the blame for his brother-in-law's murder,
Jace Denby is on the run. He must leave the ranch,
though the beauty and fierce courage of Clara Seavers
entice him to stay....

Clara doesn't trust this farm hand, but the rugged and
unexpectedly caring man ignites her spirit...and heart.
The more Jace fights their mounting passion, the more
she'll risk to make him hers forever.

Available March 2010
wherever you buy books.

Miss Winthorpe's Elopement
CHRISTINE MERRILL

Shy heiress Miss Penelope Winthorpe never meant
to wed a noble lord over a blacksmith's anvil.

The Duke of Bellston had no intention of taking
a wife. Now the notorious rake has a new aim—
to shock and seduce his prim and proper bride.

But the gorgeous duke will be taught a lesson
of his own as scholarly Miss Winthorpe becomes
his seductive duchess!

Available March 2010
wherever you buy books.

HARLEQUIN® HISTORICAL:
Where love is timeless

The Earl's Forbidden Ward
BRONWYN SCOTT

Innocent debutante Tessa Branscombe senses that
underneath her handsome guardian's cool demeanor
there is an intensely passionate nature. The arrogant
earl infuriates her—yet makes her want to explore
those hidden depths....

The Earl of Dursley has no time for girls!
Miss Tessa Branscombe, in particular, is trouble.
She tempts this very proper earl to misbehave—and
forbidden fruit always tastes that much sweeter....

Available March 2010
wherever you buy books.

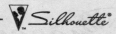

SPECIAL EDITION

FROM *USA TODAY* BESTSELLING AUTHOR
CHRISTINE RIMMER

A BRIDE FOR JERICHO BRAVO

Marnie Jones had long ago buried her wild-child impulses and opted to be "safe," romantically speaking. But one look at born rebel Jericho Bravo and she began to wonder if her thrill-seeking side was about to be revived. Because if ever there was a man worth taking a chance on, there he was, right within her grasp....

*Available in March
wherever books are sold.*

Two families torn apart by secrets and desire
are about to be reunited in

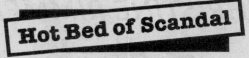

a sexy new duet by

Kelly Hunter

EXPOSED: MISBEHAVING WITH THE MAGNATE

#2905 Available March 2010

Gabriella Alexander returns to the French vineyard she
was banished from after being caught in flagrante with the
owner's son Lucien Duvalier—only to finish what they started!

REVEALED: A PRINCE AND A PREGNANCY

#2913 Available April 2010

Simone Duvalier wants Rafael Alexander and always has, but
they both get more than they bargained for when a night of
passion and a royal revelation rock their world!

www.eHarlequin.com

HP12905

REQUEST YOUR FREE BOOKS!

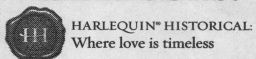

HARLEQUIN® HISTORICAL:
Where love is timeless

2 FREE NOVELS PLUS 2 FREE GIFTS!

HARLEQUIN® HISTORICAL:
Where love is timeless

The Accidental *Princess*
MICHELLE WILLINGHAM

FROM DUTIFUL DEBUTANTE...
TO PASSIONATE PRINCESS!

Etiquette demands Lady Hannah Chesterfield
ignore the shivers of desire provoked by
Lieutenant Michael Thorpe's wicked gaze.

Thrown together by scandal, a defiant Hannah joins
Michael on an adventure to uncover the secret of his
birth—is this common soldier really a prince? If so,
will the man who taught Hannah the meaning of
pleasure now make her his royal bride?

Available March 2010
wherever you buy books.

www.eHarlequin.com